PRAISE FOR *THE BORDER*

"This opening sequence—one among a handful of equally suspenseful scenes, including a car chase in the border town of Sonoyta—makes the quieter, bleaker moments that follow seem all the more intense, stressing the desperate troubles these teens endure… Brilliant."

—*Kirkus Reviews*

"This book is both eye-opening and terrifying. Schafer creates a compelling story about survival and wanting to create a better life."

—*School Library Connection*

"A thought-provoking adrenaline rush sure to satisfy fans of action and adventure."

—*Booklist*

"This story is timely and controversial because it looks at the U.S./Mexico border issue on a humane level, not a political one. Schafer aptly demonstrates the ruthless realities facing those who cross the border between the two countries."

—*VOYA*

"A riveting story of survival and perseverance along the unforgiving frontier of the Sonoran desert."

—*Summit Daily*

"Steve Schafer has given voice to a tragically common but far too infrequently told narrative of reality in towns and villages in Mexico that are controlled by drug cartels and drug smugglers. Providing legal representation for three decades to immigrants in Dallas, I have heard this same account dozens of times. Lest anyone think Steve Schafer's account is exaggeration, I can attest to the realistic depiction he provides."

—Vanna Slaughter, director of Catholic Charities of Dallas

"Steve Schafer walks us through the ebbs and flows in the lives of ordinary immigrants, the dramatic moments at the border, the fear, the yearnings, and the hope for a better future. An engrossing narrative delivered in trepidant prose."

—Mauro F. Guillén, director of the Lauder Institute at the Wharton School

"Schafer deftly brings to life the drama of unauthorized border crossing and gives a human face to those often dismissed simply as 'illegals.'"

—Douglas Massey, Henry G. Bryant professor of sociology and public affairs at Princeton University

"The four young people in this powerful story find hardship and humanity, ruthlessness and compassion without ever losing their own sense of optimism, hope, love, and goodness."

—Luis H. Zayas, PhD, dean and Robert Lee Sutherland chair in mental health and social policy at the University of Texas at Austin

the

border

the
border

UTRGV MSA

Mathematics & Science

Academy

STEVE SCHAFER

Published by Sourcebooks Fire, an imprint of Sourcebooks, Inc.
P.O. Box 4410, Naperville, Illinois 60567-4410
(630) 961-3900
Fax: (630) 961-2168
sourcebooks.com

The Library of Congress has cataloged the hardcover edition as follows:

Names: Schafer, Steve, author.
Title: The border / Steve Schafer.
Description: Naperville, Illinois : Sourcebooks Fire, [2017] | Summary: After
    the slaughter of their families in Northern Mexico, teens Pato, Arbo,
    Marcos, and Gladys narrowly escape into the Sonoran Desert, pursued by the
    La Frontera gang.
Identifiers: LCCN 2017002560
Subjects: | CYAC: Survival--Fiction. | Murder--Fiction. | Gangs--Fiction. |
    Illegal aliens--Fiction. | Voyages and travels--Fiction. | Sonoran
    Desert--Fiction.
Classification: LCC PZ7.1.S3356 Bor 2017 | DDC [Fic]--dc23 LC record avail-
able at https://lccn.loc.gov/2017002560

Printed and bound in the United States of America.
VP 10 9 8 7 6 5 4 3 2 1

For Sydney and Tyler

LA
QUINCE

The car looks suspicious. I can't put my finger on why, but I can't stop staring at it either.

We've just arrived at my cousin Carmen's fifteenth birthday party—her *quinceañera*. The street is already lined with vehicles. It's nearly dusk, and we're late. We always are. That's my dad, always behind and fine with it.

We park our truck in front of the small driveway, blocking it. My dad gets out, tucks the keys behind the rusty gas tank cover, and opens my mother's door. He takes her hand and helps her out, then strolls toward the house as though we're ten minutes early.

I follow.

"I have a surprise for you tomorrow, Pato," my dad says.

I'm not looking at him. I peer at that car parked on the street, a few houses away.

The rear bumper. That's it.

It's an older car, the kind that normally has a chrome

bumper. But this one has been painted a dull, matte black, like the rest of the car.

Weird.

"It's not really a surprise," my mom says.

"Wait, what surprise?" I ask.

"Pato is going to be disappointed if you call it a surprise," she says to my dad. "Surprises are good. This isn't. It's not bad, *mi amor*. But it's not a present."

I'm listening to my mother but still staring at the car. A pair of eyes meets mine in its side-view mirror.

Someone is in the car. Why is he just sitting there?

"Okay, Pato. It's not a surprise—it's news. It's a change. A good change," my dad tells me.

"What kind of change?"

I look from the car to my dad. I like routine. I have a way of doing things, and I like to stick to it.

"Tell you what. We'll talk about it tomorrow, okay?"

As we near the house, I can see the car from a different angle. The hubcaps are painted black too. Bumper to bumper, the entire car is black. And on the back door, I see a small dent.

No, not a dent. Is that a bullet hole?

I squint. It's hard to tell. But I can see the silhouette of the driver. He blows a thin stream of smoke out the window.

I glance at my parents to see if they notice, but they're too wrapped up in each other and all this talk about change.

Then a head pops up in the back seat and drops back down from view.

Did I imagine that?

I stare. There's no movement.

"Hey, Pato. Are you okay?" my mom asks as we arrive at the door.

"Yeah, it's just—" The door opens before we knock.

"Look who finally decided to show up!" My aunt opens her arms wide to hug my mom, while my uncle greets my father with a drink. Beyond them stands Arbo, my cousin and best friend.

As we step inside, I turn back toward the car. The driver's head rotates. It's too dark and too far away to see any kind of expression. But somehow it feels threatening.

The front door closes behind us.

— — — — — — — —

I think about mentioning the car to Arbo. Just a passing comment. He would know what to do with it—to pay attention or let it go.

Hey, there's some creepy guy in a car sitting outside your house.

But the words never make it to my lips. He grabs the conversation before I do.

"You've got to see Carmen. I didn't even recognize her."

"It's a *quince*. They're supposed to get all spiffed up," I say, though that's putting it mildly. Teenage girls are notorious for going overboard for their *quinceañeras*.

"I know. It's just weird to see my little sister with cleavage. I don't like thinking about how other people might be looking at her."

I can't imagine Carmen like that either. She's only one year younger than Arbo and me, but I still think of her as my little cousin.

"Like who?" I ask.

Arbo scans the backyard. His house sits along the edge of town. While the house itself is small, the backyard is not. One advantage of bordering the Sonoran Desert? Full access to a swath of otherwise unwanted land.

"Like that guy," he says, pointing to the other side of the yard.

Marcos.

Marcos is one year older than us and about three years cooler. At our high school, he's famous. He scores the goals. He gets the girls. For us—or for me, at least—his life seems like a fantasy. I know *of* him more than I actually *know* him.

Marcos catches our gaze and gives an acknowledging nod. Then he turns to look at the small group of girls gathered next to Carmen.

True to form, the girls teeter on too-high heels, engulfed by lavish dresses studded with sequins and beads, their faces hidden behind too much makeup. All are nearly unrecognizable from their normal selves except one: Marcos's younger sister, Gladys, who is the same age as Carmen.

Amid the *quinceañera* extravagance, she's understated, like she's not even trying. If she's wearing makeup, I can't tell. Her dress is simple. It looks homemade, but not in a bad way. There's nothing flashy about her, but she shines. I've noticed her before, though never quite like this.

She looks at me for a second, then her eyes dart away.

"*¡Una foto!* A picture!"

I'm pulled out of my thoughts. Arbo's dad and my dad are arm in arm and waving for us to join them. They're brothers, best friends, and business partners. They share ownership of the truck we drove here this evening. Like Arbo and me, they do nearly everything together.

Arbo and I cram into the space between them, their arms stretching across our backs, embracing us.

"To partners!" they say, smiling wide for the camera.

They have it in their minds that one day Arbo and I will join their construction company, and the four of us will be partners. It's a small business. They don't have any regular employees, only a few people they pay by the day when they need an extra hand. But for a couple of guys who were working in the fields and factories several years ago, they're living a dream.

The camera flashes, and I imagine another picture, years from now, with a third generation of partners sandwiched between Arbo and me. My smile lingers beyond the flash. *Who knows?*

I look around the party. They must be doing well. In

Mexico, a country of haves and have-nots, we're definitely the latter. But it doesn't feel that way tonight. The backyard is a spectacle. Hundreds of colored lights stretch across the sky like stars. Crystal vases filled with dense bouquets in a dazzling array of colors sparkle. A five-person band weaves through the yard, its harmonies surely carrying far out into the barren distance. And near the door where the house opens to the backyard, an ice sculpture sits atop a silken tablecloth. We live in a desert!

The band transitions from one song to the next. In that gap, I hear the roar of a loud engine on the street. For a second, I think back to the car.

Then Arbo says something. And the band resumes playing. My father whisks my mother to the dance floor. Then my uncle stops everything to give a teary speech about Carmen. Everybody toasts. And the celebration marches on into the warm July night.

— — — — — — — —

"Hey, Pato, let's go have a smoke," Marcos says to me, as if it's more an instruction than an invitation. I'm flattered that he's asked me, even though I know his options are limited. His family is friends with my family. Otherwise, this isn't his crowd.

"Okay. Why not?" I'm not a smoker, but I have tried it before.

I motion for Arbo to join us.

A weathered adobe wall encloses the yard, separating the house from the desert. We quietly exit through a gap in the back wall where there was once a gate. Beyond it is a blazed landscape of jagged rocks, wiry weeds, all shapes of cacti, and a host of clumpy plants that pass as bushes. It's an uninviting place. Almost everything that exists here—other than the sand—is some combination of dry, prickly, and short.

We walk along the wall, which leads to a trail that snakes through the maze of spiny plants, made visible by the faint glow of a new moon and light from a few nearby houses. Halfway down the path, I notice that Gladys is on our heels, following in silence.

We arrive at an opening in the brush about 150 meters from the house. There, in the middle of nothing, lies the back seat of a car—a long, plastic bench seat. I don't know what kind of car it belonged to, and I don't know how it got here, but I still know it well. I've been out here many times before. It's one of my favorite places in the world. Two years ago, I had my first kiss here. I was so nervous, I accidentally tipped the bench backward, and we both tumbled head over heels. This bench outlasted that relationship. Every August, this is my front-row seat for an annual meteor shower. And it's perfect anytime for watching the stars that don't fall. Arbo and I have passed many hours here staring into the cosmos in awe.

Gladys and Marcos sit on the bench, settling into the grooves where crooked springs don't poke in the wrong places.

Marcos holds out the pack of cigarettes. Arbo and I each grab one, then take a seat in the dirt, facing them. Gladys chooses not to smoke, either out of respect for her older brother or because she has better sense than the rest of us.

I've come to realize that there is a gap between doing something to look cool and actually looking cool while doing it. I hit puberty late. Very late. About a year ago. And it defines me now. My voice cracks. I'm pimpled. I have body parts that seem to have a mind of their own. Seldom do I look cool doing anything, let alone drawing smoke down my throat. It's itchy and awful tasting. My only consolation is Arbo, who is doing a brilliant job of attracting attention, so it's not on me. He coughs out a wispy stream of smoke, which rises with the lingering desert heat into a faint cloud above our heads, slowly bleeding into the sky. We laugh.

"Th-top," he says amidst a flurry of hacks. Arbo lisps when he gets flustered.

"Ooh, th-top, pleathe th-stop!" Marcos waves his arms in the air with an exaggerated flair.

Again, we laugh.

Arbo dials up his disapproval, though I can tell he's playing along. He likes the laughs as much as we do, even when they're at his own expense.

Gladys looks at me with a shy smile. And for an instant, this moment is perfect.

Then we hear a shot.

I recoil. All noise stops.

We look at one another around our circle. Their confused expressions mirror my own. Arbo starts to voice the same hope I have: "Firecrack—?"

He doesn't finish.

He's interrupted by a second shot and the screams that follow. Soon the blasts are indistinguishable, and the cries unimaginable.

Arbo stands to move in the direction of the house, but Marcos latches onto his belt, yanking him back down to the dirt with a firm "No!"

"What are you doing?" Arbo shouts.

"Shut up and get down!"

I stay frozen—from shock, from fear, from having no idea what to do. You read about outrageous situations in books and daydream about being the hero, and then you find yourself there, trembling like a coward in the darkness. Nothing prepares you for a moment like this.

I don't know how long it lasts. Time isn't moving the same. It's both the longest and briefest stretch of my life.

Then, as abruptly as it started, the gunfire ends. A sinister silence follows, pierced by what sounds like a fleet of tires peeling.

The car.

I knew something wasn't right.

Arbo rockets to his feet again, this time quicker than Marcos's reach. He charges toward the house.

I stay put. Not for fear of what might be in the backyard,

but for fear of what I know is there. The screams all stopped for a reason.

"*¡Cabrón!*" Marcos curses under his breath. His forehead buckles in wrinkles large enough to cast shadows in the moonlight.

Arbo's heavy footsteps fade down the trail. He makes it about halfway to the house before Marcos sprints into the darkness.

A few seconds later, Gladys and I relent and follow. I don't know why. We just do.

Ahead, Arbo disappears around the wall into the backyard. "*No!*"

Marcos's shadowy outline freezes. Then he turns from the entrance to the backyard and races along the wall toward the front of the house.

I don't know whether to follow Arbo or Marcos, so I do neither. I stop when the desert trail meets the corner of the wall. Gladys crashes into my back.

Marcos has already disappeared. The entrance to the backyard is paces away, and I can hear Arbo wailing.

My body goes stiff. I don't want to see what he's seeing. I don't want to scream like he's screaming. I want to go back to when I first saw that car. *I should have said something! Why didn't I say something? I could have stopped this. All I had to do was open my mouth.*

Gladys pushes into my back and tugs at my shirt, giving directions as conflicting as what's happening inside my head.

I take a slow, cautious step along the wall toward the entrance. Then another. Gladys clings tighter the closer we get, adding resistance, so each step takes that much more effort.

Step.

Step.

"Stop right there!" shouts an unfamiliar voice from inside the backyard.

Arbo shrieks.

"Where did you come from?" booms the voice.

I slide forward and peer around the wall. Arbo is lying on top of his father's body, his arms outstretched, as if protecting both of them.

The man advances toward Arbo, gun pointed, finger on the trigger, ready to fire.

"Please!" Arbo lifts his hand like a shield.

"I said where did you come from, *hijo de puta*!"

"The bathroom! The bathroom!"

The man looks back toward the house, as if questioning Arbo's answer. I inch further out to get a better view, until the gunman spins in our direction. I yank my head away and stop breathing, terrified he'll hear my gasps. I can feel Gladys—still pressed against my back—do the same.

Silence.

I listen for any sound—steps, whispers, anything.

Nothing.

"Well," he says to Arbo, "you came out too early."

Arbo whimpers.

I peek around the wall again and watch the gunman shrug his shoulders with indifference.

Arbo presses his face flush against his father's forehead. The gunman places the muzzle on the back of Arbo's head.

Everything in me tightens. I've never felt so helpless.

"I'm sorry, Dad. I'm so sorry," he sobs, barely audible.

The man rotates the weapon, back and forth, sweeping in slow circles along Arbo's head. The corners of his mouth drift upward. He's taunting Arbo. Taunting a boy who is lying on top of his dead father.

This is the Mexico we read about in the paper. We're all aware of the violence that surrounds us, but it seems more like wild lore, because it hasn't happened to us. It's on the front page of newspapers, not in our own backyards.

Until now.

Do something.

Anything!

Every scenario I imagine ends the same way—with me taking a bullet, and Gladys too. I can't risk her life.

But if I'm being totally honest, I'm using her as an excuse. Gladys pressing against me provides the perfect cover for my cowardice.

I feel my thigh go damp, and a small river runs down my leg. I'm so powerless I can't even control my bladder. If I had room for an emotion other than terror, it would be humiliation. I hope Gladys doesn't notice.

"Come on!" calls a distant voice from the other side of the house.

"I got one more," the gunman says.

"Then do it. Let's go! Everybody else left already!"

The man taps Arbo's head with the barrel, then again, presses the muzzle flush against him.

"*Adios.*"

I close my eyes. *No! No! Not Arbo! Please, not Arbo too.* I jump at the blast.

My life is disappearing right in front of me. I want to scream as loudly as Arbo had only a moment before. I want to march into the backyard for the gunman to see. What does it matter that I'm still around? What do I have left? My family is gone. Arbo is gone. Nearly everybody is gone. What do I have to lose? I'd die, but at least I'd go down swinging. At least I could tell them how brave they are for shooting up a fifteen-year-old girl's birthday party. At least I'd take a stand.

I want to do all this, yet I remain frozen behind the wall with a wet leg.

"*Oye*, Arbo." The voice is so soft I think I'm imagining it. "Arbo!" This time it's a whispery shout.

I open my eyes and peek around the wall. The gunman is no longer there.

Wait...

He is there, I realize, but he's no longer standing. He lies on top of Arbo, in an unnatural pose. Arbo's legs twitch beneath him.

Five meters away, Marcos approaches with long, slow steps, a gun drawn, aimed at the small pile of bodies.

Gladys pushes around me and runs toward Arbo. She moans, a sound between a cry and a dry heave.

Marcos shoves the gunman's body off Arbo with his foot, still aiming the gun in his hands, ready to fire again if necessary. I reach them in time to see the body roll onto the ground, neck gurgling thick bubbles of blood from where the bullet struck him.

Arbo coughs.

Arbo coughed!

He props himself up and looks wide-eyed at the three of us, then looks down. He's still on top of his father.

"*Papá.*"

"Shh!" Marcos hushes, pointing a stern finger behind him.

Before I can even focus on the house, Marcos thrusts his finger in the other direction, toward the back wall. He grabs Arbo's shirt collar and tries to yank him upward, but Arbo latches onto his father, anchoring himself.

"Idiot, let go! We need to leave now!"

The two pull in opposite directions. In the still tension of the backyard, their whispered grunts sound like screams.

I glance toward the house. There is no movement. But there is another gunman somewhere. We all heard him. It's only a matter of time before he emerges.

As I turn back to the tug-of-war, my field of vision opens, as if I'm suddenly emerging from a tunnel. All at once, I see them. Bodies. Everywhere. Some lie together, embracing each other as though they went down mid-dance. Some lie alone. Some I recognize, some I don't. These are people I know, people I love, people who loved me. This is my world, dumped lifeless in the backyard.

This is what happened while I listened. While I sat in the desert and did nothing.

As my eyes take in the scene, so do my ears. I'm shaken, not by the presence of noise, but the absence of it. Wounded people would scream, grunt, cry for help. These people make no sounds.

Why aren't there any wounded?

Then it hits me. Hard. Each person has a single shot to the head. This wasn't just murder—this was a mass execution.

I puke. Not hunched over or on my knees, but standing upright, in shock. First my bladder, now my gut. Vomit dribbles down my chin, my shirt, my leg. And I still feel cleaner on the outside than on the inside.

I hear soft sobs and turn to find Gladys weeping over a body. Her mother? One of her younger sisters? I can't tell from where I'm standing.

My mother and father lie somewhere. I don't search for them. I don't want to. I can't.

I break.

I turn to the dead gunman and kick him with everything I have left in me.

Marcos says something to me, but I ignore it. I fall down

and cry. I pound my fists into the hard-packed dirt. Dull jolts rocket back up into my arms. It hurts, and I want it to. I want the pain. I want to feel anything other than what my heart feels.

They're all gone, and it's my fault. Everyone. All I had to do was say something about that car.

Next to me, Arbo struggles—with himself, and with Marcos. Finally, he lets go of his father. With Arbo untethered, Marcos is able to pull him up. They both tumble backward onto the ground.

Wasting no time, Marcos springs to his feet and again directs us out of the yard with his finger.

Slowly, we move. Knee by knee, foot by foot, we lift ourselves from the soil, separating ourselves from our people, choosing to accept—or at least concede to—their fate and ours.

Only we're too late.

"Finish it already, Rafa! We need to get out of—" A man strides from the house into the backyard and stops.

He has some kind of rifle in his hand.

"Marcos!" Gladys screams.

Marcos doesn't need the warning. He shoots first. The bullet misses, but it sends a message.

Rather than return fire, the gunman runs for cover. Marcos shoots again. This time the bullet hits him, right in the knee. The man stumbles and drops his rifle. He howls, rolling and clutching his leg, then he pops back up and lunges off balance on his good leg toward the small, stone-stacked wall of an outdoor cooking pit. Marcos fires again, but misses.

A stream of nearly indiscernible cursing and threats spews from behind the low barricade.

Marcos is half-crouched, thrusting the gun outward with two stiff arms. He steps toward the gunman slowly, oozing determination.

I wonder why he approaches so cautiously. We can all see the man's rifle, out of reach and useless. Then I get my answer. A small handgun rises over the pit and fires a blind shot toward us.

Marcos stumbles backward and fires. The handgun launches more bullets in our direction. Arbo, Gladys, and I all charge for the back wall. Marcos is at our heels, firing twice more behind him as he runs. It's enough cover for us to clear the yard.

More bullets fly as we blaze beyond the wall.

"Come back and fight!" the man yells.

None of us, not even Marcos, turn back. We tear out into the darkness, toward the plastic bench where we'd been sitting when all this started.

"Rafa! Rafa! *¡Hijos de putas!*"

I feel a strange emotion at the man's cries. Empathy. A vicious, sinister empathy. I feel his suffering, and I enjoy it. The dark hope that we're leaving his world empty fills me. I nearly smile. A hatred swells in me that I've never known before.

"You're dead! Marcos, I know your name. You're dead! All of you!" The man's roaring threats fade as we flee.

We stop when we reach the car seat, far enough from the house that we can continue running if he starts chasing us with his wounded leg, yet close enough to keep an eye on what's happening at the house.

Panting, my hands on my knees, I see one of our cigarettes, still burning, smoke drifting up at the base of a long trail of ash. I'm struck by how suddenly my whole life vanished.

"You killed my brother. *¡Mi hermano! ¡Pinche culeros!* You're dead! *¡Muertos! ¡Muertos! ¿Me escuchan?*"

We hear him. But none of us acknowledge his screams, at least not to each other. I can barely stomach it. His attack wiped out my whole family, and he's upset that his brother died as a result?

We hide behind the bench seat and watch the gate to see if he tries to follow us. He doesn't. Several minutes later, a car door shuts and a revving engine fades into the night.

We wait for a few more minutes, but nobody arrives. No police. No ambulances. No neighbors. Nobody. Fear rules. And we are alone in our fear.

WHERE
TO
GO?

We need to run, but where? None of us have an answer. So none of us even ask the question. We are paralyzed, each trapped in our own abyss, trying to gauge its depth as we fall. To call this shock feels like an understatement. If you break a finger, you can go into shock. Grief, rage, confusion, disgust, fear, regret, hopelessness, isolation, fatigue—they all overtake me until I'm numb. It's like some heinous grand finale of emotional fireworks, marking the end of everything that was important to me.

Marcos lies flat on his back in the dirt, staring into the emptiness above.

Gladys is turned on her side, curled next to Marcos, her head resting on his chest. I can't see her face, but from her sniffles, I can imagine her tears.

Arbo sobs on the bench with his head buried between his knees. His body convulses, staying still for several seconds, then balling up in a spastic but muted wail, as if he's stuck in a loop of denying and remembering what has happened.

As for me, I'm embarrassed to admit it, but I just want to die. I don't want to be here. I have nothing, not even the will to push beyond this moment. It's ironic. I survived because I was a coward, and now this same lack of courage has taken my desire to live. But I'm not going to grab the gun from Marcos to end it. Not now, at least. I don't have that kind of determination. I don't care about anything. I can't even move.

I don't know how long we stay here. One minute? Ten minutes? If I were alone, I'd probably stay here forever.

It's Gladys who finally speaks.

"We need to go somewhere safe."

"Like where?" Arbo asks. "Your house? How long do you think it'll take them to find out where that is and bust in looking for our *pistolero*?" He looks toward Marcos, who still grips the gun in his hand.

"You were a second away from having a bullet in your ear," Marcos says.

"I know. I wasn't blaming you…"

"Good. Because they're not looking only for me."

"I was just saying that they know your name."

"They'll figure out who all of us are."

Marcos's words linger as we think about this. He's probably right. He slaps his hand against the dirt, causing Gladys to jump, and says, "I should have shot him. I should have snuck back to the wall and put a bullet in his forehead."

"You were the only one of us who did anything," Gladys says. "So stop. But we can't stay here."

"She's right," Marcos says to Arbo and me. "We can't stay."

We don't need to ask why. When you live in northern Mexico, you come to know certain things. There is a reason why the police haven't arrived yet. The line between the law and the lawless is so thin it hardly exists. I'm not saying the gunmen were police. But the police were involved. Somehow. Through bribes or threats, maybe moles. We're taught from a young age to approach the police with the same caution as we would anything in the desert that rattles. It would be unwise to be here when they arrive.

"So what now?" Arbo asks.

"We can't go to any of our houses," Marcos says. "Or to any of our friends…or family. We can't bring this into their lives."

"So nobody we know. Great," Arbo says.

"Like we have any family left," I blurt out. I'm an only child. And now I have no family. Of course, Marcos meant aunts and uncles and grandparents, and I have those, the same as the rest of them. But as of this moment, my parents are gone. It's hard to see past that.

"Stop," Marcos says.

"Stop what? It's true," I say.

"You know what I meant. We're not talking about"—his head turns slightly toward the house—"them right now."

"Who made you king?" Arbo asks. "My family is lying dead in the dirt back there. I'll talk about whoever I want."

"*I* made me king when I was the only one with enough sense to run inside and find your dad's gun."

I had no idea my uncle even had a gun. Welcome to northern Mexico.

Marcos continues, "You think I don't get that...that"—he stumbles—"that we're orphans? Well, I do. But now isn't the time for it. We have to get the hell out of here, or we're going to join them. Does anybody have any money? Maybe we can get a place for the night."

We check our pockets. Altogether we have about fifty pesos, not even enough to buy four tamales.

We sit in silence for a few minutes, thinking through our lack of options. As we do, our gazes turn toward Arbo's backyard, as if we're all considering the same question that no one wants to ask.

The police will steal whatever money they find on the bodies, but even so, there are limits to what we're willing to do.

Lights from the neighboring houses begin to flicker on, as silence and curiosity lures those who had not attended from the safety of their homes.

"We can't let the neighbors see us," Marcos says. "We don't know who talks to who around here. We need to leave. Now. I don't care where we go."

Marcos waits for someone else to contribute. I have an idea, but planning our escape feels too practical right now. I'm not ready to move.

"Come on, Gladys," Marcos says. He stands and pulls Gladys up with him. They take several steps along the path.

Arbo looks to me to move. I don't. He elbows me, beginning to panic as Marcos and Gladys leave us behind.

I break.

"I know where we can go," I offer.

"Where?" Marcos asks, turning.

"Arbo, do you remember Señor Ortíz? What do you think? Would he help us?"

"If he's still alive," Arbo says. "Maybe. I don't know."

"How do you know him?" Marcos asks.

"School sent us to his house on one of those volunteer days. He lives by himself outside of town," I say.

About two years ago, our school sent groups of us out into the community to help others. Most kids went to churches, homeless shelters, or other organizations, but Arbo and I went about ten kilometers outside of town with one of our teachers to visit an older man. I think his wife had died a few years before. He put us to work tending a few animals and the small plot of land he farmed. He worked beside us, and we spent much of the afternoon talking. He seemed lonely.

We promised to visit but haven't been back since.

"Would he tell anybody?" Marcos asks.

"I don't think he has anybody to tell." The parallel between our situations occurs to me, and I feel guilty for not having visited.

"Okay, next question. How do we get there?" Marcos asks.

"I know the way. We should drive. The truck is in front of the driveway."

"And the keys?"

"*¡Dios mío!*" A shrill cry comes from the backyard. The neighbors have discovered the scene. More screams follow. "*¡Qué demonios!*"

My pulse quickens. Their cries sound too familiar, like ours only minutes ago. I lose myself in them.

"The keys, Pato! Where are they?"

"They're behind the gas tank door," Arbo says.

I nod.

Marcos stands and we follow. Arbo takes the lead, and we sneak along a separate desert trail that winds behind several other houses, eventually dumping us into the street.

As we approach the truck, I see several neighbors cautiously approaching the backyard. I look away. I can't watch. Marcos grabs the keys and jumps in the driver's seat, while Gladys gets in the front passenger seat. There is no back seat, so Arbo and I climb into the rusty bed of the truck. I open the small window in the back of the cab so we can give Marcos directions.

He starts the engine and we crawl down the street. A few blocks later, we pass my house. As it disappears into the distance, I watch one more piece of my life slip away. We turn toward the desert and ride into the void ahead.

FINDING
PURGATORY

Arbo and I lie flat in the bed of the truck, as hidden as possible. We share a rolled-up tarp as a thin headrest and try to lose ourselves in the starscape as we ride beneath it.

We don't talk. I don't know what to say. To talk about my loss would seem to lessen his, and to talk about his loss would be to ignore everything I'm thinking. And to talk about our collective loss is too big to handle. So I don't try. I assume he agrees. I suppose that's a sign of true friendship—knowing when to be quiet. We pass the ride with our shoulders pressed against each other, letting the small warmth remind us that we're not completely alone.

I gaze up at the sky, my thoughts spiraling, tormenting me. How can the trillions upon trillions of stars, planets, moons all appear exactly the same night after night, while my life is nothing like it was yesterday or even an hour ago. High above me hovers Scorpius's tail. It looks as it always does, its stinger angled right at me. My eyes search for one single difference. None. Nothing has changed. I know it's not true, but it looks that way. It's like seeing yourself in the mirror from one day to the next—you age, but you don't notice. It takes a haircut for you to feel any different. The universe looks boundless as always, but I feel bald.

"¡*Oye!*" Marcos calls for my attention from inside the cab. "¿*Adónde?*"

I sit up and point him left. We're outside of town and only a few kilometers from Sr. Ortíz's house.

"Go slowly," I say, minutes later as we approach. "Stop here and let us out. We'll go knock."

He stops about thirty meters before the house. It's exactly how I remember it. A small house built from large concrete blocks—like dusty Legos—with a sheet metal roof.

Arbo and I hop out of the truck bed. We walk slowly.

We step in front of the headlights, and our tall shadows loom before us, ominous, as if they might rise up and strike us down.

"What if he has a gun?" Arbo asks.

"Then we quickly remind him who we are."

Arbo's question rattles around in my head with each step, along with others that I opt not to share with him.

What if Sr. Ortíz doesn't remember us? What if he doesn't even live here anymore...and somebody else does?

I hadn't thought through our arrival until now, and as we creep through the dark, I'm scared—and becoming more frightened the closer we get. I've seen what guns can do.

And I doubt Sr. Ortíz gets many visitors, let alone unexpected ones late at night. No lights were on when we pulled up, and no lights come on as we approach. I don't like that we'll be subject to his gut reaction as he's startled out of bed.

Arbo looks at me as we reach the door. I can't tell if he's shaking or if my own trembling is skewing my vision.

"I guess we knock?"

Arbo nods.

I tap at the door.

Nada.

I tap again. Harder this time, but not so hard as to seem aggressive.

Again, nothing.

I press my ear against the door. Still nothing.

I scan the area again. The house looks occupied. A small bucket sits several meters from the front step. I walk to it and give it a light nudge with my foot. It shimmers. Water. My stomach drops.

I go back to the house. We need the help of whoever is on the other side of that door.

I knock louder.

"Sr. Ortíz, it's Pato and Arbo. We were here about two years ago with our teacher, Sr. Valle. Do you remember us? We need help."

No response.

"Sr. Ortíz, *está allí?*"

Stronger knocks and louder words still go unanswered.

We go back to the truck.

"Is the door unlocked?" Marcos asks.

"I don't know," I confess.

"Try it."

"We can't just walk in there. It's his house."

"Then give me a better option."

I can't.

"If he slept through your pounding and yelling, he's not going to wake up when you walk inside," Marcos reasons.

"Then how do we wake him?"

"Carefully."

Neither Arbo nor I move.

Marcos steps out of the truck.

"Wait, he doesn't know you," Arbo says.

"Then you go."

After a brief standoff, Arbo says, "There's a flashlight in the glove box."

Gladys finds it and hands it to Marcos, and with reluctance, Arbo takes it.

We return to the front door. I try to remember what it looked like inside, as if that might somehow prepare me to go in. I recall it being a simple, two-room interior—a kitchen/living room in the front and a door to what I assume is a bedroom in the back.

I take a deep breath, grab the knob, turn it, and push. A long squeak fills the silence as the door swings inward.

I can tell from the smell why our knocks went unanswered.

A pungent, putrid odor seeps into my lungs, making me nauseous.

Arbo points the flashlight inside, swinging the beam across the kitchen in front of us and into the living room to our left. There, my suspicions are confirmed. On the coffee table sit one empty and one half-full bottle of tequila.

"It smells like crap," Arbo whispers.

He holds the beam on what is clearly Sr. Ortíz, lying motionless on the couch. I recognize his slender frame and ears, which slant away from his head, like they're propped out by toothpicks. He looks more than a few years older than I remember him, as though this place, this life, has aged him beyond his years.

"Sr. Ortíz," I say.

No response.

"Shake his arm," Arbo tells me, as if his holding the flashlight prevents him from doing this himself.

I walk toward the old man, stopping at the farthest point where I can still lean over and touch him. I poke a finger into his arm, and he lets out a tiny grumble.

"Sr. Ortíz."

I poke him a few more times, harder, until I finally do what Arbo suggested—I grab his arm and shake it. He jerks his limb back with an angry groan. Vile breath fills the air.

I jump. But it's for nothing. His arm lands in a near-dead flop, and the groan ends as quickly as it began.

I point to the door, and Arbo and I go outside to regroup.

Marcos approaches, and we explain the situation.

"I don't know what to do," I say. "He's not going to wake up."

"Well, we can stay in the truck or we can stay in there. Either way, he's going to wake up to four strangers on his property."

Arbo and I look at each other, as if the other will provide the answer.

"*¿Lo conocen bien?*" Marcos asks us.

"Like I said, we met him once, two years ago."

"Here's how I see it," he says. "No matter where we are when he wakes up, he's going to be hungover, confused, and trying to figure out who the hell we are. I really don't think he's going to wake up and shoot us. But I'd rather we be in the same room with him. That'll at least give us a chance to explain."

"So we just wait for him to get up? Do we stay awake?" Arbo asks.

"If you can sleep, go right ahead."

None of us respond.

"I hope he doesn't mind, but I think I need something of his right now." Marcos grabs the flashlight from Arbo, walks inside, and returns with the half-full bottle of tequila. He turns it upside down and takes a long pull. Then he holds the bottle out for us to do the same.

Gladys reaches for it, which surprises me. I don't know why. I don't know her well. Like Marcos, she hoists the bottle in the air, but there is something tremendously sad in watching her do it. I'm probably being *machista*, but where Marcos seemed defiant, her turning the bottle skyward is like a surrender.

Like I'm in any position to judge. I'm next in line.

I'm not uptight, but I don't drink. I've tried it—I just never liked it. Especially tequila. It tastes awful, it burns, and I don't have much stomach for it. But tonight, under these circumstances, I can't find a good reason not to drink. I don't take the bottle because I like alcohol—I take it because I want punishment. I don't know why I survived when so many others died, so I might as well suffer. And if the tequila somehow dulls my senses, that would be a welcome change.

I get the hurt I was looking for. Less than a minute after muscling down the drink, an even greater force launches it back up. I turn and spew what little remains in my stomach. Then I step outside the reach of the headlights and drop to my knees. I flop to my side and surrender. I cry tears I didn't think I had left in me. I cry for my mom. For my dad. For me. For Arbo. For my aunts. For my uncles. For my cousins. For so many people. I try to remember who was there and who was not. I cry for not having mentioned anything to anyone about that damn car. I cry for the "surprise" my dad will never be able to tell me about. I cry for a world where something like this could happen, and for a future where I'm stranded alone in it.

Arbo comes over and sits down next to me. He lays his face, wet and warm, on my shoulder. We cry together.

Arbo is my best friend, but this is not something we do.

"What are we going to do?" he asks, in snivels.

"I don't know. I don't know." I repeat it a few more times, but I'm no closer to an answer.

"They're all dead."

"And it's my fault," I say.

"What do you mean?"

"I saw a car. When we first got to the party. A creepy, black car was parked outside the house. Someone was sitting in it."

"Just one person?"

"I don't know. I saw the driver, but I thought I saw someone in the back seat too. And I didn't say anything. To anybody. Nothing! I almost did. Like that helps. And now they're all dead."

"What were they doing?" Arbo tenses. He lifts himself off my shoulder and sits fully upright. Our bodies are once again separate.

"Just sitting there, smoking and looking threatening."

"Threatening *how*?"

"I don't know. Just threatening."

"You don't know that it was them," Arbo says, slumping back onto the ground.

"Really? Who do you think it was? The backup band?"

My sarcasm lingers in the air. Arbo doesn't answer for a while.

"Maybe it was. Besides, what would it have changed?"

"Everything!"

"How?"

"I don't know. Maybe we could have stopped the party?"

"Because of a weird car?"

"Maybe somebody would have gone outside to scare them off," I argue.

"Whatever. These people aren't even people. They're animals. Nothing would have scared them. They don't care. You saw what they did. And there were more than two people. It was going to happen. You can't change that."

There isn't a good way to respond, so I don't.

"I'm scared, Pato."

"I am too."

"*Why?*" He stretches out the word, and I know that he's referring to the bigger question.

"I don't know."

"I don't understand. We're not in their stupid, crappy world. We're not narcos. We're good people. It was Carmen's *quinceañera*. A fifteen-year-old girl…" His voice fades as he buries his face in his hands. "She was so excited. It was all she could talk about for weeks. And now… She's gone. Forever. It was a birthday party! *No lo entiendo.*"

"I don't get it either."

"I want to kill them."

"I know."

"No, I *really* want to kill them. I'm not just saying it,

like something you talk about but won't do. I—want—to—kill—them," he says, sitting more upright, as if each word inflates his pudgy frame. "I'm going to kill them."

"Yeah."

"Let's do it. You and me."

"What? Kill them?"

"Yeah. Let's make a pact. We kill every one of those *cabrones*."

He holds out a hand. I don't know if I'm supposed to grab it, shake it, pound it, or what. I just stare.

"Are you in?" he asks.

As if two high school kids are really going to take on a gang of drug-trafficking thugs. *Narcos*. It's not going to happen. But Arbo doesn't really mean it. I know he's just blowing off steam, and I should let it go. Still, I can't. There are too many thoughts swirling around in my mind to control any of them.

"What's the point?" I ask.

"What do you mean?"

"I mean, who are we going to kill?"

"What do you mean, 'who'?"

"*Who* are we going to kill? Who is 'them'?"

"The *hijos de putas* who killed our families, who do you think?"

"But who *are* they?"

"I don't know. We'll find out. What are you getting at?"

"Nothing," I say. "I just… I don't see how that makes it

any better. And it's not like we're after one person. Or even two people. You heard what it was like—it sounded like there were ten of them, twenty of them. That's more than we can shoot."

"So we kill five of them. That's better than none."

"And after that, then what?" I ask.

"Then the world's better off."

"Is it?"

"Yes!"

"What world? *Our* world? The one where we still can't go home because we've killed five more of them, which only gives them five more reasons to kill us. It doesn't stop. It doesn't solve anything."

"Why are you standing up for *them*?"

"I'm not."

"Yeah, you are. You should be saying, 'Arbo, I want to shoot these guys between the eyes, just like they shot my mom.'"

"Screw you." I shove him. Instantly, I regret it.

"Screw me? Screw you." He jumps up and shoves me back. "What do you think our families would want?"

I don't like the answer I'm about to give.

"They'd want us to live."

"Like cowards?"

"Like people who stay alive."

"I don't give a crap. They killed our families. We can't just do nothing. It's not fair!"

"And I don't give a crap either. You want to know what I wish? I wish I had been in the backyard. I wish I had jumped in front of my mom to stop a bullet, even if the next one was going to kill her. I wish I were dead. Not here, not with you, not with Marcos and Gladys, not having to deal with any of this. What do I have to live for now? The hope that I might kill a couple of bastard *narcos* before I die? What a happy life. And I thought I was living a fairy tale before." I stand up and walk out into the desert. "I'd rather be dead."

It's not fair to lay that on him. I knew it as the words were coming out of my mouth, and that's all I can think as I walk away. Still, I walk.

Several minutes later, Arbo follows me. I knew he would, just as I would have followed him.

"Truce," he says.

"I'm sorry," I reply. "I don't know how we do this. I mean, look at us. We're in the middle of the desert and the only person in the world we can turn to is a drunk. And we don't even know if he'll help us."

Arbo nods. Then he says quietly, "I'm glad you weren't in the backyard."

"Same."

I wipe away tears with my knuckles and we pound our wet fists.

We walk back toward Sr. Ortíz's house and sit down in the perimeter, where we had been before the fight, while Marcos and Gladys remain on the front stoop, with the door open to keep an eye on Sr. Ortíz. I don't hear much of their conversation. They speak softly, so I don't try. We give them their space, as they give us ours.

The hours pass. Like hands on a clock, conversation moves forward, but keeps sweeping back to the same places, over and over.

Sometime before sunrise, exhaustion overpowers grief, and we sleep.

— — — — — — — — —

"Get up," Gladys whispers.

It's shortly after sunrise. She points to Marcos, who is at the door.

"He's waking up," he mouths.

We tiptoe to the door and peer inside. Sr. Ortíz lies with his back toward us, his face buried in the couch. His shoulder tilts and his arms stretch upward. He's going to roll over—and see us.

Marcos nods to me.

"Sr. Ortíz," I say, in the most unthreatening tone I can summon.

He turns over with a shimmying roll. It's not slow, and it's not hurried. It's unnaturally normal, as if he had asked me to wake him up at this time.

He stares at us with warm, questioning eyes, more bewildered than startled.

"It's Pato. I came here about two years ago with—"

He holds up a hand for me to stop, then presses his fingers to his temples and squints. It's hard to tell if he's thinking or massaging a headache.

"Not so loud, please." He looks to the coffee table as though he wants to reach for the bottle. Only the empty one remains. "You came here with"—he squints at Arbo—"this young man and your teacher. I remember you. Is this your new teacher?" He nods in Marcos's direction.

"No, it's my friend Marcos. And that's his sister, Gladys."

"So, should I ask why you're in my living room, or is that part of what you're about to say?"

"Sr. Ortíz, we're in trouble. We're in a lot of trouble..."

I let my tongue loose. I don't hold back on anything. I give him grizzly details I don't want to relive. Ever. But I do it because I need him to feel what we've been through. This is our one pitch for help. If he says no, then we'll be cast out into the desert at daybreak, without shelter, to be hunted.

Halfway through, he moves to one side of the couch, making room for me to sit. As I continue, his eyes glaze over, and I know he sees our world through the same sorrowful filter I do.

"I'm so sorry," he says. "All of your parents... They're all...?"

We all nod.

"I'm sorry we came here like this," I say. "We didn't know where else to go."

"We couldn't go to any friends or family, because if they're looking for us, they'll look there," Marcos adds. "We had to go someplace where they wouldn't connect us."

"*Narcos*," Sr. Ortíz says in a scornful tone. "They're not people. They're pests. No, they're a disease. An incurable disease we all suffer from."

He pauses and looks around at us, as if we might inspire the right words. After a long silence, he appears to let go of what he wanted to say and settles with, "They chased my children away. You can stay. As long as you want."

LA
FRONTERA

"I'm a drunk who lives by himself in the desert," Sr. Ortíz says. "Nobody in that bar is going to think I'm doing anything. That would require them to think about me to begin with—and they don't."

Behind him, the sun has dipped into the earth, lobbing its serene glow above the horizon, catching drifts of sand and clouds that burst like fireworks frozen in the sky. From where I sit, the sunset looks as if it emerges from Sr. Ortíz's silhouette, like a radiant spring.

We have been here for a day. An agonizing day of nothing to do but think about what happened. I've asked Sr. Ortíz for chores—something, anything to help keep my thoughts at bay. But he seems to feel bad putting me, or us, to work. So his respect for what we've been through sentences me to a full day inside my head.

What's worse, we know little more than we did when we left. Most people I know don't have Internet in their house—Sr. Ortíz is no exception. He's not even on the electric grid, so no TV either. None of us owns a cell phone, and even if we wanted to call someone, I doubt there would be any service out here. And the radio in the truck stopped working years ago.

But none of this really matters anyway. They don't report much here about the *narcos*. To dig inside their world is to put yourself at risk. Journalists have seen firsthand what these thugs are capable of. These truths are only whispered. It's for this reason that Sr. Ortíz volunteers to leave us, to head out into the night to listen to those whispers.

"Where is this bar?" Marcos asks.

"Nowhere you would know... People there talk." He stretches out the space between the sentences. He does this often, as if the right words, no matter how simple or complex, are always just out of reach.

"What kind of people?"

"The kind of people who drink too much and talk too much."

"Have you been there before?"

"Not in a while. I stay out here."

"You can't say anything about us. *Anything.*"

"I won't need to. I'm just going to listen. Almost forty people died... They'll be talking about it."

"And you don't think that your showing up will make anybody suspicious?"

"No. Why would it?"

"Are you sure you're okay going?" I ask. "You don't have to do this."

"Look, I know you're nervous. Nothing is going to happen. I'm an old *borracho* at the bar. A drunk. They don't even see me. Why do you think I stopped going?"

For the first time since our arrival, I look beyond myself and see a different kind of sadness—his. I think of the chores he wouldn't let us do today, and it occurs to me that this is a job he wants to take on. It's a chance to break free from whatever keeps him out here.

"Okay. Thanks for going," I say.

Minutes later, he unchains a rusty motorbike, which is leaned up against an equally weathered barrel. He climbs on and snaps his foot down on the kick-starter. Blue smoke peppers the air, popping in an irregular sputter. He waves and zips down the road, bouncing beneath a rising trail of dust.

"We're really lucky we found him," Gladys says.

Lucky.

It's a strange word to use. I wonder if this is how it happens. If this is how you go on. If you simply decide that, in some small way, you got a break. That in spite of nearly everything that could have gone wrong, that did go wrong, a few of the cosmic dice have rolled in your favor. Enough to get by. Enough to leave you with a splinter of hope. And you build from there.

I don't want to agree. I want to hold on to self-pity and

loathing. They comfort me, warming me with the tearful memories of what was.

Still, I nod, like the others, and wonder if they're thinking the same thing.

— — — — — — — —

I'm nearly asleep when I hear a soft sputter in the distance. We all hurry outside and watch as the lone, dim headlight comes toward us, zigging and zagging more than is necessary to avoid the shallow trenches in the rutted road.

As Sr. Ortíz pulls into the yard, his bike slows down and begins to wobble. He puts both legs out to brace himself, but teeters too far to his right and tumbles into the dirt. We race over to him.

"It's not good," he slurs.

"Are you okay?" I ask.

"I'm fine. But it's not good."

Marcos pulls the bike off him and puts him on his feet, which are stable enough for him to stay upright in a continual sway.

"What's not good?" Marcos asks.

"All the rumors. There are a lot of rumors."

"What are they saying?"

"We need to go inside. I need to sit down."

"No, tell us now," Marcos insists.

"How long do you think I'm going to stay standing?" His

words are drawn out, but they lack his normal hesitation. He speaks fluidly, as if the tequila has removed his filter.

We help him back into the house, then carefully guide him around the coffee table to the couch. We sit in the same places where we sat this morning, silent, fearing the worst. And Sr. Ortíz delivers it.

"The gang that did it was La Frontera…" he says, holding on to the slur at the end of the sentence, indicating there's more. But this is enough bad news to process.

La Frontera. The Border. Among the cartels, they have a reputation for being the most violent and aggressive. They don't just kill—they maim, they mutilate, they disrespect every aspect of their victims' lives. And they don't hide it. They flaunt it. They want the attention, the respect. Even their name is arrogant, as if they own and control everything in this unfortunate stretch of land we call home.

"And they're looking for you," Sr. Ortíz continues.

"Are you sure? How do you know?" Marcos asks.

"Because there's a reward."

"For us?" Arbo asks.

"Dead or alive."

"How do they know who we are? There are four of us. Do they know all of us?" Arbo asks.

Sr. Ortíz reaches into his pocket and unfolds a page torn from a newspaper.

"It's from the front page," he says.

He holds it out for us to see. It features a picture of

each of us below the headline DESAPARECIDOS. The edges are jagged where the paper was ripped, as if it had been tacked onto the wall in some *narco* den. Which it surely is somewhere. Not only do the *narcos* know our names, but they now have thousands of papers across Mexico helping them search for us. The headline might as well read WANTED instead of MISSING.

Maybe our photos were published in a genuine effort to find us, but it's much more likely that the *narcos* run the newspaper or that they have influence over those who do.

The photos are our school pictures. I look at mine with envious eyes. I was a different person then, with a different life I desperately wish I still had.

None of us speak. A quiet whimper from Gladys is the only sound. Then Marcos grabs the sheet.

"Where is the article that goes with it?" Marcos asks.

"I just tore off the picture," Sr. Ortíz answers.

"Why did they do it?"

"Because they're *narcos*."

"What does that mean?"

"It means that nobody knows."

"*Somebody* knows."

"I'm sure they had some senseless reason, like wanting to show how tough they are. They're *narcos*. They're not like you and me. They don't have morals. They don't think, they just do, and they don't care who they hurt."

"Are you sure about the reward?" Arbo asks.

"I asked a few people, and they all said the same thing."

"You *asked*?" barks Marcos. "You were only supposed to listen."

Sr. Ortíz shrugs. "I asked a few people I know."

"I thought you didn't know anybody," Marcos says.

"I used to. They're old frien...people I used to know."

"And you don't think that coming out of your hut in the desert to ask them questions about what happened looks a little odd?" Marcos's tone grows angrier.

"Here's what you're not getting—it's what *everybody* is talking about. If I hadn't asked, it would have been strange." He flops his head back onto the pillow behind him.

"And what if you're wrong?" Marcos asks.

Sr. Ortíz tries to stand, but a misplaced hand on the arm-rest lands him back in his seat. Unfazed, the kind wrinkles vanish from his face and he glares at Marcos.

"Look, you little *pinche pendejo*, this is my house. Not yours. You think you're the only one in trouble here? If they come to get you, what do you think they're going to do to me? I'm not a drunk idiot. I'm just a drunk. And I got you answers. So if you want help, then here's what you should say: 'Thank you.' Then shut up."

Marcos turns and walks out of the house.

Sr. Ortíz drops his head back onto the pillow again and that's the end of it. Or nearly the end. One question remains.

"How much is the reward?" I whisper.

He doesn't open his eyes to answer.

"Twenty-five hundred...*dollars*," he says. "Per person."

The reward for the four of us is more than some people make in an entire year.

I don't sleep that night.

ON
EDGE

The four of us sit outside, bleary-eyed, staring at the sunrise.

I doubt that any of us slept. I heard movement all night. Tossing, turning, getting up, walking outside, lying back down, sobs, sighs. Every time I was on the cusp of sleep, the noises would merge with my imagination and jolt me awake. At one point I could swear I heard a car approach. Sure that La Frontera was about to burst inside and gun us down, I stared at the door, trembling in the darkness, waiting for the end. But nothing happened. My eyes closed again. Then the cycle would repeat.

It was the second-worst night of my life.

"We can't stay here," Marcos says. "They have the whole country looking for us. They'll find us. We may be in the middle of nowhere, but it's also the middle of their hive. Somebody's going to notice something. It's not a matter of 'if,' but 'when.'"

He pauses. No one says anything.

"The way I see it, we have three options. One, we can go to whatever family we have left and hope...that things have calmed down...that they'll protect us. But I don't have that much hope, and I don't want anybody else to get hurt."

He holds up two fingers.

"That leaves us with two options—north or south. South is easier. A lot easier. Gladys and I have some cousins in Puebla who could help us, and I don't think the gangs are strong down there. But we'd still be in Mexico. We'd still be within their reach. We'd have to live every day looking over our shoulder. I don't want to live like that. Which leaves us with one option." He points north. "We cross the border."

"Aren't they building a wall?" Arbo asks.

"Who knows. And even if there is one, then we climb it. Or we go underneath it. I don't know how people get to the U.S., but they do it. Every day. And once we get there, we're free. We leave this *chingado* country and the gangs behind."

He looks at me, then Arbo.

"You guys need to decide for yourselves, but Gladys and I are going."

"When?" I ask.

"I'd leave now if we could, but it's too risky. We were on the front page of yesterday's newspaper. I don't like it, but we're stuck. We have to chance it here for a few days."

We both nod.

"Sleep on it," he says. "But you need to decide soon. For

now, we need a couple of rules. First, same as when we got here, no contacting anybody. No friends, no third cousins, nobody. If one rumor gets out, we're toast. I don't like that Ortíz was out hammered and chatting people up, but I guess it was necessary. Second, stay on the lookout. For anything. Nothing happens out here, so if something does, we have to act. If somebody drives up that road, we leave. At that moment. Car keys stay in the car. We keep an emergency bag packed—food, water, other supplies. Whatever you're doing, be ready to run."

— — —— — — —— — — —

Arbo and I sit with legs dangling out of the back of the truck.

"What do you think?" he asks.

"I'm not thinking. I don't want to. I can't," I answer.

"I know."

We fall silent, listening to the tiny squeaks from the lip of the truck bed as we swing our legs.

"This is home. It's hard to—"

"Don't worry," he cuts me off. "*No te preocupe-th.*" Sometimes he makes fun of his lisp to lighten the mood. I think this is one of those times. "We're good. We don't need to talk about it. Any of it. Right now at least. We're either dead, running for our lives, or we have a few days to decide."

"I'm hoping it's the third option," I say.

We hear the hum of a small, low-flying airplane. We both jerk around and watch intently as it passes in the distance.

"Yup," he answers.

— — —— — — —— — — ——

I wake from a nap that afternoon and walk from the shelter of the house into a flood of sunlight, reflecting off nearly everything, smacking me like it always does at this time of day.

Gladys sits alone near the edge of the garden, beneath a slender overhang of shade from the roof of the well.

She has mixed fertile soil from the garden with other crushed leaves into three small piles of different colors. On the cracked dirt in front of her, she spreads these out with several small branches into a canvas of desert landscape.

As she does this, a beetle walks onto her hand. She slowly raises it to eye level and watches as the insect skirts through her fingers.

She isn't like other girls. Not in a tomboy kind of way, she just seems free-spirited. And quietly confident about it.

Watching her, I'm reminded of a time a few years ago when a group of boys found a toad outside of our school. First, they put it in a girl's backpack. She screamed until they removed it. Then, they chased other kids as the frightened animal peed in the air. And finally, they tossed it back and forth as if it were a ball. I just watched. Not Gladys.

She stepped into the middle of their game, marched toward the boy who had caught the toad, and simply held out her hands. He handed it to her.

"Hey, where are you taking it?" one of the boys asked.

"It's not a toy," she said. She walked to the edge of the schoolyard and released the toad.

I always wished I had done what she did. It was the right thing to do. Gladys has her own compass. That's not easy, especially where we're from.

I snap back to the present. She's looking at me. I have no idea how long I've been staring. But I'm busted.

I walk closer.

"That's amazing," I say.

"Thanks," she answers. The beetle is gone, and she grabs a fistful of the darkest soil. She drops it in front of her, then brushes it upward with her finger into the sweeping arm of a cactus.

"Where did you learn to do that?"

"My sister. She called it sand-scaping. I paint, so she wanted to find something of her own." She pauses and looks down at the work. "She was a lot better at it."

"I'm sure she was."

Neither of us speak. All conversations now have these awkward pauses, when we mention someone we lost and none of us know how deep we want to go.

"But this is really beautiful. I can't do anything like this," I say.

"Sure you can." She pinches a few fingers full of the lighter-colored soil and dribbles it into the corner of her piece. "Do what I did. You can put it right next to where I dropped that dirt."

I lean into the shade and follow her instructions, creating a small pile of soil next to hers. She grabs a stick, flicks it out and upward from her pile about a dozen times, then hands me the stick and tells me to do the same.

When I finish, two wiry shrubs sit side by side on the dirt.

"The real talent is figuring out how to do it the first time. Once someone shows you, it's not that hard," she says.

"Says the person whose little shrub looks much better than mine."

"They look the same."

"What do you do with it now?" I ask.

"Nothing."

"You just leave it?"

"What else can you do?" she asks.

"Nothing, I guess."

"Right. So you keep it in here." She points to her head. "That's the only place you can hold on to some things."

As if on cue, a small gust blows some garden debris across her earthen canvas, skidding through the scene as though the wind itself were now captured.

We both stare at the ground.

"Are you guys going to go with us to the U.S.?"

I pull out of the shade.

"I don't know. I…" I still don't know what to say, or how to think about it.

"I'm sorry. I wasn't trying to push. Or maybe I was, and I shouldn't have been. It's a hard choice. Let's not talk about it." She's quiet for a moment. "I'm doing this to take my mind off of everything. I mean, what else is there to do, other than go crazy, thinking about what happened, reliving it, regretting it? I'd rather create something and get lost in it. What do you do?"

"I don't know. I don't, I suppose."

"So you just think about what happened?"

"Pretty much. Over and over."

"I'd cry myself to death," she says.

"That doesn't sound so bad sometimes."

"What do you like to do?"

"Play soccer, read."

"Sr. Ortíz found a soccer ball. Marcos plays. Why don't you play?"

"It doesn't feel right to play. That's something you do to have fun. I don't want to have fun. I shouldn't be having fun."

"Do you think I have fun when I do this?"

"That's different. It's like…being creative. You can be sad and artsy, but you can't be sad and play soccer. They're different emotions."

"Soccer isn't an emotion," she says with a slight smile.

I frown back. "But it's enjoyment. That's not where I'm at."

"Can you be sad and read?"

"Yes."

"Then read."

"Show me a book and I'll read it." Sr. Ortíz is apparently not a reader. I haven't seen a book in days.

I get that feeling you have when you're being watched, that itch from the fringe of your awareness. I turn back toward the house. Marcos. His cheeks pulse as he clenches his jaws. He locks eyes with me for several seconds, then he turns and walks inside.

— — —— — — —— — — ——

Later, in sight, but too far away to hear, Marcos and Sr. Ortíz talk. I pull my hand to my forehead to shade my eyes. Marcos throws his arms in the air. They're arguing. I stare for a few seconds, cupping one ear to listen. I still can't hear anything. Then they see me. Their discussion quickly ends.

They know something we don't. I can tell. It's more than an argument. It's a secret.

Marcos says something and walks toward me. Sr. Ortíz looks concerned. I make eye contact with Marcos. His lips purse as though he's about to say something but is waiting until he's close enough to share it. Then, before reaching me, his intent vanishes. He nods at me and looks away, as if he changed his mind from one step to the next. He strides past me and enters the house.

Sr. Ortíz stays where he is. I take a step toward him. He drops his head, turns, and walks to the shed.

I let him be.

— — —— — — —— — — ——

"You guys remind me of my sons," Sr. Ortíz says to Arbo and me.

The normal early evening wind is nowhere to be found, leaving the heat of the day like a blanket on top of us. Arbo and I sip some *horchata* that Gladys made from a cool pail of well water. Sr. Ortíz has moved on to the fermented stuff, but he isn't wiped out yet.

"How?" Arbo asks.

"A lot of ways. Pato, you look like my oldest. In fact, we almost named him Patricio too. But there's more than that. It's the way you get along. I watch you talk. I see how you appreciate each other's company. Your families were close, weren't they?"

"Our dads were brothers and best friends."

"I knew it. You learn how to act like that. Someone has to teach it to you," he says, with a somber tone.

"So your sons are friends?"

"They're best friends. They live together. They work together. You can't pull those two apart with a crowbar."

"Where are they?" Arbo asks.

"Far from here."

"In the U.S.?" I ask.

"Farther. In Canada. They're good boys, like you two. Always have been. Though they're not really boys now. They're men."

"How old are they?"

"Not that old, but probably old to you. Ignacio... Iggie is, well, let's see, he has to be about thirty-one. And that would make Mateo twenty-nine. No, wait." He sucks in a gulp of air and chases it with a swig of tequila. "I still mix them up." He stops and closes his eyes. "Mateo's twenty-seven."

"Mix up who?" Arbo asks.

"I have another son. No, I *had* another son."

"I'm sorry," I say.

"For what? You didn't do anything. It was those *cabrones* who killed your... It was the damn gangs. They did it all."

The conversation falls silent. You don't ask about these things. I know far too well. People tell you when they're ready.

"I have to go," Sr. Ortíz says.

He stands, leaving Arbo and I sitting by ourselves. He hovers over us for a few seconds, then sits back down.

"No, you know what? I never talk about it. I never have anybody to talk about it with. And now you're here and... You two, I'm so sorry to say, know exactly what this is like."

We nod, not knowing exactly what's coming, but in what direction it's headed.

"I had three sons. And a daughter. She's fine. She lives in Canada with Iggie and Mateo. So, four kids in all, and they were all good kids. Kids who knew right from wrong and did the right thing. Or at least that's what I thought. Diego was the second. Right between Iggie and Mateo. He was smart—too smart sometimes. I used to tell him he should be a lawyer. He was so good with words. Maybe that's why it took me so long to see it. I should have seen it sooner. Maybe I could have done something about it."

He speaks like we aren't even here, head tilted upward, as if looking at his thoughts drifting across the evening sky.

"You know what I hate most about telling this story? It makes Diego seem...like he was just another one of them. Another *chingado* gang member. He got caught up in it. I don't know how. And I was so slow to figure it out. He always had an explanation. And I always bought it. I even took his dirty money. You never think that someone in your own family, someone you love more than yourself, could lie to you. Or could do things that you would hear about on the news and wonder what kind of parents had raised someone like that."

He continues staring into the sky.

"One day, Diego never came home. By that point, I'd found out what he was doing, and he knew that I knew. We argued about it. A lot. I figured he'd moved out. But a week went by. No Diego. A month went by. No Diego. Six months. Every day, I'd sit outside at dusk and wait. I'd look out at the horizon—for hours—and scan it back and forth, sure that he'd appear. He was my son. He couldn't just be gone. If you look out there long enough, you imagine things. I saw him come home a thousand times, but he never did. He never—"

His voice cracks. I turn away. I can't watch him. I'm already tearing up. From the corner of my eye, I see him wipe his arm across his face.

"You know what's funny about when I would imagine him coming home? It was always as a little boy. He used to drag his feet and kick up dirt as he walked, no matter how many times I asked him not to. That's what I'd see. Little puffs of dirt coming closer and closer until I could almost hear that little kid talk, and talk, and talk. I guess that's how I thought of him. Or how I wanted to think of him—as my innocent little boy. I couldn't think of him as a *nar*…as one of them. Knowing what he was… It's a curse. It's my biggest regret. I couldn't change him. I tried. I wish I'd never found out. Do you have any idea how awful it is to have your memories spoiled? It's like losing him twice. I don't want to think of him that way. So most days I don't. He's my little boy who will never come back. Mateo and Iggie tried to find him. They got shot at three times, and the last time, they were warned to stop looking and to leave Mexico."

He refills his glass with a hefty pour.

"So they did. They left. Within a year, I lost all my sons. And two years later, my daughter, Lupe, went to join them in Canada. She said she couldn't stand living in a war zone. I don't blame any of them. Once this hits home, it's never home again."

He swirls his drink around in his glass.

"My wife died a year after Lupe left. They said it was a heart attack. I didn't need a doctor to tell me it was her heart. Now my kids want me to move to Canada, but I know what they went through to get there, and I'm too old for it. No, actually, I'm not. I'm too stubborn. This is where I've lived my whole damn life. The *narcos* stole so much from me already. I'm not going to let them take my home. What's left of it anyway."

I put an arm around his shoulder. Arbo does the same.

I want to ask him about his argument with Marcos, but he didn't want to talk about it before, and I'm not going to press him after the story he just told. I let it go. For now.

The final traces of light dwindle, and I stare out into the darkness, wondering what's left of my home.

_ _ _ _ _ _ _ _ _

I wake early the next morning and step outside. The sun sits like half an orange on the horizon, turning the dwarfed desert plants into a field of lengthy shadows. There is a faint beat and familiar sound coming from behind the house. I peek around the corner. Marcos is juggling a soccer ball.

He doesn't appear to be aware of my presence. He's in the moment. His eyes, narrow and determined, never leave the ball. Left-left-left-right-right-right. The ball leaps from foot to knee to head to chest as though this were the final cut of a how-to film on grace with a soccer ball. He's no less of an artist than his sister, his canvas is just a soccer field instead.

But the longer I stare, the more I see beyond the grace. I see what fuels it. With each tap of the ball, he pops a crisp and rigid breath, as if releasing a tiny sliver of anger and frustration. Soon the grace falls completely from view. All I see is his rage as he attempts to slowly bleed it dry.

For an instant, his eyes dart toward me. The ball falls to the ground. He taps it in my direction.

I walk-dribble the ball over to him.

"You can do better than that. I've seen it," he says.

"You've seen me play?"

"A couple of times. You play midfield, right?"

"Yeah."

Marcos is the star of our varsity team. I play on a much lesser team. I don't stink, which is about as much as you can say. I'm in the middle of the pack.

I'm surprised and a little flattered that Marcos knows even this much about my game. Where we're from, everybody (okay, everybody except Arbo) plays soccer.

"You're fast, that's a big help there. And you handle the ball well. I saw you score a goal against Dorado. That was awesome."

That was my shining moment of the season. My lone goal, and against our rival high school. It was a long bomb over my head from our defense, which I chased down past our offense. One fake-out later, it was only me and the goalie with a few seconds remaining in the game. I nearly bungled it by jamming it into the goalpost, but the ball ricocheted in.

Marcos saw my goal. My chest puffs out, as if I'm holding a deep breath of confidence.

"Oh yeah, I remember that one. Thanks."

"Of course you remember it. You won the game. You don't forget those."

Coy never did work well for me.

"So, let's see what you've got," he says. He pops the ball into the air, taps it short with his left foot, and then bumps it off the side of his right foot over to me.

I knee it into my nose.

He chuckles and I turn red.

"Relax."

Again, he kicks the ball into the air toward me. This time, I receive it with my right foot and bounce it high. I tap it three times with my forehead, then back down to my left foot and over to Marcos.

"Nice," he says.

After that, I relax. I even enjoy it. I feel guilty using the term "fun" with anything right now. But this moment at least feels not un-fun. That's as far as I'll go.

After about fifteen minutes, Marcos drops the ball into the dirt and speaks in a low voice.

"I don't like you talking to Gladys."

"What?" I ask, though I heard it perfectly.

"I've seen you talking with Gladys—a couple of times. I'm asking you, as a favor to me, to please not talk to her."

"We're the only five people out here."

"Then act like we're four," he says.

"I'm not trying to do anything. We're just talking."

"Look, you're a nice guy. I know that. And we've all been through a lot of... I don't even know what to call it. But I'm the one looking after her now, and she doesn't need any of this."

"What's 'this'?"

"Don't play stupid. I see the way you guys talk," he says.

Gladys and I have really only had one meaningful conversation. Otherwise it has been a few words here and there. But I don't think it's worth arguing that point.

"I'm not trying to do anything."

"Good. Then it shouldn't be a problem to stop." He knocks the ball toward me. "I'm going to grab something to eat. You should keep playing. That's when I get the best practice—when it's just me and the ball."

Only moments before, it had occurred to me that I could learn to like Marcos. That feeling vanishes.

He nods as if he hasn't asked me for something ridiculous, then strolls back toward the house.

"What were you and Sr. Ortíz arguing about?" I call after him.

"Lunch."

I punt the ball over his head to the other side of the house.

— — —— — — —— — — ——

"I need for each of you to grab a leg," Sr. Ortíz says, as calmly as he would ask us to hold a glass of water.

I've been rehashing my conversation with Marcos most of the morning. This quickly pulls me back into the present. The cow lies on her side, panting heavy puffs of snotty air. Arbo and I gawk at the gooey hooves poking out from under her tail.

"Come on, you can do it," Sr. Ortíz says, running his hands in long, gentle strokes along the cow's belly.

As I grab a hoof, I notice the calf's black nose, like a turtle's head, slowly sliding outward from sloppy folds of what look like guts. *¡Qué asco!* I look away. But as my face twists and my stomach churns, a voice inside my head chides me. I've seen the gruesome end of life, which I will never forget. I might as well give myself the chance to see, in gory detail, the beauty of how it begins.

I look back down and firm my grip.

"Ready?" I ask.

"*Sí,*" Arbo says.

"A short, smooth pull," Sr. Ortíz says. "It'll take a couple of times for him to come out."

With each pull, the calf glides outward. Not at a steady pace, but in spurts, punctuated by squishing and slurping sounds. A thin, milky film runs across the calf's partially exposed body like a torn blanket. Everything is slimy. And stinky.

On the fourth pull, the entire back half of the calf

emerges with a gush of internal juice that hits my leg so hard it splashes up to my shirt.

The calf opens his eyes and lets out a tiny squeal.

My nausea is gone. This isn't revolting. It's amazing.

— — — — — — — — —

"Quick, get inside!" Marcos shouts.

"Why? What happened?" I ask.

"Someone's coming! Get inside!"

"Shouldn't we drive away?" Arbo asks, panting mid-stride. "I thought that was the plan."

"Gladys is sleeping. There's no time!" Marcos barks back. "Get inside. And hide!"

We zip by the side of the house near the garden and fly through the front door. As we do, I see the trail of dust in the distance. A car is approaching. It's still far enough away that I question whether we could have been spotted.

Sr. Ortíz goes outside to meet the car. We wake Gladys and take turns peering through a small crack between the door and wall. Although we can't all see what's happening, we can hear it quite well.

"Pablo, how are you?" the man asks.

"Good. I was hoping it might be you," Sr. Ortíz says.

"You been playing soccer?" he asks.

"No. Why?"

"I saw a soccer ball."

"Oh, that. Um, well, I found it...out in the desert. And it seemed like a waste. So I brought it back."

"Okay. I thought maybe you had visitors. I thought I saw somebody else as I was driving up."

"Somebody else here? No, no. Must have been a skinny cow."

"Yeah, must've been. Did you get a new pickup truck?"

"Oh yeah, yeah, I did," Sr. Ortíz stutters. "I've been thinking about building onto the house and I needed something to haul materials."

"It's nice to have that *gringo* money coming in."

"My family is good to me."

"Are you feeling okay?"

"Yeah, I feel fine. Why?"

"You seem a little on edge."

"I don't know. I guess I'm excited every time you show up and bring me something."

"I won't hold you in suspense any longer then. I've got two for you this time. One came in a few days ago and the other one came yesterday."

They chat a bit more before the man departs.

Sr. Ortíz comes inside.

"He knew we were here," Marcos says.

"No, I don't think so," Sr. Ortíz answers.

"He knew someone was here. I don't like this."

I don't often agree with Marcos, but I think he's right this time.

"He's a nice man. He stays and talks with me every time he brings me a package. He doesn't have to do that."

"How long does he normally stay?" I ask.

"Twenty minutes maybe. I usually ask him inside for some *horchata*."

"And this time, you didn't," Marcos says.

"No, but—"

"He knows something is different," Marcos interrupts. "The question is whether he puts it together and if he talks about it. And we're not sticking around for that. We're leaving tomorrow."

"It's too soon," Arbo says. "Our pictures were in the paper two days ago."

"Do you want to wait here until the next car drives up? How quickly did we escape? Because that was the plan, remember? And we didn't. There wasn't time. We hid, and we didn't even do a good job. If we try that when the *narcos* come, it's over." He stares at Arbo, then me. "Gladys and I are going. You guys need to decide by tonight if you are coming with us."

— — — — — — — —

I knew—we all knew—this moment was coming. The visit this afternoon only triggered the inevitable.

Arbo and I shuffle away from the group silently, toward the truck. Neither of us want to be the first to speak. As I scoot onto the edge of the truck bed, Arbo picks up a small rock and points to a cactus about ten paces away.

"If I hit it, we go. If not, we stay."

He hurls the rock. He comes closer to hitting me than the cactus.

"Maybe you should try," he says.

"What do you want to do?" I ask.

"What do *you* want to do?" he asks back.

We both know the answer and neither of us like it. We catch each other's gaze and look away.

I see a small pad of paper lying behind us in the bed of the truck. It's ancient. The pages are so old they've yellowed. There is a drawing on the top sheet, sketched in blurred pencil lines.

For as long as I can remember, Arbo has drawn a cartoon series of a character he invented based on his one childhood fascination—wrestling. His name is El Revolucionario. The Revolutionary. Or Revo, for short. At eight syllables, it takes a hefty breath to say it. Arbo was so young when he named him that merely pronouncing it was an accomplishment. El Revolucionario rides bulls, travels the world, plays the drums, explores caves on the moon, fights crime, builds skyscrapers from clay, and more. He is a catchall for anything Arbo wants to do. But he mostly wrestles.

What El Revolucionario is not is well drawn. Arbo struggles with stick figures. It's his curse. He knows it. He's taken plenty of grief for it. And it's one of the things I admire most about him. This inability has never stopped him.

I stare at the paper. El Revolucionario is in the backyard. I can't tell exactly what is happening, but it looks like a different turn of events. Stacked bodies lie in a pile beneath a sign: La Frontera. Crowds cheer. Among them, a man with a T-shirt that reads *Papá*.

"It's my backyard," he says.

"I know."

"It's this pencil." He points next to the pad. "It's older than I am. It makes everything I draw look like crap." He smiles. Slightly.

"You should ask Gladys to draw some Revo stuff for you. I think she's good at it."

"I talked to her about it. She said no. She said wrestling is violent."

I don't ask if he showed her this particular work.

"I miss my dad," he says. "It's not fair. He was a good guy. Everybody liked him. And he worked his ass off...for everything. His business, that *quinceañera*, his family. Then somebody comes and takes it all away from him. No warning. They just take him out. And now he's gone, and everything he worked for."

"I know."

"I mean, I miss them all, but I really miss my dad."

"I miss mine too," I say. "We had a lot of good times, us four."

"We were going to be partners," he says.

This hurts. To the core.

"I know. I guess you and I still can be," I answer. It's more head than heart, but it's the side of the conversation I'm on.

He nods. "Do you remember how my dad used to joke about how they switched us?"

"Yeah, every time the other person would win at something."

"Which was usually you."

"Not always."

"Which is why I said 'usually.'"

"Oh, is that what that word means?"

"But really, do you think he was joking?" Arbo asks quietly.

"Are you serious?"

"Sort of. I mean, we're kind of shaped differently. I'm pudgy like your dad and you're skinny like mine," he says.

We are shaped quite differently. The name Arbo actually comes from his nickname, Arbusto. He's short and round, like a bush.

"We come from the same gene pool. It all gets swapped around," I say.

"Maybe."

"And then we got the other half from our moms," I add.

"Did you just call my dead mom fat?"

I did. "Ummm."

"Are you serious?"

If someone had asked me minutes before if I thought I would be capable of laughing at any point over the next year, I would have said no. And yet here I am, on the verge of callously snickering about one of our dead parents. There are some moments for which I have no explanation.

"*Cabrón*, there's a boundary," Arbo says. "You can talk about how you were my dad's lost son, but when you call my mom pudgy…"

"That was your word."

"So, you admit it? You just used a different word."

"What are you talking about?"

"That's it. I'm going to ask her spirit to curse you."

"Just don't ask her spirit to sit on me," I say, rolling onto my side in the bed of the truck and crying. I put my hands up in a defensive position, fully expecting him to hit me.

"If you were Marcos, I'd kick you in the balls."

"And if I were Marcos, you'd hurt your foot." I take my voice an octave lower. "Remember, 'I'm the only one who thought to grab a gun. My balls are like steel-plated steel.'"

"Shh. He can probably hear you. I bet he has super-hearing."

"No, he can't hear us. He's too busy listening to his own brilliant thoughts."

"'Look how beautifully I juggle the ball.'"

"I bet Marcos could kick Revo's ass," I say.

"And now I *am* going to hit you."

He doesn't.

"By the way, he told me not to talk to Gladys," I say.

"At all?"

"Yeah."

"Why?"

"He thinks I'm trying to hit on her."

"Why?"

"Because I talked to her," I say.

"I talked to her too. There are only five of us out here."

"That's what I said!"

"You didn't do anything else?"

"No. Like what?"

"I don't know. Anything," he says.

"No. Nothing. You know him, he's intense."

"Yeah. That's how he is." He draws in a breath and holds it, as if deciding whether to continue on with his thought.

"What?"

"Nothing," he says.

"'Nothing' means you're lying. What?"

"I never told you... I used to have a crush on her."

I knew this was what he was going to say—and I already regret asking the question.

"Gladys? When?"

"Last year."

"No, you never told me."

I leave it there. He doesn't give any more information, and I don't ask for it.

We hear a noise and turn. Sr. Ortíz has opened the shed and is handing a few things to Marcos and Gladys, presumably supplies for the trip.

"We need to decide," Arbo says.

"Let's each say our answer on three, whatever it is."

He nods.

I hold out my hand and begin to count. "*Uno, dos...*"

"U.S.," we say together.

For me, it comes down to this: I understand the power of revenge. If I had the opportunity, I'd shoot everybody in the gang. Twice. I'm not proud to admit it. I'm not that type of person. But I still would do it. I'd do it for my family. I'd do it for Arbo's family. I'd do it for Sr. Ortíz's son, even though I know he was part of the machine, part of those who took my life from me. That's what's twisted—revenge lacks precision. It's a hurt that wants to lunge in any direction to hurt back.

Because I see this in me, I know that Rafa's brother won't stop. He'll hunt us for the rest of his life, and if he can't hurt us, he'll hurt those near us. I need to put as much distance as I can between me and anyone I know. I'm a liability in my world. I need a new one.

— — — — — — — —

Within a few hours, we have a plan. Sr. Ortíz shows us letters from his children describing how they crossed the border. They even sketched a crude map. They wanted Sr. Ortíz to join them and provided the name of the *coyote* who guided them across the border from Sonoyta, the closest border town. Our hope is to drive there early tomorrow morning, find this man, and pay him with the pickup truck. None of us know how much a rickety, old truck is worth in the world of human smuggling, but it's all we have.

Sr. Ortíz loads us up with all the supplies he can, then makes a quick trip to town to buy a few extra items—flashlights, canned food, matches, and water jugs.

We're packed and ready to leave before the sun goes down.

I go to the garden to weed one last time. It doesn't need it, but I do. I need a moment to myself.

Within seconds, I'm holding dirt-ridden hands to my eyes, filled with a storm of memories and the realization that I'll never again see my one true home.

I hear steps behind me.

"What's wrong?" Gladys asks.

"Nothing. I'm just thinking," I say.

She steps carefully over the rows of plants and takes a seat.

"I'm going to miss it all too."

She puts an arm around me and lays her head against my shoulder.

This is the first time we've ever touched. It's electric, but not in a romantic way. Her embrace feels so maternal, so unconditional. It's a shocking feeling from where I was only seconds before.

"What?" she asks.

"I'm thinking about my mom. She loved to garden. She had patches of herbs and peppers around the yard. And she put so many plants inside the house, my dad started calling our living room the jungle."

"I always liked your mom. I mean, I didn't really know her, but there was something about her. Some people give you a good vibe. She was one of them."

Whatever sadness I had been feeling vanishes, and I hold on to a separate set of memories—warm, delicate, peaceful. I submerge myself in all of the reasons why I loved my mom and my home. Nobody can take those memories away.

I don't know what to make of this nostalgia, so I don't try. I just let it happen.

Gladys leans in a little closer. It feels wonderful, but I can't fully enjoy it, mostly because of two people who I'm sure are watching carefully.

SONOYTA

The wind flaps the tarp like a drum, booming at a techno music pace just above our heads. We lie in the bed of the truck while Sr. Ortíz drives us to Sonoyta. The ride takes a couple of hours. I think of us—Marcos and Arbo flanked by Gladys and me—like those little hot dogs you get in a can, lined head to toe in perfect order and pressed tightly together. The only other image in my mind is of us in a giant coffin. Hot dogs seem like a more pleasant alternative.

We stop.

"*Ya llegamos*," Sr. Ortíz announces as he unties the tarp.

I pop my head up. We're in an alley, shielded from the border town hustle that hums in the distance.

"*Rápido*," he says, as we all jump out of the truck.

My stomach tightens. We are wanted and our pictures have been published across all of Mexico for all we know. But our options are limited. It's too hot to stay in the truck, too suspicious to sit in an alley, and too obvious to stay together. Well-intentioned Sr. Ortíz bought several cheap wigs during his supply run yesterday, but they only make us look like we're trying to hide. So the plan is for us to split into our natural pairs and blend in the best we can. Sr. Ortíz will find the *coyote* and negotiate our deal.

We plan to meet back in the alley in three hours.

We wish each other luck, then Sr. Ortíz drives away. The four of us quickly pair off and walk in opposite directions.

Sonoyta is just a car ride from home, but I've never been here. I've never been this far away. I've heard stories. Some good, some bad. I've seen pictures. I've dreamed of what it must be like. But I've never experienced it.

I want to enjoy it, but I can't. I feel neon. All eyes seem to land on me—shop merchants staring through their windows, schoolkids giggling in their gray-and-white uniforms, locals going about their business, tourists snapping photos, everyone. I'm $2,500, walking down the street, waiting for someone to snatch me up.

"I feel like someone's going to recognize us," I say softly.

"You're paranoid," Arbo says.

"¿Y tú no?"

His answer lags a few seconds, as an armored police car that looks more like a tank rolls down the street. We both turn and face the window of a small convenience store, watching the reflection of the vehicle slowly pass.

"No, I'm thirsty," he says.

"We don't have any money," I remind him.

"No, but we could ask for water."

"I think we should get off this street and go someplace where nobody's going to see us."

"You're overthinking this. We're just two kids. Look around. There are people everywhere. Half of them aren't even from Mexico. Nobody is going to recognize us," he says. "If you're worried about it, we could get you that enormous sombrero."

He points across the street to a tourist stand that has colorful sombreros as large as umbrellas.

An SUV stops in front of the stand, and a few people who I assume are tourists on their way to our beaches step out of the car. With their flip-flops, bright shirts, enormous icy drinks, and fists shoved deep into tall bags of chips, they look like they're from another planet.

"They think we actually wear those sombreros." He smiles. "You could pull it off, I think."

"Okay. You're right," I say. "Let's ask. I'm thirsty too."

We walk inside the convenience store. The clerk glances up at us, then looks back down at the counter, to whatever he was reading.

"Excuse me," I say. "Can we get a cup of water, please? It's really hot outside."

"Sure," he says, without looking up. "The faucet is in the back."

Arbo and I find the water, fill cups, and return to the front.

"Thank you," Arbo says.

"You don't want to buy anything? Chips? Candy?" he asks. His head stays down while his eyes roll up toward us.

I'm about to answer when Arbo jabs me in the back. I turn to look at him. He's wide-eyed.

"No thanks," he says. "We're in a rush. We have to meet our parents."

He tugs at my shirt, looks at me, and then slings his gaze to the counter for a fraction of a second. Long enough for me to follow his eyes.

My stomach drops.

Spread out on the counter is a newspaper. Even upside down I can read the giant headline: STILL MISSING. Our four pictures hover just beneath his nose.

"You guys okay?" the clerk asks.

"Yeah, yeah. We're fine. We, um, we're late," I say, scooting toward the exit. I bump into Arbo and nearly spill my water. "Thanks again!" I say as we fly into the street.

Without speaking, we speed walk to the nearest corner.

"One point for Pato," Arbo says.

"I didn't want that point."

We round the corner and walk in no specific direction, other than away from any kind of action. Eventually we find a small park with a bench in the shade and a distant view of the highway border crossing. We take a seat.

We're close enough to the United States that we can see the other side. Cars stop, documents pass back and forth, and the cars disappear quickly into the distance, requiring no more effort from their drivers than the mere press of an accelerator. And here we are, on the cusp of trying to cross fifty kilometers of desert by foot. If we're lucky, we'll make it in three days— according to their letters, that's how long it took Sr. Ortíz's children. These people could reach the point where we'll exit the desert in less than thirty minutes. Assuming that highway even leads in the direction we're going, which is nothing but a wild guess. I know little about where we're headed.

I wonder what life might be like had I been born over there. If I were the one sitting in the SUV with a frosty drink in hand, on my way to play at a fancy resort. Would I have noticed me watching from the sidewalk? Would I have merrily taken pictures while armored police cars rolled down the streets? Would my life have been better or just different?

In a way, it's hope. For a blissful moment, I'm looking at the finish line and not focusing on the road to get there.

"*Algún día*," says Arbo.

I guess we were thinking the same thing. *Someday.* My dad used to say that Arbo and I shared a brain, or at least borrowed each other's thoughts.

"What do you think it'll be like?" he asks.

We've both seen dubbed TV shows and movies from the U.S., and we live close enough to the border that we've heard stories about people who crossed and now live over there, but none of that says much about what *our* lives will be like once we get there.

"Peaceful. I hope," I say.

"Yeah, me too. But, I mean, other stuff, like where do you think we'll live?"

"I guess we'll *have* to get an apartment."

"Where?"

"I have no idea."

"I've heard people say Seattle is a good city."

"I don't even know where that is."

"I think it's close to Los Angeles. That could be another option."

"Sure."

"What about Canada?"

"Maybe. Let's take it one border at a time."

"Good point, but wherever we end up, we should live together," he says.

"Definitely."

"Are you ready for it? Not the crossing part, but once we're there. Once we leave. We're never coming back here again. It's all gone."

"I don't know if I'm ready for it, but I'm ready to move on," I say.

"Everything's going to be different. I think. I don't know anything about the U.S.," he says. "I don't play soccer, but at least I know *how* to play. I don't know anything about basketball, American football, baseball. I don't know English. I don't know if the people will like us. I don't know if I have to go to school. I don't know if I *can* go to school. I don't even know if I *want* to go back to school. Do you?"

"I suppose I want to go. But I don't have a good reason other than school is the only thing I know that might be the same. Math is the same here and there. Science is the same. Like you said, everything else changes."

"But won't classes be in English?"

"Good point. I guess we should have paid more attention in English class. We'll have to learn fast."

"I think I want a sports car when we get there," Arbo says.

"Where did that thought come from?"

"Right over there," he says. "I want something like that one." He points several cars deep in the line on the other side of the border. I have no idea what kind of car it is—it's shiny, red, and much lower than everything else. "Only I want it in yellow," he adds.

"You'd barely fit in that thing."

"Shut up, *flaco*."

"Well, if you get that car, then I'm going to get a truck."

"We have a truck here."

"No. A really nice one. Like the kind that has a back seat."

"That's just a bigger truck."

"I like trucks," I say.

"Why not get something better?"

"Why?"

"Because you can."

"Okay. Then you can. Have your fancy yellow car. Just don't park it behind my truck. I'll run it over."

"We'll need a house with a big driveway then."

"And a swimming pool."

"And a huge yard."

"And statues."

"And a big gate."

"And guard dogs."

"And a butler."

"And a maid."

"Who only wears bikinis."

"Then we'll need two of them."

"And a helicopter."

It's my turn. I pause. "Seriously, we're not going to have anything. We're going to get there with nothing."

"Like I said, I don't know anything about the country, but why do you think so many people try to get over there? Maybe not everybody is rich, but"—he turns toward the line of cars at the border—"a lot of them are."

We spend well over an hour in banter between reality and fantasy, at times pleasantly unsure of which is which.

Arbo checks his watch.

"Time to go?" I ask.

"*Sí.*"

We're the first to arrive in the alley. Within a few minutes, Gladys appears. She's alone, holding a small plastic bag looped around one of her wrists.

"Where's Marcos?" I ask.

"Who knows," she says.

"What do you mean?"

"He said he had something he wanted to do." Her eyebrows push together and slant down, forming a *V*.

"Like what?"

"I have no idea."

"So you've been by yourself the whole time?" I ask.

"For most of it," she says. "It was okay. I like exploring."

"What's in the bag?" Arbo asks.

"Wouldn't you like to know," she says.

"What, are you trying to imitate your brother?"

"Ha, ha," she says in a dry tone. "It's something for Pato."

Arbo turns to me with an annoyed expression.

"And nothing for me?"

"Well, I almost got you a wrestling outfit. You know, to cross the desert in style."

"Ha, ha," he says.

"So, you want to see it?" she asks me, as she dips her hand into the bag.

"*Sí.*"

She pulls out a book and hands it to me.

"*Las aventuras de Huckleberry Finn,*" she says.

"What is it?" I ask.

"It's a gringo book. I think it's about a boy who leaves home to go on an adventure. It's not exactly the same as us, but what is? I thought you might like something to read."

It's beyond thoughtful. If Arbo weren't here, I might have teared up. We've passed the it's-okay-to-cry phase, but not when it comes to something like getting a book from a girl.

"Thank you," I say.

Wait. Something occurs to me—and because we share a brain—Arbo asks the question before I can.

"How did you get this? I thought none of us had any money."

"I just did," she says.

"What do you mean you 'just did'?"

"I mean, you don't need to know about everything that I do."

"You stole it?" Arbo asks.

"No, I didn't steal it."

"Well, then how else did you get it?"

"That's none of your business."

"*Dios mío*, you're just like him," Arbo says.

"What's that supposed to mean?"

"What do you think? Full of secrets, just like your brother. Pato and I sat on a bench and laid low for three hours. And, by the way, our pictures are still all over the newspaper. But that didn't stop you. You were off robbing bookstores and doing who knows what."

Throughout our time at Sr. Ortíz's house, there wasn't much space to hide emotions, whatever they were. But I've never seen Gladys truly angry. Until now.

And in this anger, I see something else for the first time— Marcos. She doesn't look like him, and it's not just that she's being secretive. She projects him. Her jaws press together, pulsing her cheeks outward. Her pupils dilate and she stares at Arbo as if the rest of the world doesn't exist.

I hold my breath.

Then, as quickly as he arrived, Marcos vanishes, like some inner demon she has learned to control.

"Okay. You really want to know how I got it?"

Arbo nods. He's as taken aback as I am.

"Here's what I'll do. I'll tell Pato. But he can't tell you anything, except that I didn't steal it."

I both love and hate this plan.

"He'll tell me," Arbo says.

"No, he won't."

Both look at me. This is the part I hate.

"I…" I freeze. There is no right answer. Either choice is wrong. Still, they stare at me, each expecting me to support their side.

Arbo finally does the humane thing and bails me out.

"Fine. Tell him. I'll let it go."

He's lying. We all know it. But it gets me off the hook.

I follow Gladys around the corner. Her eyes, which had been so fierce only a moment before, now look at me playfully and send my stomach into a free fall. In an instant, I forget about Arbo. I forget about the deal. I just want to be here.

"So, you want to know?" she asks eagerly, suggesting that all along, she really wanted to tell.

"Of course."

She checks in both directions to make sure no one is around, then smiles somewhere between bashful and proud.

"I showed my boob," she says.

"You what? To who?"

"To the guy at the bookstore."

My mouth hangs open, but nothing comes out.

"Well, he wasn't a guy," she continues. "He was a kid. He was about twelve."

"Why?"

"Duh. To get the book. I didn't have any money. He said I couldn't take it. It was a store, not a library. So…"

"So, what? Did he ask you to do it?"

"No. There wasn't anybody else around so I made a deal. He was just a kid, and I'm never going to see him again. And you got a book!"

I'm part touched, part flabbergasted, and part…envious.

"I can't believe you showed your boobs to a twelve-year-old."

"Just one."

"One what?"

"One boob."

"Why?"

"I didn't need to show both."

"Don't they look alike?"

"Wouldn't you like to know."

I look right at them. Then I look back up at her eyes, unsure of what's going to happen next. I can feel each beat of my pulse surge through my body.

She simply shakes her head. "You got a book out of it."

I've never felt worse about literature.

Gazing at her, I'm struck by how differently we reacted to this day. I hid. She exposed herself—literally. We faced danger in opposite ways.

I think back to when we were outside the wall that night, Gladys pressing against my back, listening to Arbo scream in the backyard. There was comfort in having two of us there, both afraid to run into the madness. It was an unspoken empathy. And, apparently, one that I had only imagined.

I had been holding her back, wet leg and all.

This is the second time I see Marcos in her. Only this time, it makes me want her. In a way that I shouldn't, just days after losing my family. And it makes me want to be someone different, someone more than I am.

"Remember. You can't tell Arbo. Promise me."

"I won't."

She walks past me and I follow her back into the alley. As we turn the corner, she gives me a smug grin, half for me and half for Arbo. Arbo eyes me like he can't wait to get me alone. Fortunately, before we get close enough to speak, Sr. Ortíz drives into the alley.

"So?" I ask.

"Good news and bad news," he says, stepping out of the truck.

"What's the good?"

"They looked at the truck and said it's probably enough."

"Probably?"

"That's the bad news. I didn't talk with our *coyote*. But

I did find some people who know him and can get in touch with him," he says.

"So what do we do?"

"We wait."

"In Sonoyta?"

"Or we drive back. I don't know which is better or safer."

Both the *narcos* and the police have been known to stop people on the highway, for no good reason. All of us are aware of this.

"How long do we wait?"

"They think they can reach him by *mañana*."

Tomorrow. Arbo and Gladys deflate, the same as me.

Mañana doesn't usually mean *mañana*. Just like *un momentito* can stretch into hours. It's a lie we tell ourselves and others when we don't know.

Still, it's tempting to believe. It's what I want. Today I saw the United States. I was close enough to breathe the foreign air. And in my mind, I've already said goodbye to Mexico. I'm ready to start the journey.

"Where would we stay?" I ask.

"They gave me the name of a motel."

"How much is it?"

"It's not much," he says. "Don't worry about the money. My family has been good to me."

"We'll pay you back for all of this," Arbo says.

"Get across safely. That's all you have to do to pay me back."

We wait another thirty minutes for Marcos, until Gladys finally gets concerned. She and Sr. Ortíz leave the alley to see if he might be somewhere nearby, which gives Arbo his opportunity to corner me.

"So?" he asks.

"So, what?"

"Come on."

"She made me promise not to tell you," I say.

"So that's how it's going to be now?"

"What do you mean?"

"Is she your new best friend?"

"Come on," I say.

"What?"

"You want me to break my promise?"

"I don't have any secrets from you," he insists.

"None?"

"None."

Our eyes lock. He's telling the truth, which makes me feel that much worse about what I'm about to do. I've never lied to him. Never. Until this moment.

"Sr. Ortíz gave her some money."

"So why didn't she just say that?" he asks.

"Because he asked her not to tell anyone. I guess she looked hungry. I don't know. I wasn't there."

Lies. *Mentiras y más mentiras.*

Arbo cocks his head slightly and bites his lip. He's trying to read me. "You remember I told you that I like her, right?"

"You said you *liked* her."

"What's the difference?"

"As in, you *used to* like her."

"Well, I still do."

"Okay... Well, I still didn't do anything."

"Well, you're not acting like that."

"She got me a book. I didn't ask for it."

"Right."

There isn't a good, natural end to this conversation, so I'm thrilled when an unnatural one turns the corner.

Marcos walks toward us. Gladys and Sr. Ortíz are at his side.

"Did you get done what you needed to do?" Arbo asks in a bitter tone, still riled up.

"What do you mean?"

"Gladys said you had something you wanted to do."

He glances quickly at Gladys.

"No. I didn't think we should be walking around together," he says.

We all know it's a lie, but his tone makes it clear that this is the end of the conversation.

We return to the bed of the truck and huddle in a hot, agitated mass beneath the tarp.

COYOTES
ARE
DOGS

After less than five minutes of driving, the truck stops.

A half-dozen men line the porch of the motel. They watch us climb out of the truck, as if it were nothing out of the ordinary. They smoke cigarettes, talk quietly, and mostly ignore us.

I take one look at the motel and have a good idea why they are on the porch and not in the rooms. It's filthy. Most of what could be broken is. Railings bow outward and dangle from the second floor, one threatening to fall with the next gust of wind. Whatever paint remains on the outside is coated with uneven splotches of dirt. Several windows are busted out, leaving empty frames with a few lingering shards of glass. Boards are rotting or already rotted. This isn't a motel. I may not have stayed in one before, but I've certainly seen them, and they don't look like this. This is somewhere you're told to wait. For as little time as possible. A place so unwelcoming you can happily walk into a miserable desert and never look back.

I look again at the men on the porch. They are us, and we are them. Our stories are different, but we are the same. We are all waiting to cross.

Sr. Ortíz waves us toward what should have been the front door but is only the front doorway. The door itself is gone.

As we approach the steps, a truck pulls up behind ours—a flatbed—the kind usually used to haul equipment. The porch empties quickly, leaving only one man behind. The men pile onto the back of the truck, pull their hats low, and ride away. I watch them with envy. I want to start this trip now, not wait around this…whatever this place is.

I make eye contact with the one man remaining on the porch. He nods, and I nod back.

We get a key and climb the stairs to the second floor.

The inside of the motel matches the outside well. There are two mattresses, both of which lack frames. Lying on the ground, they're more inviting to bugs than people. A lone bulb dangles above our heads. I'd sooner cross the border twice than touch the wires that support it. And the toilet, it flushes. That's the nicest thing I can say about it.

We open a door to a balcony, which overlooks an alley behind the building. The whole balcony slopes downward toward an iron railing with flakes of rust that flap in the wind. None of us step outside. We keep the door open for the breeze.

We return to the truck to gather our supplies and carry them to the room, unsure of when *mañana* might arrive.

Marcos and Gladys lie down on one of the mattresses,

eyes closed, surely trying to imagine they are elsewhere. Arbo does the same, though I think he's mostly trying to avoid talking to me. Sr. Ortíz takes the truck to get some food from a market we passed a few blocks away.

Which leaves me alone with my new book. I can't concentrate, with the heat, smell, and mood in the room, so I leave to find a better spot.

I walk downstairs to the porch. The man I had nodded to earlier is still there, alone. I walk to the opposite end and take a seat on the floor, settling into a creaky wooden plank. I open the book.

"*¿Qué lees?*" he asks.

"*Las aventuras de Huckleberry Finn.*"

I know I shouldn't be talking to anyone, but it seems more suspicious to get up and leave.

"Never heard of it," he says.

"Me neither. A friend got it for me."

"Well, it's good to have something to do out there. Something to take your mind off the heat." He crosses to my side of the porch and holds out a pack of cigarettes.

"No, thanks."

He lights one.

"You're young to cross."

"How do you know I'm crossing?"

He laughs. Quietly at first, then louder, turning his head from side to side as if wishing someone else might appear to share in this gem.

"*Claro*. You're on vacation and this is your favorite hotel."

"Are you waiting to cross?"

"I'm waiting to meet up with a friend. And then, yeah, we're going to cross. This is number four for me," he says.

"Wow."

"Do your parents know what you're doing?"

I don't answer.

"Mine didn't the first time I went," he follows up. "I was older than you, but I wanted to prove I was a man. Send them money, you know. Prove I could make it. On my own. I did."

"My parents already crossed over," I say.

"Both of them?"

"Yeah."

"They left you here with other family?" he asks.

"Sort of."

"That's rough, but it happens."

"So why are you crossing for the fourth time?"

"It happens too. I've got a wife. And a daughter."

"So I guess the trip isn't that bad?"

"*No seas pendejo*. It's an *hijo de puta*." All pleasantness falls from his face as he chides me. "People die. You've got a *guía*, right?"

I lower my voice. "We're waiting on a *coyote* to take us across."

He takes a long drag on his cigarette.

"You don't have a clue... *Ni una puta idea*," he says. Smoke chases the words out of his mouth.

I start to speak, but he cuts me off.

"*Coyotes* don't cross. They organize. They're the leaders. You talk to them, and then they set you up to cross with a *guía*. And you know what you are?"

I shake my head no.

"*Un pollo*. A chicken. Just an animal they take across the desert for money. *Y nada más*. Do you know this *coyote* you're supposed to meet?"

"He's a recommendation from a friend."

"He'd better be. If you try to find a *coyote* here, you'll be a fried chicken. That's the number one rule of crossing. These *cabrones* on the border will leave you for dead in the desert."

"Do you and your friend have a *guía*?" I ask.

"*Por supuesto*. Of course."

"Why not go on your own if it's the fourth time?"

Again, he laughs, but only for a second. He drops his cigarette and smothers it with his shoe.

"You need to listen or you could die, okay?"

I nod.

"*Necesitas un guía*."

I nod once more.

"I'm going to say it again. You need a guide. For two reasons. One, he knows the way. Once you step into that hellhole, you start dying. There's no wall out there. You know why they haven't put one up?"

I shake my head.

His eyes widen. He stares at me like he's looking deep

inside of me. "Because that wouldn't make it any harder than it already is. Are you from somewhere near here?"

"Yeah."

"Then you know how hot it gets. Now imagine it even hotter. You've never felt heat like this. It feels like your lips are going to melt off your face. During the day, it's fifty degrees, or one hundred twenty if you measure it like they do up north—I always thought that sounded hotter. And at night, when it cools down, it doesn't cool. It never gets much below the temperature of your body. It strangles you. You know how much water your body needs every day out there?"

I shrug.

"About six liters. Every single day. But you can't carry that much. So you take less than you need, and it's a race to get out. Three days, five days…seven days. How many days do you think you can last? A good *guía* will make it fast. Without him, you can walk in circles for days and have no idea. You don't find roads or water walking in circles. You die. And if not burning alive isn't a good enough reason for you, here's another—the gangs control the border. They charge you to cross if you don't use a *guía*. If they find you alive, that is. And they're looking. You don't want them to find you if you haven't paid anything."

I feel my Adam's apple move down my throat as I swallow a mouthful of dusty spit.

"So you pay either way. Might as well get a *guía*. But do you know what can really kill you out there?"

"No."

"Everything. The sun. The heat. Poisonous plants. No water. Bad water. Snakes. Scorpions. Spiders. Wolves. Cougars. Bears. *Chupacabras*. And that's only the desert stuff. Then there's the human element. If you get caught and you're lucky, you'll meet *la migra*. Their border patrol is your one-way ticket back. All it costs you is a beating. Not much. A black eye, a broken arm. Most people live through it. They're the nice ones. The people you really don't want to run into are the *gringos* themselves. You think they want you in their country? They don't. They look so friendly when they drive by on the way to the beach here, right? Well, they're not. At least not the ones you meet in the middle of the desert, when no one else is looking. They have their own patrols. They ride around in the night, looking to take out their anger on anyone they find. They know what happens when *la migra* sends you back—you try to cross again. So they don't send you back to Mexico. They send you back to God."

I let this sink in for a minute.

"If it doesn't work out with our *coyote*, do you think your *guía* could—"

"You don't get it. Don't trust anybody you meet here. You don't know who I am. You met me on a porch."

"But—"

"But nothing. I could be anybody. Everything, everyone in this town is trouble. You got it? You want to stay alive, right?"

"Yeah."

"Then wait for your *coyote*. And if he doesn't come, leave. Find another one somewhere away from here and then come back. Your mom and dad will wait for you."

I hate that he has no idea how much that comment hurts, and I can't show it either.

An enormous, dusty pickup truck parks in front of the motel. Its loud diesel engine booms with a force I can almost feel in my chest.

"Maybe that's your *coyote*," the man says.

Two men sit up front and two are in the back seat. They're all looking in our direction. They could be here for any reason, but I don't like the way they're looking at us. Or more specifically, at me.

"Relax. They never look friendly."

I don't relax. My whole body tenses. They're passing something back and forth between them. I strain hard to see what it is. Each time I'm close to getting a good look at it, it gets passed again. Finally, it moves to the driver and he presses it flat against the steering wheel.

I leap to my feet and race back into the motel, nearly knocking over the man on the porch. The dingy hallway whizzes past me in a blur. I take the stairs three steps at a time. I start yelling before I even get to the room.

"Get out! Get out!" I blast through the door. "We have to leave, now!"

All three bounce from the mattress to their feet in one fluid move.

"What's wrong?"

I lock the door and bolt it shut.

"They found us! *¡Vámonos! ¡Ahora!*" I say, charging toward the open balcony and looking out. It's a one-story drop to the dirt alley below.

"How?"

"I don't know. They have the newspaper with our pictures in it and they saw me. They're coming! Let's go! Now!"

"Here?"

"Yes! Now!"

Boom!

The room shakes from the pound at the door. It's not a knock. It's an attempt to knock it down.

Gladys shrieks.

"*¡Abre la puerta!*" a voice shouts from the other side of the door.

Marcos blows by me and onto the rickety balcony. He kicks the railing, knocking the top clear off. He kicks again at the bars and the rest of the railing swings downward, clinging upside down by its base. As it does, the entire balcony starts to fall. It stops suddenly, as if catching on something. Marcos tumbles off the balcony to the dirt below.

Boom!

Gladys eyes the balcony. It slants downward like a ramp at a loading dock. She puts a hesitant foot on it, then starts to shuffle toward the edge, to reduce the distance of the jump.

I hear a loud splintering noise. I throw an arm around her

and anchor my other hand on the side of the doorframe. I yank her back as the balcony plunges.

Marcos leaps back, and the balcony crashes, just barely missing him.

Boom! Crack!

The doorframe behind us starts to split.

"Come on!" Marcos yells. He braces himself and beckons Gladys with his arms open wide, just beyond the jagged remains of the balcony, its rusty handrail now protruding up toward the sky.

Gladys jumps. Marcos doesn't catch her but breaks her fall. Almost before they can get out of the way, Arbo launches himself into the alley. He hits hard and flat, missing the edge of the hazard by next to nothing.

He's slow getting up. I'm about to try to jump over him when Marcos yells. "My bag! Get my bag!"

The bags!

I turn, fling myself back into the room, and clutch his bag. *Huckleberry Finn* sits right next to it, where I had apparently tossed it in a panic. I grab it and am about to reach for the other bags when the door snaps open, sending tiny splinters flying across the room.

I don't wait to see who's on the other side. I bolt for the balcony and jump, without looking below. Arbo has moved out of the way, but it doesn't matter. I would have cleared him. I sail to the far side of the alley, hitting the dirt so hard if feels like it breaks my hip. There's no time to whine about it.

I pick myself up and we run. We run hard. We run like our lives depend on it, because they do.

I look back. A man appears in the open balcony door. He's heavy and older. He hesitates, then jumps. He doesn't clear the wreckage, landing on a broken piece of the rusty iron railing. It shoots through his foot. He howls.

We tear down the alley, with Marcos in the lead. Gladys and I nearly keep pace with him, while Arbo trails farther and farther back. As we approach the nearest corner, another man appears. He points a gun in our direction.

Marcos banks a hard left around the corner. Gladys and I are on his heels, but Arbo lags a few seconds behind.

"Run, Arbo!" I yell, peering around the corner.

His arms flail in random directions—left, right, up, down. His frame leans so far forward that with each step he gets closer and closer to falling facedown in the alley. It is the most ungraceful body in motion I have ever seen.

A bullet hits the corner just as he clears it.

The market is three blocks in this direction. Marcos turns up and down different side streets, making the run nearly a kilometer. We keep a pace that Arbo can hold, which still leaves us all breathless.

When we get there, Sr. Ortíz is leaving the market, walking toward the truck.

"They...found...uth!" Arbo wheezes across the parking lot.

"Who?" he asks.

"*¡Por favor!* We need…to go!"

We hurdle into the bed of the truck, crashing into the sides and one another, as Sr. Ortíz climbs in the front and starts the engine.

A thunderous motor revs on the street alongside the market. As a pickup speeds by, the driver turns and sees us.

Screech!

The truck skids to a stop, then turns around, leaving a curling trail of four black marks on the cement. The wheels spin smoke into the air as the vehicle accelerates back in our direction.

Sr. Ortíz punches the gas. The four of us tumble into the back wall of the truck. He takes us down a narrow side alley next to the market. The other truck follows.

Sr. Ortíz makes a hard, tight right around the back of the market. It feels like we're going to flip. The truck behind us tries to do the same, but it's larger and going faster. Its tail end skids and slams into a wall, stopping the truck dead. The tires squeal and spew out puffs of smoke. It buys us a few seconds at most.

We turn down an alley on the other side of the market and soon launch into the street. A block later, they're back on our tail. Within seconds it's clear that, despite their damage, they have the faster truck. Our engine howls at a painful pitch, and we're losing ground.

Marcos reaches into his bag and pulls out a handgun, the same one he used at the *quinceañera*. None of us had forgotten about it, yet we're all startled by its emergence—Arbo, in particular, as he is directly behind Marcos. He flops down low in the bed of the truck as Marcos raises the weapon.

Marcos shoots twice. Their truck swerves and the shots miss.

We soon discover the problem with this plan. An arm extends out of the window of their truck. This is now more than just a car chase.

I flinch as a bullet strikes our truck. Where, I have no idea. Marcos leaps up, fires another shot, then drops back down. I doubt he's even aiming.

I peek over the wall of the truck bed. They're less than half a block away. I glance at Marcos. For the first time, he looks shaken. Scared.

He props himself up, slowly, and raises the gun with both arms.

Again, one of their shots hits our truck. This time, there's no guessing where it strikes—a bullet hole appears just above the back window of the truck cabin, missing Marcos's head by a few hairs. He never even flinched.

Marcos closes one eye and fires.

His expression grows confident.

I pop up my head in time to see their truck swerve off the road. There's a bullet hole in the windshield, right in front of the driver. The guy in the passenger seat is grabbing desperately for the steering wheel.

Marcos remains in his pose. Rigid and frozen.

But not for long.

Sr. Ortíz turns hard around a corner, causing us all to slide into the side wall of the truck bed, including Marcos. As he tumbles, he keeps the gun raised high. When he hits the wall, his wrist smashes into the top edge. The gun soars out of the truck and into the street.

He screams in pain, clutching his wrist. "Stop the truck!"

We keep going.

Marcos steadies himself and pounds on the back window of the cab.

"Stop the truck! I dropped the gun! We need that gun!"

Sr. Ortíz fumbles with the window and opens it while racing forward.

"We can't go back!" He turns hard onto another street. Again we tumble.

"We have to go back! We have to go back!"

The truck continues.

"It's too late! They're back there," Arbo shouts.

"I shot them!"

"You shot the driver. What about the others? You think they can't drive?"

Sr. Ortíz yells, "Turning!"

We all brace ourselves again. Marcos stares at us, looking for support for his case.

It's too late. I'm not sure how I feel about this.

"How is your wrist?" Gladys asks. Marcos still clutches it with his other hand.

"I wish I could trade it for that gun," he says and slumps against the wall.

Sr. Ortíz turns down a few more streets until he finds a highway leading away from Sonoyta. He takes it and we head west, along the border.

OUT
OF
OPTIONS

"We don't have any other options," Marcos says.

"But we left everything back in the motel," I answer.

All we have is what is in Marcos's bag and the book that Gladys got for me.

"All we *need* is food and water. We can stop somewhere and buy that," Marcos says.

"With what money?" Arbo asks.

"I have some," Marcos says.

All of us are thinking the same thing. I'm surprised that Gladys is the first to ask.

"Since when?"

"It doesn't matter. I can buy us food and water."

"What do you mean it doesn't matter? You've had money this whole time?"

"No."

"Then how did you get it?" Arbo asks.

"A friend gave it to me," he says.

"What friend? When?"

"In Sonoyta."

"You broke the rules?" Gladys asks.

Marcos looks away.

"You were the person who came up with the rule," Arbo adds. "No visiting anybody we know. Remember?"

"Sometimes you have to break the rules."

"Well, nobody told the rest of us that," Arbo says.

"You can't tell somebody it's okay to break the rules. Because then it doesn't make any sense to have rules," Marcos says.

"Exactly!" Arbo answers.

"Look, you have to know when to do it. We need money right now, and I got us money."

"Sr. Ortíz could have helped us. Who do you think paid for the motel?"

"Now he doesn't have to. It was a good call. I also got a few more bullets. You want to complain about that also? Seems those came in pretty handy."

"Whatever. No wonder they found us."

"That wasn't how those people found us," Marcos barks.

"Then how did they?"

"I don't know."

"Well, that's the only thing I can think of," Arbo says.

"That's the only thing? What about Ortíz running around talking about us with *coyotes*?" Marcos asks.

"He never used our names or ages. Nothing. No way," Arbo says.

"And never mind the fact that whoever shot at us found us at the same motel that the *coyotes* recommended," Marcos says.

"He never said our names! How could they know?" Arbo asks.

"The truck," I say.

They turn to me with questioning looks.

"What?" Marcos asks.

"He showed them the truck," I say. "It's registered to my dad and Arbo's dad."

"They're not car dealers," Arbo argues. "They're a bunch of thugs. Why would they—"

"Why not? If someone was going to pay you with a truck, wouldn't you want to know if it was stolen? They probably checked."

Whether I'm right or not is irrelevant. It's spilled milk. They found us. What we need to do is stop bickering and come up with a plan. This, at least, accomplishes that.

We sit in silence for a few uncomfortable moments, delaying the inevitable. We all know what's coming next.

"Like I said," Marcos starts. "We don't have any other options. We shot a *coyote*, which means they're looking for us. The police are probably looking for us too. The gangs are still looking for us. They all know we're here and there aren't that many roads going out of Sonoyta. We need to get out of Mexico. Now."

My head is filled with one line, repeating over and over.

Necesitas un guía.

You need a guide.

"If anybody has a better plan, feel free to speak up," Marcos adds.

Nobody says anything. I want to, but I can't. There isn't a good alternative. There isn't even an alternative. I shudder every time I see a car appear behind us. It isn't a matter of whether they will find us—it's when.

Marcos sticks his head inside the back window of the cab.

"Do you know where your children crossed?"

The rushing wind in the open truck bed blurs Sr. Ortíz's response.

"But where exactly? We need to leave. What did the letters say?"

After a few seconds, Marcos pulls his head out of the window, with a flustered expression.

"Pato, you spent the most time with those letters from Ortíz's kids. Do you have an idea where we're headed?"

I read them. I didn't study them like it was a test. We didn't plan on crossing by ourselves, or leaving the letters back at the motel in a frantic exit.

"They went to a town called Ajo," I say. I close my eyes and try to remember the map. "I think it's almost directly north of Sonoyta. Maybe a little west. And we're going west now, so it's probably straight north. Maybe a little east if we go much farther."

"How far from there?"

"They said it's about fifty kilometers, but it's not a straight shot, so it ends up taking longer."

"So how long is it?"

"I don't know," I say. "The letters said it took them three days."

Marcos turns his head and looks to the north.

"We can do three days out there, guys."

A car pulls up behind us. We all tense. Nobody says anything. The vehicle lingers for a few seconds, then passes us.

"Let me put it another way," Marcos continues. "Even if we die out there, we'll live longer than if we stay here. I'm serious. If anybody's got a better idea, then speak up."

Nothing.

"Okay," Marcos says. "Then we get some supplies and get the hell off this road and out of this *chingado* country as soon as possible."

He reaches through the back window to Sr. Ortíz's shoulder, then points to a gas station in the distance. The truck slows down.

Marcos goes into the convenience store with Sr. Ortíz while the rest of us huddle low in the bed of the truck. They make a few quick trips back and forth. The haul: six four-liter jugs of water, a few smaller bottles, about fifteen cans of food, a few rolls of cookies, a can opener, and three small duffel bags to carry everything. I suppose the store is accustomed to stops like this.

We drive, again moving west.

I stare at the water and run the math. I already know we can't carry as much as we'll need, but I can't help it. All that water, and it's still only a day's worth for each person.

"Does it really matter where we leave from?" Marcos asks me.

"Anywhere that looks deserted," I say. Even if we knew the location of a trail, we wouldn't be able to take it. We need to avoid other people.

Marcos taps Sr. Ortíz through the cab window.

"Go a couple of kilometers then find a place to pull off the road. We'll leave from there," he says.

Five minutes down the road, we stop. It's disappointingly perfect. There is nothing.

The afternoon heat is no different here than it was back in Sonoyta, but I feel it more. There's no end in sight. No cool drink of *horchata* around the corner, no shady spot to sit, not even a filthy mattress to rest on while waiting out the fever of the day. We're climbing into an oven. You can see it. The ground shimmers in waves, like the earth has taken in too much heat and can hold no more, sending it back to the sun, roasting us in two directions. I sweat from everywhere. I hoist one of the duffel bags full of cans and water over a shoulder and feel a bead of sweat roll off my nose. I'm already losing precious water.

Arbo slings his bag over his shoulder. The weight causes him to lean to one side. His expression says the same thing I feel—we haven't even started and the load is uncomfortable.

Marcos removes several items from Gladys's bag and adds them to his load. Then he ties two water jugs to the bottom straps of his backpack. If the weight bothers him, he doesn't show it.

Cars whiz by on the highway, each one bringing a potential threat and reminding us that we don't have time for a lengthy goodbye.

"You're going to make it," Sr. Ortíz says.

"It's only a couple of days," I say.

"That's right. A couple of days. You can do it."

He reaches into his pocket and pulls out a slip of paper with an address and phone number on it.

"In case you lost it with your bags, hold on to this. I don't know if you'll make it to Canada, but even if you don't, get in touch with my children. They're good people. And you can consider them family. I'm sending them a letter. They'll know you're coming and they'll find a way to help you."

Gladys had it right from the beginning—we are amazingly lucky to have found Sr. Ortíz. It just took me longer to see this. I don't know how much farther we'll make it from here, but one thing is certain: without his help, we wouldn't have made it here at all.

"Thank you," I say.

"Write me a letter. Let me know when you get there," he says.

"We will," Arbo responds.

As I'm about to step away, something occurs to me—Sr.

Ortíz is staying with the truck. How could I have been so selfish?

"Sr. Ortíz, they're looking for that truck, you have—"

He puts a warm hand on my shoulder and interrupts. "I'm going to drive it back to the gas station and leave it. Somebody will give an old man a lift back into town. Don't worry about me. Worry about you. Get there."

"Thank you. We need to go," Marcos says.

"He's right. Go," Sr. Ortíz answers. He looks at me once more with watery eyes, turns, and goes back to the truck.

Seconds later, he drives away.

This is it. Goodbye Mexico. Goodbye family...what's left. Goodbye old life. Goodbye everything. All of this flashes through my head, but I can't give it much attention. I'm overwhelmed by what lies in front of us—or rather, what doesn't—a boundless emptiness.

We walk into the desert.

And I mean "into," not "through." There are no trails. It's an endless maze of twists and turns to avoid getting poked and scratched. All the vegetation is armored, like each plant is at war with everything else in the desert. Spiny, prickly, thorny, scratchy limbs reach out in all directions. We weave our way through the gaps, sometimes wide and sometimes narrow, trying as best we can to maintain a straight line to the north. Which is an estimation anyway. Among the items left back in the hotel room is our compass. Not only do we not have a *guía*, but we don't even have a tool to point us in the right direction.

At least not during the day. Our only saving grace is that Arbo and I have stared at the night sky enough to know how to find north. For now, we march toward a mountain peak in the distance, which is more or less the direction we want.

Necesitas un guía.

Necesitas un guía.

Marcos takes the lead. He walks fast.

"We need to get out of sight of the road," he says, several times. The two jugs on his bag swing like giant bull testes behind him, clanking together with dull thuds.

The shrubs thin and thicken along the path we make, leaving us exposed to the road some of the time, and shielded at other times.

Gladys walks behind Marcos. Arbo trails her and I bring up the rear. I watch Arbo shift his bag from one shoulder to the other, then back again, as I do the same. We finally settle on putting both arms through the straps and using the bag as the most uncomfortable backpack ever. The thin straps dig deep into my shoulders, grinding back and forth with each step. I try to fold my shirt over several times where the straps press against me, but it never holds. Within minutes I can feel my shoulders getting raw. I can't imagine how I'm going to keep this up for days on end.

Noise from the highway soon fades, and so does our view of it.

Marcos slows.

"We're here," he says.

"Where?"

"Welcome to the United States, *amigos*," he says, pointing to a low fence in the distance. We've walked no more than ten minutes.

"That's it?" Arbo asks.

"Yup."

It stands no more than shoulder high, with posts several body lengths apart and thin strands of barbed wire running between them. I wasn't expecting a wall, but I was expecting something more than this. This fence looks like it would barely keep cattle from crossing. The cacti will slow us down more than this fence.

It feels underwhelming. Way underwhelming. And the more I stare at it, the smaller it seems. Its puny frame is engulfed by the desert. It's inconsequential. It's nothing.

Then I get it. I think back to what the man on the porch said, and I see his true meaning.

The fence is insignificant because it can be. It's a warning. I can almost hear those who built it say, "We don't need a barricade here. Look around you. You don't know what you're up against."

The closer we get, the more worthless and more threatening it becomes.

Necesitas un guía.

Necesitas un guía.

The rusty wire stretches wide as Marcos puts a foot on one strand and pulls up on another.

Gladys ducks and glides through in a quick sweep. Arbo passes through next, though being Arbo, he finds a way to jab his side with a barb. He yips, rips his shirt, and takes his first step into the United States with his chin.

All four of us are soon across, looking at each other as if something monumental has happened. Marcos picks up a rock and wings it back across the fence.

"Screw you, Mexico!"

We watch the rock disappear into the brush.

"Yeah, screw you, Mexico!" Arbo yells. He throws a rock over the fence, then does a small, uncoordinated jig.

Gladys giggles. Arbo's smile widens.

"*¡A la mierda!*" Marcos curses.

"I'm standing at the *frontera*, so you can bite me, La Frontera!" Arbo kicks the dirt at his feet, sending a cloud of dust through the fence.

Marcos throws his chest out, then leans his neck back and pipes a rolling-tongue screech into the air, "R-r-r-r-r-aaaa—haaa!"

Gladys's arms shoot high in victory.

I try to smile, but my nerves take over. I look around to see if anyone can hear us. We are right on the border. *The* border. Of story, of legend, of dreams. But we might as well be on the moon. So famous, yet so desolate.

A few tossed rocks later, our feet move, but the celebration continues.

"Are we U.S. citizens now?" Gladys asks.

"No, that takes eight years," Marcos answers.

"I heard it was five," Arbo says.

"I think it used to be, but they changed it," Marcos says. "It's not as easy now."

"So, if we stay there for eight years, then we're citizens?"

"Yeah."

"But how do you prove you've been there for eight years?"

"I think you take a test."

Pause.

"But why not study hard and try to take it after a year?" Arbo asks.

Pause.

"Then that's what we'll do!" Gladys says.

"You know what I'm going to do, Pato?" Arbo asks me.

"Dance more?"

"Please!" Gladys says.

"No! El Revolucionario is hereby an official U.S. citizen. No test. No eight years. He crossed and he's in!"

"Can you make him stop wrestling?" Gladys asks.

"I second that," Marcos says.

"No! That's what he does. Why should he be any different? He changed countries, not superpowers."

"Wrestling isn't a superpower."

"It's his."

"Fine, then you should also make him rich if he's coming to the U.S. with us," Marcos says. "Unless you want to kill him. I'd be okay with that too."

"No! He can't die. And not everybody there is rich."

"*Órale, güey...* They buy all the *mota* the *narcos* can send them and everything we make in the factories. And everybody I've heard of that moves there sends money back home. So what do you think?" Marcos asks.

"So, does that mean we'll be rich?" Arbo asks.

"In eight years," Marcos says.

"Unless we study hard for the test," Gladys adds.

"I'm studying," Arbo says, then he throws both arms out to his side. "Wait, they don't give you money when you pass the test. Do they?"

"No! The money's not free, you *payaso*," Marcos says. "We'll have to pay our dues for a couple of years, but there's opportunity. Maybe it's three years, maybe it's eight. But if you work hard, you'll get there."

"I don't care about the money," Gladys says. "I want to be a doctor."

"Do you know how much money doctors make?" Arbo asks.

"It doesn't matter. I want to heal people."

"Good for you," Marcos says.

"You know what, I think El Revolucionario should be a doctor, too. Yeah. He's an American doctor now."

"No. You can't just make him a doctor," Gladys says.

"Why not? I just made him an American."

"He can't be a wrestler and be a doctor. Wrestlers put people in the hospital. Doctors get them out. They do opposite things."

"No. There's good and there's bad. That's it. El Revolucionario does good and so do doctors. Same team. And if he puts some bad guys in the hospital, then he'll be a busy doctor...and make lots of money!"

"Ugh," Gladys groans.

They continue their banter as we trudge onward. I zone it out. Crossing the border for them was like some kind of drug. It's as if they forgot about all that we're up against, or why we're crossing in the first place. Not me. I can't, no matter how hard I try. We're twenty minutes into a three-day slog, if we're lucky. The bag feels heavier with every step, the sun pushes against me like a blistering headwind, my neck is scratched from multiple branches I've brushed up against, and I'm already thirsty. Whine, whine, whine. I'm out of sync completely, and I know it. So I keep to myself and stay in the back of our line.

"A toast," Arbo says, grabbing for his bag.

"No," Marcos says.

"Why?"

"We haven't even been walking for half an hour. We drink every hour."

"Who made you God?"

"I'm not God, I'm reason. We have to make it last," Marcos says.

"I'm only going to take a sip," Arbo says.

"On the hour."

"I'm carrying it. I'm going to do it," Arbo says.

"Don't."

"Or what?"

We stop. Gladys stands between the two of them, their eyes locked on each other. Neither move.

"Or we'll end up like whatever's over there," I say, pointing to a group of vultures circling in the distance.

Both turn to see.

"Yeah," Marcos says. "Like that."

Arbo scowls. "Fine."

We start to walk again.

"I want to see what it is," Arbo says.

"What are you talking about?" Marcos asks.

"I want to see what the buzzards are circling."

"Why?" Marcos asks.

"Why not?"

"It's not where we're going."

"It's just off to the side," Arbo shouts back over Gladys's head.

This is a detour from the straight line toward our mountain peak, but not by much. And we're not walking in straight lines anyway.

"It's more or less north," Gladys says.

"Fine," Marcos replies.

Our zigs and our zags curve to our left and the conversation stops. I watch the vultures slice effortlessly through the wind, rising and falling on the current of air drifting up from where we are, from where it feels still and suffocating.

Never in my life have I so wished I were a bird, even one as disgusting as a vulture waiting to eat rotting meat.

Soon they are high overhead and our steps soften, each of us looking for the unfortunate creature that's meeting, or has already met, its end.

"Oh my God," Gladys says.

"Oh boy," Marcos follows.

Through the wispy brush, I catch a flash of dark blue beneath the speckled shade of a lonely mesquite tree. I squint, trying to figure out what it is. I put a hand to my forehead to shade my eyes. Then it hits me.

Blue jeans.

We all freeze, waiting for the legs inside those jeans to either move or stay put. They do the latter.

Marcos puts a finger to his lips, motions for us to stay where we are, then crouches and moves slowly through the brush.

I stare at the body. I'm thinking two things. One, I hope the person is dead. And two, what an awful person I must be to think such a thing.

Marcos stands tall and waves us over.

With each step toward the tree, the scene becomes clearer. A dark red stain covers his belly and has soaked through his plaid shirt. He lies next to the tree, his head propped up against the trunk with his body stretching away like one of the roots, ending in a tall pair of tan boots, which are laced up high. The legs of his jeans are bunched upward, as if he slid down the trunk of the tree. A large stick runs along the length of his body—maybe this was how he got here, or maybe this was why the buzzards weren't here yet. Enough flies dance across his face to produce a quiet hum. His lips are cracked. They look dry, almost wooden.

Marcos lightly kicks at his leg.

Nothing.

I stare at his face. *Who was he? How did he get here? How did he die?* Then a wave a fear runs through my body. *He looks like Marcos.*

I look at Marcos, then back at the body. I wouldn't have mistaken him, but they have similar features. He looks a year or two older than me, has a lean and muscular frame, strong jawline, wide nostrils, a thick buzz cut of hair, and a sparse mustache and beard...waiting for age to thicken it.

Was this supposed to be Marcos? Did he die because of us? What if they're here, watching us right now?

I turn away from the body and begin scanning the land around us. The rising heat makes everything move in a menacing sway.

"*¿Está vivo?*" Arbo asks.

"I don't think so," Marcos says. "But he hasn't been dead long."

Almost in unison, the others turn and do as I do, search for any sign of company.

"How long?" Arbo asks.

"Not very long."

"About two hours," I say.

Eyes that were scanning the horizon turn back to me.

"Look at the shade," I say. The shadow from the tree slices across his body at an angle, leaving most of it exposed to the sun except for his head and part of his upper chest. "He was trying to stay in it...until he died."

"Well, professor," Marcos says, "that's pretty good. What else do you have?"

"He looks like you."

I wasn't going to say it. Why mention it? What good would it do? Scare the rest of us? But his smug delivery knocked the restraint right out of me. I almost felt like I was hitting him when I said it.

"No he doesn't."

"Oh my God, he does," Arbo gasps.

"What, because he's got short hair?" Marcos asks. "He doesn't look anything like me. And so what if he does?"

"So what? So why do you think he's dead?" Arbo asks.

Gladys turns away, cupping a hand to her mouth.

"See? She even thinks so."

Marcos stares down at the body.

"We need to go," he says.

"Hell yeah, we need to go," Arbo answers.

"Now," Marcos says.

"Wait," Gladys says. "We need to find out who he is."

"What?"

"He's a person. He has family somewhere," she says.

"No. We need to go now," Marcos says in a low voice, as if to make the point that we might not be the only people in the area.

I think of Sr. Ortíz's son. I look up at the vultures, and I consider where we are—in the middle of nowhere. Whoever this is will never be found, at least not by somebody who cares.

"She's right. We need to look," I say.

Marcos huffs. "Then go for it, *güey*." He motions toward the body with a sickly gesture.

I kneel over the man and swat at the flies. They storm my head, trying to enter me like they had entered him. I hold my breath and pat lightly against his front pockets. Nothing.

I know the next place to look, but I back away before doing it.

"Come on. We need to go," Marcos says.

"Hold on." I take a deep breath, move in, grab his belt and his shoulder, and pull. His body rolls toward me with a sucking pop, as if it has been baked into the desert floor. Caked blood and dirt cover his backside. I cringe and poke a delicate finger at his back pockets, hoping I'll find something and fearing I'll have to fish it out.

My fears win. He has nothing. I roll him back over. His head knocks against the side of the tree and I almost say, "Sorry." It's hard to think of this as merely a body. A person yesterday, a corpse now, and a ghost tomorrow. Known to nobody.

A murky river of thoughts washes over me. All at once, I

see the backyard, Sr. Ortíz's son, even the driver of the truck that chased us in Sonoyta slumped over the steering wheel.

It's overwhelming.

How many people have to die? How many people die like this? Alone, devoured in the belly of the desert, leaving nothing except haunting questions for others. Hundreds? Thousands?

Will I be one of them?

I gaze at his boots and think of the care that went into lacing them, the thought that went into picking these for his trip. All for nothing. They aren't shoes you wear to the store. They're for a long, rugged journey. I wonder if it occurred to him as he threaded them up that it might be the last time.

"Hey, we have to go. You understand?" Marcos says.

"Just give me a *chingado* second. Okay?"

I grab the young man's hand and clutch his rigid fingers tight in my palms. In my mind, I swear I'll try to help him. But I know I can't. I can't ask him his name. I can't take his picture. Even if by some miracle I were to talk with his mother, I doubt I could describe him well enough for her to be certain it was him, or even begin to guide her back to the spot where he lies.

This is his funeral.

Gladys places a hand on my shoulder. It's time to leave.

We walk away and a few minutes later take our first sips of water, with Marcos's guidance on how much we should drink. We are all still thirsty.

"Hey, Pato, do you really think they killed that guy because they thought it was Marcos?" Arbo asks in a low voice as we continue our march.

"No," I say. And I believe it. "But someone killed that guy, and that person is out here. And so are we."

After that we prod along in silence, taking advantage of a dipping sun, listening to the sounds of the Sonoran wild... and listening for any other sounds too.

BONDED
BY
BLOOD

Marcos takes the knife from his bag. A sliver of moon hangs low near the horizon, giving enough light to guide him as he makes a small slice in his index finger. He hands the knife to Arbo to do the same.

"You can pass diseases doing this kind of thing," Arbo says.

"That's what you're most worried about right now?" Marcos asks.

I don't like to admit when Marcos is right, but it's a valid point. Given what we've seen and where we are, this is the least of our worries. We risk more by not pledging ourselves to each other.

Arbo doesn't answer. Marcos reaches for the knife.

"No, I want to do it. I'm just saying…"

"Then do it."

Arbo winces and cuts. He hands the knife to me, and I gently slide the blade across my finger. It's not easy to cut deep enough to draw blood, but shallow enough to stop the loss quickly.

Gladys follows.

We each squeeze a few drops onto a bent tin lid from the can of beans that was our dinner. Marcos delicately swirls the mixture together, then visits each of us, smearing streaks of our communal lifeblood across our cheeks.

"To the other side," Marcos says, wiping the final streaks on his own face.

"To us," Arbo says.

"To our families," Gladys says.

"To the unknown—may we see it coming," I say.

Bonded by our blood, we all fall deep into thought. We're sitting in a circle, resting after having trudged through the last available light of the day. The stars wheel slowly around us, except one.

"Which one is it?" Gladys asks, looking up, breaking the silence.

"That one," I say, taking my finger out of my mouth to point to a bright spot dead north in the sky. "It's called Polaris."

"How do you know that's it?"

"You know what the Big Dipper is?"

"Yeah."

"Draw a line from the two stars on the right side of the cup. Find the brightest star on that line, and that's it."

"Where did you learn that?" she asks.

"My dad," Arbo answers. "He used to say that if you only knew one star, that was the one to know."

"It's good that you know it. We're going to have to do most of our walking at night," Marcos says, like this is a command he's passing down to us. It isn't. We talked about it together back at Sr. Ortíz's house. We talked about it several times on the miserable trek out here. None of us expected how exhausting it would be to plow through the desert during the day. Even limiting our water, we drank more than we planned. And we're still thirsty. We'll boil before we make it, if we don't get spotted first by any one of the countless groups of people who are looking for us. Traveling at night is a known. Like leaving Mexico, it's our only real option. It's classic Marcos to call it out as his own decree. And I'm getting pretty sick of it.

The pale glow of the moon at my back reflects off Arbo's eyes as he rolls them at me. It's enough to calm my nerves. I put my finger back in my mouth and taste blood once more.

"We're never going to see it again," Gladys says after a while.

"See what?" I ask.

"Mexico. Home. Our families. Everything we've known."

"Whatever home was, it's not that anymore," Arbo says.

"I know," she answers. "That's the saddest part."

Heads nod, but none of us answer.

"I'm trying to be positive, but...it's hard," Gladys continues. Her voice shakes. "I can't stop thinking about that guy under the tree. Who was he? Where was he from? Was he feeling the same things as me? Trying to let go of his past? Trying to find a way to move on? Because it didn't make any difference. Someone shot him and it was over."

"We don't have to let go of the past," I say.

"Yeah. You're right."

"There are some things we can only keep in here," I say, pointing to my head. "But they're still there. You know who told me that?"

"Yup. That makes it a *really* good point," she says. "I have an idea. We should each say one of our favorite memories from back home."

"Anything?" Arbo asks.

"Yeah. One thing that you can think back on and always smile about because nobody can ever take that moment away."

No one speaks. I suppose it's one thing to mash our blood together and wear it, but it's another thing to actually open up to each other.

"Okay. Fine. I'll start," she says. "My mom sewed. She loved to sew. She would make these beautiful dresses. I know you guys know that." She looks at Arbo. "She made Carmen's *quinceañera* dress."

Arbo nods and bites his lip.

"That was her favorite thing to do. Somebody would tell her about their daughter's *quince* or wedding, and she'd immediately smile. You could look at her and tell she was thinking about how to make the perfect dress for that person, for that special moment. She'd be so excited, she'd stay up half the night working on it. I used to stay up with her to watch. The way she worked, the joy that would pour out of her, the different music she would listen to for different dresses, the smile she had when she hummed along, the dancing with the cloth to make sure it felt right, the way she stored clips and pencils in her hair like a tool belt, the way she'd always lose something up there too, and it didn't bother her because *she* was lost in what she was creating... Then she'd shake her head and a pair of scissors would fall out, and we'd laugh about it. It was art. I was watching an artist. She would tell me where to sew a button or what type of stitch to use, and most of the time, I'd do it. Because it was right. But sometimes, I'd see it differently. And she'd listen. And then it would become our dress. Our art. Something we made with each other and nobody else in the world. She'd make me part of it."

I'm entranced. She sniffles and wipes her nose along her sleeve. I've never seen her so beautiful.

"That's my moment. No matter what happens, I'll always have that. It's the perfect way to remember her too. It's so...who she was. I didn't have a *quinceañera*. I didn't want one. It's not me. But I was so nervous to tell her. I was sure she had been dreaming about the dress for years. And when I finally built up the courage to tell her, she almost looked happy. She said that anybody who makes art—of any kind—should listen to themselves first and do what they think is right. I miss her."

"I remember hearing Arbo's mom tell someone about it," I say. "She talked about how happy your mom was because you made your own choice."

"Thanks. I know she was happy."

We sit in silence, waiting for someone else to step forward, which isn't easy with a story like that to live up to.

"Mine is easy," Arbo says. "It's the day I came up with El Revolucionario. Which was also one of the worst days ever. Everything about that day sucked. I got made fun of because of the way I talked. One of the teachers said I was too *gordito*, and she took away part of my lunch in front of everybody. We played some stupid game after school and divided into teams. I wasn't even the last person picked. I wasn't picked at all. We had an odd number, and I was the only person left at the end, so I couldn't play. I just sat on the sideline like a loser until somebody kicked a ball and it drilled me in the head."

We all laugh. He means for us to. Nobody can talk down about Arbo like Arbo can. I think it's a defense mechanism. He beats people to the punch.

"I got home, found a flashlight, and crawled into a closet. Which was great, until about five minutes later when I started to get bored. But I didn't want to leave. I didn't want to see anybody. Plus, I had told my mom I was never going to come out. I couldn't give up after five minutes. So I looked in my book bag and found a pencil and paper. It was like, here's something I can do. Here's somebody who's not going to make fun of me. And if anybody does, here's somebody who can kick their butt!"

Again, he gets a laugh.

I turn to Marcos and Gladys as they react to Arbo's story. I smile. What I like most about this moment is that they're learning to appreciate Arbo for who he is. Not everyone does. Not everyone gives him a chance.

"I know he's made up. Duh. But he's also not. I don't think of him that way. I think of him as somebody I know. A friend. Family. Someone like that. It's almost like he talks to me sometimes. Even though I know it's only me talking to me, it feels different. Anyway, that day—the second half of it—that's my moment."

"Okay. Fine. I'll draw him for you," Gladys says.

"Really?"

"Yeah. You told that story just so I'd offer to, didn't you?"

"No. But I should have!"

"When we get out of here, I'll draw him. I promise."

"You'd better. He can't wait."

"Oh boy," Marcos sighs.

"I've got mine," I say.

They all turn and look at me.

"One time I stayed at Arbo's house, and we spent all night on that old back seat in the desert behind his back-yard. It was almost three years ago exactly, because it was right after Carmen's birthday... We snuck into the kitchen at some point and ate the rest of her cake. We spent the whole night on that bench, counting shooting stars, making up stories about what Revo might do if he went to the moon, looking for eyes in the dark, scared that some *chupacabra* was going to leap out and eat us. We talked about life, about girls, about how far away the stars were but how we could still see them, and about how close the beach was but neither one of us had ever been to see it. It was the best conversation of my life, with my best friend."

Arbo nods next to me, as if this easily could have been his favorite memory too.

"Then we fell asleep. When I woke, it was just before dawn. Right when you can see only a tiny glow of light. Arbo was still asleep. I didn't wake him. I had seen sunrises before, but I had never been in the middle of one like that. I had never listened to it. It was like the earth was waking up. Things rustled, little things, tiny animals running from one bush to another. I saw some, but I didn't see most. Birds started chirping. Slowly. Softly. Like they were warming up, one at a time. I saw a rattlesnake—a big one—sliding along as though he was taking his usual morning stroll. I didn't bother him and he didn't bother me. It was like I was watching all of this, and my presence wasn't disturbing any of it. I remember thinking, this is how it happens every morning, only I'm not here to see it. It was like walking into your house and finding another room you had never seen before.

"Then I heard footsteps. It was Arbo's dad coming out to us. I thought he might be mad, but he wasn't. He waved and took a seat. Arbo woke and the three of us watched the sun come up. He said that he and my dad had done the same thing one night when they were about our age. That's the first time I remember thinking about how much I loved where we lived. Because it was our home. It was where we belonged. And I had this vision of me walking outside one morning to my son and Arbo's son, watching the sun rise over the desert. And now. Well, you know..."

I stop. I don't want to make it about what can't be. That's not the point. It's about what we remember that's good.

"It's still a great memory," I say. "The best. It doesn't get any better than that night and that morning."

Gladys puts a hand on my shoulder. Real or imagined, I can feel both Arbo's and Marcos's expressions shift.

Marcos clears his throat to speak. I can hardly wait to hear what game-winning goal he's going to share to enlighten our lives.

"Our dad played soccer," he starts.

Oh boy.

"And he was good. No, he was great. When he was a couple of years older than me, he played for Morelia for a season. Midfield. He could score, but more than that, he was fast. When I'd meet the guys he played with, they'd still talk about how fast he was. They called him Humo—they swore he left a trail of smoke behind him. Morelia put him in the starting lineup. He traveled all over Mexico. The guy came from dirt. He didn't even have a toilet in his town where he grew up, and here he was signing autographs, staying in fancy hotels. His life was about to take off. Then a defender slid into his knee during a game. Sideways. Broke everything. In a second, his career was over. The next year, he's back in a town without a toilet. The only good that came out of it was that he met my mom."

Gladys is crying softly. He puts an arm on her shoulder.

"I promise, I'll get to the good part. So, I'm the only son. I've had a soccer ball near me since I was born. Dad put one in my crib. Seriously. I didn't have a teddy bear. I had a ball named Don Balón. Don't get me wrong, I love the game. I do. When I'm out on the field, it's like... I'm a better me. I'm doing what's in my genes. I'm at my best. But that—my best—was never enough. In seventeen years, my dad never said I had a great game. Not once, no matter how many goals I scored. No matter how hard I ran. He always said, 'Here's what we need to work on.' '*Nosotros*,' he'd say. It wasn't me. It was *us*. I was playing for us. And for my dad, that was never as good as him playing for him.

"Then you know what happened? It was like he knew. I don't know how. But it was like he could tell what was coming. Right as we got to that *quince*, he pulled me aside. He said he never told me how proud he was of me before... and that was a mistake. He said the way I played the game made him proud. Right there, that was the best moment of my life. And then, two hours later..."

He stares deep into the space between us all. I know

that space. I look into it often, reliving little moments, over and over.

Gladys slides over to him and wraps her arms around his midriff.

None of us respond, because none of us know how to.

I'm torn. It makes me want to think differently of him. It makes me want to read into other things he does and understand where he's coming from. It makes me want to like him again.

Then there's the other side of me.

I think for Marcos, this was just another competition. And he won.

WALKING
BLIND

The mountains that were once in the distance are now much closer. Their shadowy outlines linger like dark teeth rising out of the horizon, blocking the stars and drawing us further into the belly of the desert. Their growing presence is our only sign that we're making any progress.

The moon has dipped from sight. Among the more important items left back at the hotel are three of our four flashlights. From one perspective, it's a nonissue, because we shouldn't be using any lights at night. Lights can be seen by others.

However, we quickly discover the other perspective. And it's a painful one.

We're not on any kind of trail. We're surrounded by a random scattering of cacti and other prickly cousins that plague our path. It's like we're walking through a minefield. All of us get scraped and prodded. Slicing our fingers to draw blood now seems less like a bonding experience and more like an exercise to prepare us for what was to come.

The letters from Sr. Ortíz's children made no mention of this hazard, which slows our pace and makes the walk miserable. They must have followed some kind of trail or a river bed, or had a bright moon to light their travels, or hiked through a different, sparser area of the desert. But wondering about what they did is a moot point. It only frustrates me and distracts me from what I should be paying attention to—each next step.

Marcos remains in the lead. He rips a branch from a mesquite tree and waves it along the path in front of him, like a white cane. This helps, but it's not a foolproof method. It's only a matter of time before one of us takes a real hit.

"Ouch! Ow! Ow!" Marcos hollers. He crashes with a heavy thud into the dirt.

Gladys drops to his side. "What happened?" she asks.

"My leg!" he groans. "My leg."

He turns on the flashlight and shines it down. If anybody is nearby, they'll know exactly where we are, between the screams and the light. But this is a problem we don't have the luxury of worrying about at the moment.

As I peer around Arbo, I see the culprit. Next to Marcos is a barrel cactus—a round, stubby plant with firm spines like razors. I cringe and crane my head farther around Arbo to get a look at Marcos. He's lying on his side. His knee is bent and he's grabbing his shin. His face is tightened in a frozen wince. A small cluster of spines poke out of his jeans, a fist or two above his ankle.

Gladys grabs his leg. He rolls his head back along the desert floor near Arbo's feet and draws in deep, noisy breaths, blowing them back out with the same fiery force.

"Shh," she says. "Shh. Relax. We're going to get them out."

She touches one of the spines.

He yelps. "Stop!"

"Okay. Okay." Gladys strokes his hair, while his head wags back and forth as if trying to deny the pain.

We all give him a moment.

He groans through a loud exhale and props himself up on an elbow.

"Help me get this backpack off. I need to get the knife out of it," he says.

Gladys helps him slide the pack off, then Marcos fumbles through it and pulls out the knife we used to cut our fingers.

He thrusts the flashlight at Arbo.

"Shine this on my leg."

We all lean in. There are four needles piercing through his jeans, though they are not all the same height. One appears half as tall as the others.

Marcos gently slices the cuff of his jeans and works the knife upward. As he does so, it tugs at the fabric pinned against his skin by the spines. He moans, low and determined.

Gladys reaches for his leg and he flinches.

"I'm going to press the jeans against your leg so they don't move."

He concedes with a nod.

Carefully, she places several fingers on his leg, on either side of the spines. Marcos continues to cut until he reaches halfway up his calf. He grabs the flashlight from Arbo, asks Gladys to move her hand, then slowly lifts up the flap of denim and shines the light around at different angles.

I take a delicate step around the cactus to get a better view.

"Most aren't that deep," Marcos says. "I have to pull them out." He says this more for himself than for us.

He stares at his leg. We stare too. Seconds later, he snatches the top of a spine and yanks it out.

"Mmmm," he grunts, his face bunching together, stifling a scream.

Twice more he repeats this drill until all that remains is the shortest of the spines. He inspects this final wound, shaking his head back and forth, looking at it from one side, then the other, then back again.

"*Está bien metido*," Arbo says.

"Thanks for the reminder. It's in *my* leg. I can tell it's deep."

"You want me to pull it?" Arbo asks.

"You touch my leg and you're going into that cactus."

Marcos slides his hand down his leg and grabs hold of the spine. He pauses. His eyes squeeze shut and his jaws clench. He rocks forward, then jerks upward on the spine.

It goes nowhere.

He continues to tug, his upper and lower halves pulling violently in opposite directions. The white of his teeth emerges beneath snarled lips. He growls. He sounds like some kind of animal.

Gladys presses back into me and reaches for my hand. She wraps my fingers in her palm and squeezes. My knuckles dig into each other as she crushes my hand.

Marcos gives one final heave. His leg kicks out and his torso slams into the ground. His hands hover over his body, clutching something. Arbo shines the flashlight on his bloody fingers. He's holding the spine, but only the top half of it.

Gladys releases my hand and drops back down to his side.

"I broke it. It's still in there," Marcos says. He sounds defeated and exhausted.

"We can't leave it like that," Gladys says.

Marcos slowly pushes himself back onto his elbows. He extends a hand out to Arbo.

"Let me see the flashlight," he says.

He shines it along his leg. The jeans are no longer pinned down. He pulls them up over his knee, revealing his bloody shin. He slides his fingers in soft circles around the area, flinching several times.

"There's nothing to grab," he says.

"We need to get it out," Arbo says.

"I said, 'There's nothing to grab.'"

"We still need to get it."

"How?" Marcos snaps.

Arbo looks down at the ground. We all track his eyes to the knife.

"You touch that knife and—"

"Arbo's right," Gladys says. "It'll get infected."

"No. It'll work its way out."

"Marcos, we—"

"I said no! Nobody is digging a hole in my leg with a knife." He says it to all of us, but mostly to Gladys.

I look at Arbo. He seems to feel the same as me. This is between them.

"Can you even walk?" she asks.

"Yes," he says, his voice thick with defiance. He rolls up the flap of his jeans, leaving the bloody mess exposed, then turns onto the knee of his good leg. He looks up at us as I hold out a hand for him to grab. He ignores it. He pushes himself up and balances on one leg.

"We should at least wrap your leg with something. You're still bleeding," Gladys says.

"I don't want anything touching it. It's done bleeding. It'll scab over."

Gladys starts to say something.

Marcos cuts her off. "Let's just go, okay?"

He places his wounded limb in front of him and leans on the mesquite branch to help support his weight. As he takes a quick, gimpy step forward, he lets out a barely audible groan, then looks back at us, as though this proves his case. He punctuates this by reaching down, grabbing his pack, and slinging it over his shoulder.

"You know I'm not trying to hurt you, right?" Gladys asks.

"Yeah, I know. Let's walk."

So that's what we do. Slowly. Our already sluggish pace is halved, partly for Marcos's benefit and partly because we know what can happen if we try to move too fast. Gradually, the grunts and groans fade, and we hear nothing from Marcos. I can tell he's in pain from his limp, but he's not going to let us hear anything more about it.

Several times, Gladys suggests we stop, but Marcos insists we move on. "It only gets hotter and harder from here," he says. So we continue.

_ _ __ _ _ __ _ _ __

Clouds move in. If it were daytime, this would be a gift from above. But it's not. It's as if the desert has attacked us with a new weapon. At night, the clouds knock out the only tool we have to point us in the right direction.

It's not even kind enough to rain. It drizzles a light mist that's impossible to collect to restock our dwindling water supply. It's just enough to make the desert feel swampy. It doesn't cool here at night—it just becomes less hot. The warm droplets dampen our clothes, making the heat stick.

We trudge along, but we have no idea if we're headed in the right direction. Furthermore, we are now walking on the slanted side of what appears to be a low hill, which pushes us along its slope. While feeling the angle of the hill keeps us from walking in circles, the path that it forces us to take may or may not be the way we want to go.

Arbo has the only watch among us. He checks the time: 11:00 p.m. We have many more hours of walking ahead of us.

"Are we going the right way? I think we're turning," Arbo says.

"I don't know," Marcos answers.

"Maybe we should stop."

"We need to make progress tonight."

"We can walk at dawn."

"We're going to do that anyway. Then we rest," Marcos says. "You'll be happier sleeping through the middle of the day than walking through it."

— — —— — — —— — — ——

It's 11:15 p.m.

"I don't think we're going the right way."

"How do you know?"

"I don't, but it feels like we're turning."

"I agree."

"Well, what do you want to do, go up the mountain?"

"I don't think it's a mountain, I think it's a hill."

"How do you have any idea how big this thing is?"

"Before the clouds came in you could see it. It didn't look that tall."

"There are mountains out here."

"I know. I don't think this is one of them. I think it's a foothill before the mountains."

"Then do you want to go up the *foothill*?"

"I don't think we should. I think we should keep going around it."

"How do we know we're going the right way around it? Maybe we should be walking the other way."

"You want to turn *around*?"

"No. I'm just saying we don't know if we're going the right way."

"It's turning us. I say we go up it."

"You want to walk up because it *might* be the right way? I guess this isn't exhausting enough for you already?"

"*¡Dios mío!* Can we please decide on a direction to walk and *go*?"

"Great idea. Anybody who can figure out the right way, feel free to speak up."

"I just don't want to keep walking just for the sake of walking!"

"So you want to stop?"

"I'm saying that we need to make sure we're not headed back into Mexico."

"I don't think we're turned completely around."

"And how do you know that?"

"Okay! Look, none of us know where we are. Let's at least admit it. We're lost."

"We're not lost. We just don't know the right direction to go."

"That's what lost is!"

"No, lost is when you don't know where you are. We know where we are."

"Please, do tell. Where are we?"

"Stop! Stop!"

"We are stopped."

"No, stop talking! Okay. Let's make a decision."

Our group falls silent, which is both disheartening and pleasant. Marcos takes off his backpack.

"So, we're stopping?" I ask.

"I'm at least going to take this sack of bricks off and sit for a moment." It's the first time he's hinted at how heavy the pack is. "And we should have some water. If it rains harder, we can fill the jugs."

No one argues with this. We take off our bags, sit, and drink more than we should, hoping that the taunting clouds will deliver.

Then we wait. We wait for someone to speak up, to push us on. No one does. So we sit, consumed in our thoughts, or lack thereof.

I reach into my bag and feel for the book Gladys gave me. The cover is damp. It's not dripping, but it's wet from having been pressed up against the top of the bag, which has soaked up what little rain has fallen. I take it out and tuck it under my shirt, while thumbing through the pages.

My whole body relaxes in a way I wouldn't have thought possible by simply touching paper. It feels like years since I have run my fingers through pages. I love how they feel. I slide my fingers along the diagonal crease of a dog-eared page. It takes me back. I close my eyes and think of home. I'm suddenly whisked back into my bedroom, reading by the light of a lone lamp. My head flush against the pillow, my mind somewhere inside the pages and far outside the room, all from the comfort of my bed...until my eyes can no longer stay open, and I fold a page over to mark my spot for the next night. The same place, the same routine. The pages turn, the books change, but everything else stays the same.

I smile. Then I think about who gave me the book and how she "bought" it. I smile even wider. I could stay lost in that thought all night, but I open my eyes. Sitting and thinking won't get us anywhere.

"If we could see Ajo, then we'd know the right direction," I say.

"What do you mean?" Marcos asks.

"In the letters from Sr. Ortíz's kids, they said they could see the lights of Ajo from far away."

"I don't see any lights."

"That's my point. We need to get up higher to see them. They're probably blocked by this hill."

"Or mountain."

"Well, whatever it is, we can't see around it. If we can

spot Ajo, we can at least know what direction we should head," I say.

Marcos thinks for a few seconds before answering. "How long do you think it'll take to climb up there?"

"I don't know. Thirty minutes maybe. But if I went alone, I could do it a lot faster. Probably in half the time."

"No, we're not splitting up," Marcos says.

"I'll go with him," Arbo says.

"I don't think that's a good idea."

"Why not? What else are we doing? Just sitting here," Arbo says.

Again, Marcos pauses and thinks. He looks at his leg. He won't say it, but I can tell he knows that it makes no sense for him to go up a hill on a hunch.

"We're not going to go far. You keep the flashlight. If we're not back in half an hour, then shine it up every few minutes. We'll see it and know where you are," I say.

"How are you going to see?"

We hear a beep from Arbo's wrist, and a tiny blue light beams out. He holds it up to his face and smiles. Then he waves it away from us, out toward the brush. It's dim, barely bright enough to light up a step or two in front of him, which makes it perfect.

"Why didn't you tell us about that before?" Marcos asks.

"I forgot about it."

Marcos shakes his head back and forth. It's not hard to connect the dots crossing his mind.

"Look," I jump in. "We'll be back in thirty, okay? We'll leave everything here. We'll walk faster without it."

I take the book out from under my shirt. Rather than tuck it back inside the bag where it might get wet, I cram it into my back pocket. It's a tight fit, but I don't mind. I'll keep it dry, and I feel better having it on me.

Arbo takes the lead, using his watch to light our way. His steps are broad and confident. Compared to how we were shuffling before, it nearly feels like we're running. And without the weight of the packs, moving uphill hardly feels like a challenge.

We'll be back in twenty minutes, I think to myself, as though I have something to prove.

Ten minutes later, Arbo stops.

"I need to catch my breath," he says.

I do too. The memory of our lightened load is already fading, and the slope feels as though it's becoming steeper.

"Are you sure it's only a hill?"

"No, but let's walk a little farther," I say. "The higher we get, the easier it will be to see the lights."

We resume. I trace Arbo's footsteps, as they wind to the left and right, dodging the thorny land mines that dot the slope. It's a dizzying trek that rarely leads us straight uphill. Birds can move in straight lines here—everything else must negotiate.

Five minutes later, the slope begins to level out. We sense that we're near the top and press on with renewed drive.

Over the next fifteen minutes, we have the same conversation three times.

"Just a few more minutes."

"We should think about turning back."

"I think we're almost there."

Then it steepens again. Each new step is more up than forward. Loose, sharp rocks roll beneath our feet sending us crashing into the slope.

In my mind, I envision this as the final grueling ascent. Each step we take could be the one that reaches the top and...

And then what? If we see Ajo, what do we do? Can Marcos even walk up this slope right now? It would take all of us to carry him. So, do we try to walk around it without getting lost again? How likely is that?

"Pato, we need to go back," Arbo says.

I drop down onto the rocks, exhausted. It's been more than forty-five minutes since we left. All for nothing. It's not even cooler up here than it was where we started below. If anything, it's worse. The steamy wind feels like hot breath, as gusts sweep up dust and drive it through the buttons and holes of our shirts, mixing with our sweat and caking onto us, like a gritty paste.

"You're right," I say.

He gives me his watch, and I lead us back down. It's impossible to retrace our steps while zigzagging around every obstacle we come across. The best we can do is walk in a direction that feels like we're moving straight down the...mountain.

The wind rushes up the slope, forcing me to squint just enough so I can see each step ahead without letting sand fly into my eyes. I fail several times. Each instance requires us to stop so I can blink my dry eyes clear.

I pass the time by not thinking about the walk. My head is elsewhere. I feel like I've failed. This was my idea. My plan that got us nowhere, that didn't take thirty minutes, but more than an hour. And—if I'm being honest—what I'm really dreading is telling Marcos that he was right. With Gladys there to hear.

"I don't see the flashlight," Arbo says.

I snap out of my wandering thoughts.

"How long have we been walking back down?"

"You have the watch," he says.

"Right. About forty-five minutes. We should be getting close," I say.

"We've been looking down to walk. Let's stop for a few minutes and watch for it."

"Good idea."

We see nothing.

We yell into the darkness, but our shouts are swallowed whole by the wind now whipping around us.

"Do you think we passed them?" Arbo asks.

"I don't know."

My stomach tightens. We're in trouble.

TWO
BY
TWO

We walk back up. Nothing.

We walk back down. Nothing.

We repeat. Nothing.

We shout. Nothing.

We walk back and forth along the slope of the mountain.
Nothing.

Hours pass. Nothing.

We try to think of anything else we can possibly do.
Nothing.

We remind each other of exactly what we have with us.
No food. No water.

Nothing.

We cry. Together.

"We're screwed," Arbo says.

"Yeah," I answer.

"I don't know what else to do."

"Me neither."

"What time is it?"

"It's almost three."

"We've been looking for them for *two hours*?"

"Yeah."

I hear his head hit the ground in frustration.

"We should wait until dawn," I say.

"And do what?"

"Sleep? Lay here? We should be able to see them in the morning. They've got to be down there. Maybe the flashlight isn't working."

"Yeah. Maybe."

We hike back up the slope so that we'll have a good view, and we lie down on the dirt. Not long after we settle in, the clouds begin to slide mockingly out of the sky, revealing our map above. North lies somewhere between the slope of the mountain and the angled path I think we had been walking along. Where that puts Marcos and Gladys is beyond me right now. My head is spinning.

I close my eyes and fester. I'm angry. At a lot of things. First, at myself, for getting us into this mess. At La Frontera, because they are going to win—they'll get us, and they won't even have to pony up the bounty. At the sky, for betraying me—how many nights have I spent staring into it with wonder, and the first time I call on it for help, it leaves me. At Marcos, for finally letting go of control long enough to allow me to fail.

It's a giant swirl of bitterness.

And I feel guilty. Very guilty. I look at Arbo. If we don't get out of this, I will have killed him. My foolishness will be to blame. And to make it worse, he never says so. He never blames me. I wish he would. I wish he would lash out at me, call me names, and put me on the defensive. Then maybe I could throw some of the blame back outward. But he won't. That's not him. So I'm forced to swallow all of it whole.

On the very dim bright side, my body is drained, so as much as I want to beat myself up, I can't stay awake to do so. Even with a mattress of rocks and a book for a pillow.

— — — — — — — —

"Hey, Pato."

I feel a tug at my sleeve. I try to open my mouth and my eyes—both feel glued shut. I raise my palms to my eyes and gently rub them open. They are greeted by the soft glow of morning.

"Hey."

I sit up. If this were any other circumstance, I could stare at the scenery for hours. We are in the shade of what I can now safely call a mountain. Its mighty shadow bulges outward toward the horizon, skirted at the top by a narrow, golden strip of sunlit desert, which fades into the dark blue of the western sky.

"How long have you been awake?" I ask.

"A couple of minutes."

"I'm guessing you haven't see them yet."

"No."

We both scan below for a few more minutes.

"I don't get it. We didn't walk that far," he says.

"I know. Do you think they moved?"

"No. They said they were going to stay right there. Why would they move?" His voice trails off, and I can tell that the same thought has entered both of our heads.

"They could have moved for a lot of reasons," I say.

"Like what?"

I can't come up with any.

"I can only think of one reason," Arbo says. "Do you think it was because of the flashlight?"

Again, my idea.

"I don't know, Arbo. We don't know that somebody found them."

"But if they did, then they also found our packs. They know that we're out here too!"

"Okay. We need to calm down." I'm speaking as much to myself as I am to him. "We don't know anything. We're only guessing."

"But we need to know."

"Why? We just have to look for them, okay?"

"No. If somebody found them, then they're looking for us, and we need to hide. We're on the side of a mountain. Anybody down there can see us. But if nobody found them, then we need for them to be able to see us. See? We need to know what happened."

He's spot on. And completely wrong.

"Okay. You're right," I say. "But we have to assume that nobody found them." I pause to think through how to soften my next line. I give up. "Because if someone found them, then we're dead. Whether they find us or not. We need that water, Arbo. We're not going to last a day without it." I pause. "I'm so sorry I got us into this. I thought—"

"Stop. It's not your fault. And you're right. Let's assume they're okay. They probably are," he says.

"You think?"

I look into his eyes. He's lying.

"Yeah. They're probably down there looking for us and asking themselves the same questions."

"Then we'd better find them before we lose our shade."

———————

The sun breaks over the ridgeline and greets us like a torch pressed to our skin. We've scoured the mountainside and can't find any trace of Marcos and Gladys.

The inside of my mouth feels like cotton. I don't know how we'll make it through the next few hours, much less the rest of the day. Or beyond. I've never known thirst like this before. Arbo sits in a disappointed slump beneath the flame.

I'm feeling the heat, but I look at him and can tell he's doing much worse.

I spot a small desert willow below, offering slivers of shade beneath its skeletal frame.

"Come on, Arbo. We need to get out of the sun."

I give him my hand and hoist him to his feet. We stagger down the slope to the tree and take a seat in the thickest line of its bony shadow.

Arbo's lips are cracked and red. His whole body looks flushed. He takes off his shoes and socks. His feet are swollen and his left foot is blistered in several places along the outside edge. He flops his body back into the dirt, closes his eyes, and groans.

"We should take off our clothes and put them in the tree. That'll give us more shade," I say.

He nods but doesn't move.

I stand on unsteady feet and remove my clothes. Bracing myself against the trunk of the tree in my underwear, I'm suddenly aware of how little I have left. With each step forward, I'm further stripped of everything in my life. Until finally—soon—I'll be naked, alone, and dead.

I hang my clothes on the low branches and turn back to find Arbo in his underwear as well. His shoulders are raw, like mine, from the backpacks we so desperately miss right now. He hands me his shirt and jeans.

We sit across from each other, waiting for the other person to say something, anything.

"You look like crap," he says.

"I'll take that. I thought I looked a lot worse."

"You do. I was being nice."

"How does your foot feel?" I ask, pointing to his blisters.

"Like the rest of me. At least we're not walking."

Which also means we're sitting still...letting the desert slowly suck us dry.

"What are you thinking about?" he asks, breaking me from my darker thoughts.

"Water."

"How good would that taste right now?"

"I don't even want to think about it."

"But you are."

"I can't help it," I say.

"Do you ever wonder why water doesn't taste like anything?"

"Not really. I guess that means you do."

"Think about it. Everything else we put in our mouth has some kind of flavor—sweet, bitter, spicy, horrible..."

"I don't think horrible is a flavor," I say.

"You know what I mean. But water has no flavor. Try to describe it. You can't. And it's the one thing we need the most. Why not give it flavor?"

"Maybe that's why. Because we need it so much. What if it had a flavor and you didn't like it? Then you'd be screwed."

"But you could always put other flavor in it, like how coffee has water in it, but it tastes like something else."

"But that's because it doesn't taste like anything to begin with. What if you poured coffee on your eggs?" I ask.

"That'd be disgusting."

"Exactly. So it tastes like nothing."

"Hmm. You're a smart guy, Pato. I've never told you that."

"If I were smart, we wouldn't be talking about water. We'd be drinking it."

"This isn't your fault," he says.

"Yes, it is. First, for not saying something about the car, and now this."

"Stop it with the car. And this isn't your fault."

"Whose idea was it to leave them *and* leave everything we had with them?"

"It made sense."

"If you're stupid."

"Are you calling me stupid?"

"No, I'm calling *me* stupid."

"But I agreed with you, so you can't call yourself stupid without calling me stupid."

"Then... I'm calling me stupider."

"Well, I'm not mad at you," he says.

"I know you're not."

"Good. I just wanted you to know."

"You're... You're better at that than me. I'd be mad at you."

"No you wouldn't."

Maybe he's right.

I look down at myself, then back at him. Squeezed into

the small slab of shade, we're as close as we can get without being pressed against each other, in nothing but our tighty-whities. We deserve each other. In the best of senses.

That I can still shed a tear feels both surprising and wasteful.

"What's wrong?"

"I'm just glad you're here with me. I wouldn't want to be out here with anybody else," I say.

"Almost naked, under a tree in the middle of nowhere?"

"Yeah. Almost naked. If we have to lose these to make more shade I might change my mind."

We laugh, as much as we can. We try to hold on to the feeling, pushing each other with half-forced chuckles, until we can do it no longer.

"This isn't good, Pato."

"I know."

"We should write a note."

"To who?"

"Whoever. I'm thinking about that guy we saw, and how you searched over his entire body and couldn't find out anything about him. Nobody is ever going to know who he is. I feel like we ought to write something down about us."

"We're not done yet," I say.

"I know. But just in case, we should do it."

"What? Write our names?"

"And why we're here."

"Why? What good is it going to do?" I ask.

"What harm is it going to do, and what else are we doing right now? You never know who might find it and what they might do with it. Maybe they'll tell people back home. Think about the family we've got left...*abuelita* Marisol, or *tío* Carlitos, or all the kids from our school, our teachers. We still have people back there. They don't know anything about us now. I know that was the plan, and I know it has to be that way, but it still feels wrong. If something happens, they should find out what we did."

I know I was the one who was so interested in finding out the dead man's name, but I still think it's unlikely that writing our names will accomplish anything. But that's not what bothers me about it. If we don't make it out, I'd rather La Frontera never know. I'd want Rafa's brother—that *cabrón*—to spend the rest of his days wondering if the guys who killed his brother were enjoying the good life in the glorious North. I'd rather leave a note saying, "Whoever finds this, please send a postcard to La Frontera from the United States, care of Pato, Arbo, Gladys, and Marcos. We miss you. Give Rafa our best!"

But, more than all this, I want to make Arbo feel half as good as he makes me feel.

"Okay," I say. "That's a good idea."

"I still have the pencil in my jeans. We can write it in the cover of your book."

"What about Marcos and Gladys? Should we write their names also?" I ask.

The question hangs over us, like the clothes on the tree.

"Like you said, it's not over yet. This is just in case. We're still in this together," he answers.

I fish the pencil out of his jeans and sit back down.

Daniel ("Arbusto," "Arbo") Luis Ortega Romero—16
Patricio ("Pato") Juan Manuel Ortega Maqueda—16
Gladys Solange Salvador Guerrero—15
Marcos Edgar Salvador Guerrero—17
On the run from La Frontera, who murdered our families.

I put the pencil in the inside seam and close the book around it.

"I'm going to try to sleep," Arbo says. "Please don't leave. For any reason. We're staying together, right?"

"Until the end," I say.

Arbo closes his eyes and falls silent. I watch his chest rise and fall. I'm not expecting it to stop yet, but that thought is not far off. Maybe a few hours, maybe longer.

I close my eyes and try to join him.

— — —— — — — —— —

I can't sleep. I'd blame the heat, but the real culprit is me. I can't turn off my mind. It's the same swift current of thought as always.

As I sit up, I discover that the shade has slid past most of Arbo's body. The midday rays blast into his chubby frame, which now sports a red line, seared on a diagonal. I want to kick myself for letting this happen. I rearrange our clothes so he is once again covered, and I vow to keep watch on our shifting shelter.

I don't feel much like reading, but Gladys's gift to me is the only escape I have from my own discomfort, outside and in. I open it and dive with pleasure into somebody else's misadventure.

Of all places, this story happens on a river! I feel a cool trickle of water in my mouth. I didn't know a person could drool for water. All my life, I have been accused of becoming so absorbed by books that the outside world vanishes. People call my name, I don't hear them. Time passes, I don't realize it. I become entranced. Never has this been more of a gift than now. My mind sets sail along the cool, fresh water of the Mississippi.

And in Huckleberry and Jim, I find Arbo and me, and the others. I'm not suggesting it's the same. Nobody here is anyone's slave. But there are striking similarities. They lose their home. They're forced out into the unknown to find a new life. There's a bounty on their heads. They get in gunfights. They have to work their way through untrustworthy criminals. They even find a dead man…shot, abandoned, and unknown.

I zip through the pages at a pace as blistering as the light that makes me squint to read them. What strikes me most is Huckleberry's attitude. To him, it's an adventure, and he embraces it. His tragedies, his flight from home, all the unknowns, his narrow escapes from death—these are all part of the journey, and he presses forward, shaping his travels as much as they shape him. You even get the sense that it's fun.

¿Divertido? No, this isn't fun. It's tragic. It's appalling. Huck hasn't suffered a loss like I have. He doesn't even like his home all that much. Still, there is something in this for me. I can't put my finger on it, but it's there...

"How's the book?" Arbo asks in a low, throaty voice.

"It's good. I've only read about half of it. It's interesting. It's... Do you ever wonder what we'll think about this trip later on?"

"If we make it?"

"Yeah. If we make it."

"I think we'll always wish it never happened, no matter how good it gets."

"You think we'll ever laugh about it?"

"Some of it. Maybe."

"Like what?"

"Well, we are in our underwear," he says.

"Yeah, I guess that's an obvious one."

"We'll definitely laugh about Marcos. But only when he's not around. Unless we want him to punch us."

"I'd let him punch me right now, if it meant I could see him with a big jug of water," I say.

"He probably drank it all already."

"Are you kidding? No, they've probably had five sips each, every two hours and seventeen minutes."

"Yeah. We'll definitely laugh about that," Arbo says. He struggles to prop himself up on an elbow and his expression turns serious. "She likes you more, you know."

"She likes us both, but that's the last thing—"

"Stop," he says. "We both know it. It's not worth arguing about. If I stood in the way, I'd only be doing it to be bitter. And that's not right. Besides, I could use a little sister. I miss Carmen." He looks down for a moment, and I reach out to him. He regains his composure. "What I'm saying is that if we find them, don't worry about me. I want you to know that I'm okay with it."

"And what I'm saying is that we're in the middle of an oven, and that's the last thing you or I should be thinking about," I say.

"No. It's one of the first things. I'm sixteen, *güey*, and I've never had a girlfriend. And there's a good chance I never will."

"What about Daniela?"

"She kissed me once and then broke up with me two days later. That doesn't count. So, if we're going to die out here, we'd better start making things count. If we find them, go for it. You owe it to me. Because finding them doesn't mean we get out of here, it just means we might, and we get a little extra time if we don't."

I'm not sure how to respond.

"Besides," he says. "It'll make Marcos mad, so it's not like I won't get any fun out of it."

"Okay. You got a deal," I say, as if any part of that is a deal.

The shade threatens to leave us again, so I stand and rearrange our clothes.

"*¿Te duele la cabeza?*" he asks.

"No."

"Ugh. My head is throbbing."

This is the worst part of our situation. He hands over his ego to me, and I can't do anything in return except shuffle some laundry on a tree.

"Maybe you should sleep. It might feel better when you wake up."

"Yeah, maybe."

He closes his eyes and goes silent. Again, I watch his chest rise and fall.

I look out beyond our tree and think about Gladys, wondering what she's doing right now. I miss her. I miss her playful smile. I miss the way I feel when I'm around her. I miss her perspective. I need it. If she were here, she'd be sand-scaping or doing something to search for the positive in all of this, not eyeing our situation up and down and seeing nothing but a bleak and hopeless mess.

I grab the book once more. I turn to the inside cover and look at our scribbled names above the measly sentence about us. *Is this it?* ¿Es todo que somos? *Just names scribbled on a page?*

What if we make it?

I consider this possibility.

If we make it across, it should be more than a mad dash that almost killed us. It should mean something. But what?

There are several blank pages in the back of the book. I grab the pencil and write. I write about our bond and the events that fused us all together, even if we're separated at this moment.

I write, not in case someone finds us—I write in case we make it.

BENEATH THE WILLOW

I watch Arbo's brown skin begin to lighten, like a chameleon placed against a white sheet.

I tap on his arm. He doesn't budge. I put my hand on his shoulder. I'm startled by how cool it feels. I shake him, softly at first, but soon I'm tugging in near panic.

He makes a noise.

I let out a long, deep breath of air I didn't realize I had been holding.

He rolls slowly onto his back.

"Arbo?"

"Mmm."

"Arbo?"

"Mmm."

"Arbo!" I shake his chest.

His eyes open and turn in my direction. I've never looked at a pair of eyes before and been able to tell that they were out of focus. His are.

"*¿Qué hora eth?*" he asks, in a lisped draw.

"I don't know. You have the watch," I say.

"*Ah. Sí,*" he says and holds his wrist up over his head, swinging it around in unsteady circles.

I grab his arm and hold it still. "It's two o'clock," I say.

"Can you pathhh me the water? My throat is tho dry."

"We don't have any water, Arbo," I say.

We haven't had water in about fifteen hours.

He cocks his head and stares at me as though I'm lying. Then his neck goes limp and his head slumps back into the dirt.

"Ohhh, that's right. Nooo water."

"Arbo, are you okay?" I ask, like I don't already know the answer.

"I think… *Thólo nethethito dormir.* A little sleep. Just a little more…" He closes his eyes again.

"We have to go find Marcos and Gladys," I say. "We need water."

"Yeah, waaater…"

I grab his arm and pull up.

"Come on, Arbo. Let's go find them."

He swipes at my arm.

"Arbo. We have to look."

He props himself up on an elbow, with his head swaying back and forth. He turns on to his knees and tries to push himself up to stand. He doesn't even make it halfway. With his face down, he blindly points a finger outward. I look. It leads to the middle of nothing, the same as it would in any other direction.

"Water..."

"There's no water, Arbo. We need to find Marcos and Gladys. Revo wants you to get up right now, Arbo. Think about it. What would Revo do?"

"Sleep a little more. It's too hot. *Solo...una...hora...más. Qué calor...*"

I'm crying. Again.

"I'm going to go look now, okay? I'm not going to go far."

His lids spring half-open.

"Nooo. You can't leave me. We can't split. Okay?"

I don't answer.

"Okay?"

I nod.

His eyes roll backward as they shut.

"Just a little more sleep..."

He's asleep in minutes.

The sun is high above us, and it feels like it's still getting hotter, if that's possible. I look around us. Nothing. No one. Anywhere.

I roll back onto the ground. I consider breaking my promise and leaving. Then I fall asleep too.

— — — — — — — —

"Arbo?"

I look at his watch. It's four o'clock. I grab his arm and shake.

"Arbo."

No response. Again, I start the fearful, wild tugging.

"Mmm," he says.

"How are you doing?"

"Waterrr."

"There's no water."

He shakes his finger. "Waterrr."

"We'll get some in a little bit, Arbo. Okay?"

He puts his thumb up. Then he goes limp again. "Mmm."

I watch his chest. Still moving, though it's slower. I don't know why he is fading so much faster than me, but he is. Arbo is dying. And all I can do is watch. Well, I won't. I accept that among my final words to him, I may have lied.

I put on my shoes and stand. I reposition the clothes so he'll stay in the shade, and I stare at him. *How long will he last? Will I come back to find him dead?*

I want so desperately to do something more, but I can't. I have nothing to offer.

Or do I?

Living near a desert, you hear stories of desperation. Of nearly doomed people who do outrageous things when there is almost no hope left.

Our hope is dwindling.

I have an idea. I don't know if it's a good one. I don't even know if it will help. But I'll do whatever I can to try to keep Arbo alive. For at least a few more hours. I need time to find water.

I don't have a cup. I need a cup. It doesn't work without a cup.

I reach for the hole in my underwear.

He'll never take it.

I could just put it there.

Who am I kidding? He'll never drink it. If he wakes up and sees what I'm doing, he'll freak. Wouldn't I? And if he doesn't wake up, then he won't drink.

I kick at him lightly. No response. I repeat. No response. He's still breathing.

I settle for the next best thing. I pull down my underwear and aim. I know it's warm, but so is sweat, and sweat cools the body. I need to cool him down.

I release.

I haven't peed since we left Marcos and Gladys. It's a dark yellow. It splashes against his body, mostly dripping into the sand below. I squeeze and stop the flow.

This isn't working. It's not sticking to anything.

I know what I have to do.

I aim at his head and douse it. His thick locks of hair soak it up. His hand moves up to brush at the drops, but he doesn't wake. As far as he knows, it's raining.

"I'm so sorry. I swear I'll come back."

I turn and walk up the mountain. I don't look back. I can't. I need to focus on moving forward.

The western sun slams against my bare back, feeling more like noon than late afternoon. The slope, having faced the sun for hours now, is like a frying pan. Each step burns through my shoes. I take quick, little hops to try to defeat it, but it only wears me down, leaving me doubled over, huffing breaths of sweltering air. Breathing habanero mist wouldn't burn this much. I lick my lips and my tongue nearly sticks to them. My mouth feels like it's coated with clay. I couldn't spit if I wanted to. I look down at my hands—they're swollen. It doesn't make sense how I can feel so thirsty, yet my fingers can be so plump with fluid.

My head soon begins to throb. I think of Arbo's comment about his head only hours before. *Am I merely a few hours behind him? I can't go crazy out here. I need to make it back to Arbo.*

I stop my march upward and turn around. I can still see our tree, baring the small tapestry of our clothes on its branches. I study the view. I won't make the same mistake twice. It's the only willow I can see, but I need more of a reference. I spot a saguaro cactus with a broken fork near the top of one of its tall arms, thrust high into the sky as if reaching for rain.

I look back up the mountainside. I find a boulder that's split in half, like an egg dropped from above.

Up the slope from the split cactus and down the slope from the split boulder. I repeat it over in my head.

I decide I'll only walk in two directions—I'll start along the slope to the south, then retrace my path and head north.

I turn south and start walking. It's the loneliest and most scared I've ever felt in my life. But the fear isn't dying.

The fear is losing my way. My pounding headache gets worse with each passing minute. Confusion lingers so closely that I can feel it creeping into my wandering thoughts, causing me to question what landmarks I've seen and in what sequence.

The fear is that I will exhaust myself and will be too far away to go back. Every step I take I'll have to match on my return. My legs wobble more each minute, making me worry I won't have the strength to do it. And stopping provides no rest. I can't sit on the scalding ground in my underwear. The heat doesn't quit.

The fear is that even if I am strong and aware enough to return, Arbo will have woken to find that I'm not there, so he will stumble out somewhere in the brush to die on his own, his last thoughts being that his best friend abandoned him.

I press as far as I can. I find nothing. No Gladys. No Marcos. Only a long stretch of one disappointing step after the next. I turn around in defeat.

The sun dips lower on the horizon, like an hourglass. The softer light does not relieve my distress. The lower it gets, the more concerned I become.

Will I make it back by dark?

What seems like hours after I began my hike, I find the

cracked rock and the split cactus. I stumble back to the willow and collapse underneath it with Arbo. I've achieved nothing but exhaustion. There is an hour of daylight left at most.

He is curled on his side. I rest my forehead on his shoulder.

"Mmm," he says.

"Hey, Arbo."

"Mmm..."

That's the most I'm able to get.

This is how it ends.

I place my hand on his back so I can feel him breathe, and I close my eyes.

I won't leave him. Now. Or later. I won't abandon him. What good would it do anyway? He may get there sooner than me, but we're both near the end. There's not much point in dropping dead a few kilometers away from him. This is our fate. Together.

I begin to feel my own clarity slipping away. My thoughts scatter. I'm not scared. I suppose I've had a few days of warm-up for death. There's a numbness to it. A resignation. Even a curiosity for what, if anything, lies beyond.

But I'm disappointed. In myself. In how quickly the desert devoured us. And in life in general—ironically, for the lack of adventure I've had, until now.

Through my eyelids, I can sense the light retreating from the sky. I think about my parents and the others from the backyard and wonder if it would be better to go suddenly, or have time—as I do—to sit and reflect on it all.

I don't come to an answer. I wait for the stars, hoping that I'll go beneath their twinkle, rather than face the fury of the sun one more day.

— — — — — — — —

A guttural roar echoes off the mountainside.

I open my eyes. The sun is gone and its dwindling reflection against the sky is all that remains, leaving everything a dull tan.

I listen for the sound again.

Silence.

A dream?

I close my eyes once more.

"Auuggghhhh!"

I spring up. I know that voice. And this time, I hear where it's coming from.

"Arbo?" I say, tugging his arm.

Nothing.

No! No! Please no!

I put my hand in front of his mouth and nose. He's breathing. I don't bother checking any further. I stand and sprint south, trying desperately to listen beyond my huffing. I don't know where this burst of energy comes from, and I don't question it.

"Marcos!" I yell. "Gladys!"

I stop and cup my hands around my ears.

"Pato! Pato!" It's two voices. One high and one low.

I race forward.

We scream each other's names until, finally, I see them.

Gladys charges toward me, wraps me in her arms and kisses me. On the lips. It's glorious. Absolutely glorious. Marcos is in the distance, but not that far away. I'm sure he sees it.

"I thought you were dead," she blurts out through sobs.

"No. We're alive!"

"Where's Arbo?"

"We need to get back, now. Get water!"

"What's wrong?"

"He's not good. We need water!"

"How far away is he?"

"A couple of minutes."

Gladys motions and we run back toward Marcos and the supplies. He's on the ground with his leg in the air. His hands are wrapped around a small, bloody cloth, pressed against where the cactus speared him.

"What's wrong?" I ask.

"His leg got infected," she says, while running.

"Is he okay?"

She doesn't answer. She speeds up and I struggle to keep pace. We reach him before I have the chance to ask again.

He sits up and wraps a bone-crunching arm around me. I wasn't expecting it.

"I didn't think we'd see you again," he says.

He shoves a jug of water in my face.

"We need to get Arbo," I say.

"Drink. We'll get him," he says back.

I place the jug to my lips and chug. Screw conserving. I fill my stomach like an empty sponge. Water has a flavor—it's sweet, like I've never noticed before. It's a primal taste, like a *chupacabra*'s thirst for blood. I gulp it down like a savage animal.

I pull my mouth away and a small drop dribbles down my chin. I wipe it with my wrist and lick it, leaving a glistening trail. My wet tongue against my skin feels almost icy. I lick my lips just to feel the dampness inside my mouth.

"What the hell happened to you?" Marcos asks. It's a different tone. One I don't know from him. It's the first time I've ever seen him smile at me.

"We couldn't find you. We've been looking... We have to get Arbo!"

"Okay. We'll talk about it later," he says. "Where is he?"

"I can show you."

He moves, as if to stand.

"No, we'll go. You should stay here," Gladys says.

I look at the bloody cloth draped over his leg.

"What happened?" I ask.

"I had to cut the spine out," Marcos says.

I notice the bloody knife at his side. It's flanked by small chunks of sandy flesh and a piece of cactus spine as long as the tip of my index finger.

"We're going to get Arbo and come right back," Gladys says.

"I can walk," he says.

"I know you *can*. So can we. You're still bleeding. Press," she says, motioning to the cloth on his leg.

Reprimanded, he nods slightly. Gladys and I stand. I grab the water and we run back toward Arbo. I scan the horizon, searching for our tree.

I don't see it. I stop, breathless.

"Where is he?" Gladys asks.

"We were beneath a willow. It has our clothes hanging in it, for crying out loud. How can I not see it?" I shake my fist so hard I nearly drop the jug of water.

"There!" Gladys yells.

She's points off to the side from where I was looking. I can't believe how easy it is to get turned around out here.

She sprints once more and I follow. We find Arbo in the same position I left him in. On his back, pale-skinned, he looks dead.

"Is he okay?" Gladys asks.

"I don't know."

"What happened?"

"Nothing. We just didn't have any water. We were... No, *I* was stupid. We never should have gone. And we definitely shouldn't have gone without water."

"Is he alive?" her voice breaks.

Again, I put a trembling hand to his mouth. I don't feel

anything at first. My own heart feels like it nearly stops. But as I cup my palm closer, I feel his breath.

"Yeah. He's alive," I say. "Come on, Arbo. Please. Hang in there. We need to prop him up."

Gladys helps me pull his shoulders up, and I slide farther underneath him, so that his upper body curls into my stomach.

"Arbo?"

He lets out a grumble so faint I can barely hear it.

Gladys hands me the water, and I tilt it to his mouth. I split his lips with my fingers and slowly pour. He doesn't devour it like I did. He lets it slide in. Then he coughs and water spews back out.

"We've got to do it slowly. He'll throw it up if it's too fast," Gladys says.

I give him a few more tiny sips, then set down the jug.

I look at Arbo and run my fingers through his hair. I know what's in it and I don't care. It's thick and coarse—almost exactly like my own—but on him, it's a strange sensation, like touching a part of your own body that has fallen asleep. I realize that I've known him for sixteen years and I've never touched his hair. I've never thought about this until now. And I get why. It's intimate.

Gladys grabs his shirt from the tree. She moistens the cloth and presses it to his forehead. She pulls it away, lets the damp trail evaporate, and then repeats the drill.

"I used to help with Marcos's soccer games. Guys would overheat. I've done this before."

She pulls the cloth away and puts a hand on my shoulder.

"It takes a little while, but they bounce back. I've seen it before."

"I hope you're right."

"I am," she says.

I lean my head onto her outstretched arm.

"Pato, believe me. I wouldn't lie to you. We got him in time."

I nod. I want so badly to believe what she's saying.

"And you're alive," she says, leaning her head in so that it touches mine. "I still can't believe it. I couldn't stop thinking about you. I really thought you were dead."

"I thought about you too."

She pulls her arm away, shifts, then leans over and kisses me. And for one, invigorating moment, everything else around me fades. I'm pulled into the delicate clasp of our chapped lips, gliding across each other as if they were forever moist and silken.

She pulls away and stares at me. Her dark pupils are wide, soaking up the soft light around us.

"Do you want to see something?" she asks.

"Okay."

She presses her eyes tightly shut for a moment and draws in a deep breath, as if searching for final motivation. Then she reaches for the bottom of her shirt. She lifts it up and hooks her finger around the lower rim of one side of her bra. Her left breast rolls out with a gentle wobble.

Her eyes drift upward, like they don't want to meet mine. Not that I'm looking at them.

I freeze. I don't know what I'm supposed to do, but I don't reach for it. That doesn't feel right. That's not her intent. I just stare. It's only for a second or two, then she tucks it back in.

"If I can show a boy in a bookstore, then I can show you."

I guess we've all had too much time on our hands to think. I lean in and kiss her softly once more.

"Can I admit something?" she asks.

"Yeah."

"That was my first kiss ever."

"Really?"

"Yeah. It wasn't yours, was it?"

I shake my head no. It was my third. "Could you tell?" I ask.

"No." She pretends to push me. "Whatever. You're the *second* boy to see my boob."

I smile, as much as I can right now.

She moistens the cloth and again spreads it across Arbo's forehead. I follow with the water.

"I still can't believe you're alive," she says. "You have no idea how much we cried."

"Both of you?"

"He isn't a bad guy, Pato."

"I know."

"He's serious. But this is serious." Again, she dabs

Arbo's forehead. "We started walking a couple of hours ago, hoping we might see you. He could barely stand. But he kept going. He kept saying that you didn't take any water. It was all he could think about. He looked for you with that cactus spine in his leg until he couldn't go one more step."

"Did he cut it out himself?"

"Yeah. I don't think I could have done it. I've never heard him scream like that."

I nod.

"But I'm glad he did," she said. "You heard it. If he hadn't screamed..." She pauses and looks down at Arbo. "Well, we're lucky that he did."

There it is again—luck. I love the way she looks at life. Actually, I think I just love her. All of her.

"I'm telling you all this because I think you think he's some kind of jerk. And I know he comes across that way sometimes, but he's not. You should have seen him at home. He was such a different person than the guy out on the soccer field. You know the prickly pear, right?"

"Yeah."

"They bloom in May. He used to gather the flowers every year and bring them to my mom. For weeks. She'd have dozens inside...everywhere. She loved it. And he knew it. So he did it."

"I believe you," I say. "And really, I'm happy he's here. He's good for us. I'll give him another chance."

As if on cue, we hear his voice. Alone, with night approaching, questioning whether we're out here. Gladys looks out toward the sound and hands me the bottle.

"Arbo is going to be okay. Just keep giving him sips of water. You should drink more too."

"You're going to make a great doctor someday," I say.

She kisses me, then disappears into the desert.

Arbo and I are once again alone, under the tree.

And I wait.

And wait.

Sip after sip, he stays the same.

At last, his eyes open. Not wide. Just a sliver. Enough for him to see me hovering over him.

A tiny smile forms at the corner of his lips.

"Arbo?"

"Paat…"

Half my name has never sounded so beautiful.

_ _ _ _ _ _ _ _

It's nearly dark. I hear footsteps. They're heavy and coupled with low grunts.

Marcos and Gladys emerge from the brush. He has an arm around her shoulder, hobbling step by step. They collapse next to us.

"How's he doing?" Marcos asks.

"Ask him," I say.

Arbo's eyes remain closed, but he raises a hand from atop his chest and gives a thumbs up.

"So… What happened?" Marcos asks.

"We couldn't find you," I say.

"Well, we didn't move."

"Were you shining the flashlight?"

"Too much. How far up did you go?"

"Farther than we wanted to. I kept thinking we were near the top."

"So how far?" he asks.

I look down. I can't face him, even if I'm only staring at a shadowy form.

"About forty-five minutes."

"What? We said fifteen minutes."

"I know."

"So you probably walked two or three kilometers. No wonder. Even a little turn on the way down would have put you a long way from where we were."

"But we walked around for hours looking, and we shouted."

"At night, in the wind, when you had no idea where you were going."

"We also walked this morning, and I walked again this afternoon, for hours, looking down here for you."

"Pato, we're probably five kilometers from where you left us last night. Once you got turned around up there, you didn't have a chance. You drifted. And even if you had come across us this afternoon, you wouldn't have seen us. I built a shelter. We kept our clothes on."

I don't respond. There's nothing to say. He's right.

"You know what? Don't kick yourself. I might have done the same thing. I hate giving up."

All this time together, and this is the first real connection I've felt with a guy who's going through the exact same thing I am.

"Thanks," I say.

"No more splitting up," he says. "No matter what. We stay together."

We all nod.

"I can take over," Marcos says, sliding next to me. "It'll help me take my mind off my leg."

"Okay," I say.

"You should get dressed," he says. "There's only one of us here who wants to see you in your underwear."

We switch places, and I put on my clothes.

Gladys holds Arbo's watch in her hands and shines the soft, bluish beam on his face while Marcos guides the bottle toward his mouth. Knowing how it feels to cradle Arbo's head, it's strange to watch Marcos do it. He does it fine, which is what's odd. I'm not used to seeing him like this.

Maybe Gladys is right.

Sip by sip, Arbo improves. One syllable of my name turns into two. Other words appear. Sentences form. The lights come back on.

"You're not going to try to kiss me, are you?" he asks, as Marcos leans over to tilt the bottle to his mouth. His voice is raspy, like the first words spoken after a deep sleep.

"Oh yeah. I never knew you had such a great body until I saw you in your underwear," Marcos says.

"More water please," Arbo opens his mouth to exaggerate the command.

"Last one, then you hold it."

For a little while, it's almost like we aren't where we are.

"Let's eat something and rest," Marcos says. "Maybe we can walk some before dawn."

We open a can of tuna and a roll of cookies, and we pass them around.

MOTA

"It's a little after four. We can walk for a few hours in the dark, then once sunrise hits we'll have a couple more hours. Can you do that?" Marcos asks, directing the question to Arbo.

Arbo's energy has returned in ways I didn't think possible, and Marcos claims his leg feels better. The swelling has gone down and the area around the wound doesn't look as red, so we're hopeful the infection is retreating.

I've slept some, but not much. Enough to trudge along in the dark.

We decide to follow the contour of the mountain. It's not due north, but it's close enough, and climbing seems like too much to take on without a clear reward.

Our marching order flips. We don't discuss it, it just happens. Arbo trails Marcos, then it's Gladys, with me at the end. Gladys reaches back for my hand periodically, holding on to it for a few uncomfortable steps, then releasing it when it becomes too physically awkward to maintain.

I catch glimpses of Arbo waddling ahead of Gladys. It's hard to believe that a mere eight hours ago, I thought he was dead. He and Marcos speak in low voices. We shouldn't be talking. We should be quiet. But, like Marcos said, you need to know when to break the rules. And I'm enjoying listening to them. I thought we'd die in the desert long before I ever heard the two of them banter back and forth.

"So, I have to ask a question," Marcos says.

"Okay."

"Why do you smell like piss?"

"I've been trying to figure that out," Arbo says. "I think I was lying near where somebody peed back at our camp."

"No, you smell like piss."

"It must be my clothes."

"No. It's you. You smelled like piss naked. You sat in my lap for an hour. It's not the clothes."

Arbo sniffs his arms, then at his chest. I chuckle, loud enough that he can hear.

"Why are you laughing?" Arbo asks.

"No reason."

"You know. I know you, and that's the sort of thing you say when you know. Why do I smell like piss, Pato?"

I laugh harder. It even slows my walk.

"Pato," he says.

"What?" I ask. I can barely get the word out.

"What is it? What happened?"

"I can't," I say.

"Okay. You saved my life. Whatever it is, please tell me. I'm not going to get upset."

We've all stopped walking now. Marcos swings the blue light toward me.

"Well, the thing is..."

"Oh, come on! Just say it."

"You were passed out under the tree, and I was trying to think of ways to cool you down. And we didn't have any water, so..."

"Are you telling me you pissed on me?"

I try to hold back my snickering. I can't.

"You pissed on me. Where?"

I laugh harder.

"It was my head, wasn't it? You pissed on my head!"

"Mostly," I say.

I've never heard Marcos laugh before. It's a deep belly boom. It overwhelms Gladys's giggles next to me.

Now I start to feel bad. Just a little.

"I really am sorry," I say, though my sincerity is crippled by my continued laughter. "But you're alive."

"Yeah, thanks a lot for that," he says. "Well, I guess that means you and I have something in common then."

"What are you talking about?"

"You've pissed all over both of us now. You think I didn't notice that you hosed your pants in the backyard?"

I stop laughing.

"I mean, really, is there anybody here who didn't notice?"

Neither Marcos nor Gladys says anything.

"You reeked all night."

"The situation was a little different," I say.

"No. You have a problem with urine. Admit it."

"I don't—"

"Who here is scared that Pato is going to piss on them?" Arbo asks.

"Me," Marcos says.

"Me too," Gladys says. She pokes me in the side.

"Stop," I say. I'm talking about the poking, but I don't think Arbo or Marcos can see it.

"Or what, you'll pee on us?" Marcos asks.

I'm the butt of the joke, but I'm fine with it. I'd take it ten times over to give us another moment like this. Just for now, it feels like we're not us. Like we're not orphans, not on the run, not lost in the desert, not odd pairs forced together by tragedy. We're just friends who know how to make each other laugh.

"You'd better sleep with your mouth closed," I say.

We start walking again, but they keep it up. I pick up a nickname: P-P-Pato. I hope it won't last. Then again, there are worse things that could happen. I know them well.

We watch the shadow of the mountain retreat over several hours while we continue moving forward. As Marcos predicted, his leg has made a swift recovery with the cactus spine now removed. He's still limping, but less and less. We make more progress than any of us expected. I estimate that we cover nearly fifteen kilometers this morning. Our pace sweetens our already rejuvenated mood, giving us the opportunity to feel good about resting for the day.

"I think this should work," Arbo says beneath the low branches of a willow. It reminds me of where we sat the day before. I'm not the only one who thinks this.

"I agree, but keep your pants on," Marcos says, then turns to me. "And don't pee on anyone."

Arbo laughs.

Marcos grabs the knife out of his bag. "I'm going to cut up some bushes to hang in the tree, to give us more shade. Look for any other stuff around here we can use."

"I'll help you carry it back," Gladys says.

They walk off in the direction of some roundish shrubs.

Arbo and I briefly scan the area, then turn back to each other with empty stares. There's nothing lying around that we can put on the branches. It's the floor of a desert.

"If we emptied the bags, we could hang them on the tree," Arbo says.

"Great idea," I say. "Let's do it."

I'm standing next to my pack and Arbo's, so I begin

removing the few items we have left in them. Arbo walks to Marcos's bag and does the same.

"What the hell is this?" Arbo asks, and it occurs to me for the first time that none of us have ever been in Marcos's bag before.

He's holding a large coffee can and peering inside. He pinches a piece of plastic and pulls. Dark coffee grounds spill into the sand below as he draws out a clear plastic bag and holds it toward me with one hand.

"Is that what I think it is?" I ask.

"What else could it be?"

The list is short. The bag is stuffed with tightly knotted brownish clumps that look like shriveled-up herbs. I've never seen anything like this before, but I have a solid guess as to what it is. I'm sure some people at our school would be very familiar with this stuff. But I'm not, and I'm pretty sure Arbo isn't either.

"It's in coffee. That's what they use to hide the smell," Arbo says. "It's marijuana. It has to be."

He gapes at me as though I'm supposed to confirm this. I gape back.

"Why would he have *mota*?" Arbo asks.

"I don't know."

"Do you think he's smoking it?"

"That looks like a lot to smoke," I say.

I walk toward him and grab the bag. It dwarfs my hand. I quickly understand why it was hidden in the coffee—it reeks, like a skunk. I wrinkle my nose and look at Arbo. He doesn't look shocked anymore. He's moved way past that. Veins bulge in his neck, his fists ball up, and his eyes burn hotter than the noon sand.

"I'm going to kill him," he says.

"Let's not—"

"What? You think this is okay?" He snatches the bag from me and wraps both hands around it, as if he's strangling the contents.

"No. Hell no. Of course not. But we need to—"

"No, we don't need to do anything. This is why you don't have a mom or a dad anymore!"

I don't respond. He's right. I'm upset too. It's disgusting. But Arbo looks deranged beyond reason. I fear this situation is about to get uglier than we can afford.

"I don't understand. How could he even look at this stuff after what happened? *How?*"

"I don't know. I'm with you. I'm on your side."

"Good, because I'm going to punch him."

"Don't punch him."

"Why?"

"Because we need to stick together."

"And what happens if border patrol finds us now? We don't go back to Mexico. We go to prison. You know who's in prison? *Narcos.* How long do you think we'll last?"

"And how long do you think we'll last outside prison in Mexico?" I ask.

"That's not the point."

"Then what about this: How long do you think we'll last out here on our own? We tried that one already."

"Stop standing up for him!"

"I'm not. Calm down. You're not thinking straight. Let's talk, not punch."

He pushes me. Hard. I fall backward.

"Screw you! Screw all this! Screw Mexico! Screw *narcos*! Screw Marcos!" He takes the empty coffee can and hurls it at the tree. It ricochets off the trunk with a hollow bang.

"Hey! What's going on?" Marcos asks, hobbling toward us with Gladys chasing behind him.

"I don't know, Marcos. Why don't you tell me? *¿Qué es que está pasando?*" Arbo dangles the plastic bag in front of him.

"Why did you go in my pack?"

"Are you kidding? Yeah, that's the real question here."

"You don't know what you're doing."

"*What?* I don't know what I'm doing? Why the hell are we in this *chingado* desert to begin with? It's because of this crap! This! This is why. And now we find out you're part of it?"

"You don't know what you're talking about."

"Then tell me what I am talking about. Because this sure as hell looks like a bag of *mota* to me."

"It is. And we need it."

"Marcos," Gladys says. She's standing behind him, gazing at the bag. "That's yours?"

He looks at her, then back at us.

"What are we going to have when we get out of here? Huh? What? We'll be in another country. We won't know anybody. We'll be illegal. We'll be broke. This is to get us started. We sell it and we've got something."

"No!" Arbo shouts. "This is what started it!"

"So at least we can use it to help us."

Arbo slaps his own face.

"Oh my God. This is what you were doing in Sonoyta. You were buying drugs. You were buying stuff from the same *hijos de putas* who are trying to kill us."

"No. That's my point. I was selling them."

"What?" we all say, nearly in unison.

He looks down and shakes his head, as if in regret. Regret for having told us this, not regret for having done it.

"I bought it when we were at Ortíz's house. I snuck out one night and got it."

Even Arbo is stunned silent by this.

"You left the house and went back into town?" I ask.

"You have to know when to break the rules."

"Wait, how did you buy it? You had money to buy drugs, and you let Sr. Ortíz pay for all that stuff he bought us?" I ask.

"No. I know a guy who did me a favor. He gave it to me to take across the border and sell. I'll send him some money when I sell it, and we'll keep the rest."

"You're nothing but a *narco cabrón*," Arbo says.

"No. I'm not. I did it once. For us. What do you think

paid for everything you have right now? Every drop of water, every bite of food. Everything that keeps us alive out here. That!" He points to the bag. "I sold some in Sonoyta so we didn't have to use Ortíz's charity. And so we'd have some cash if we got in trouble. Did anybody refuse it then? No. You shut up and took it. So I'll sell the rest when we get across, and guess what? You might not want to, but you'll shut up and take it again, because we'll have nothing, and we'll need it. It's for us." He points again to the bag. "This is the only thing we'll have."

"It all makes sense now," Arbo says. "I couldn't figure it out. You're why they attacked the party. And you weren't even there. Did you know it was coming? Is that why you went outside?"

"Screw you!"

"Screw me? I'm serious. Anybody else have a better theory? Why else would they hit a *quinceañera*? Carmen's *quinceañera*? A fifteen-year-old girl who did nothing wrong! It's because of you and your *narco* friends and this...crap!"

Arbo rips open the top of the bag.

"Give me the bag."

"Hell no!"

"It's mine."

"Yours? You want to know what belongs to you? Blame. For all of this. I never liked you, but I never had a good reason before. Now I do. I hate you."

I know I should tell Arbo to stop, to let it go, but I can't.

He's acting out exactly what I'm feeling. With each revelation, I'm more disgusted than before.

Arbo takes the bag and shakes the *mota* out with wild swings of his arm. The wind, so warm it's easy to forget it exists, scatters the falling pieces.

"No!" Marcos shouts. He dives for the bag.

Arbo slips out of his path, moving deftly, in a way he seldom does. He kicks the dirt below him to spread the debris even farther.

"What the hell are you doing?" Marcos says, frantically trying to capture the pieces on the ground. "This is all we have!"

"No, no, *no*! This is why we have nothing! Why don't you just go off somewhere and die like everybody else did because of this crap."

"Stop, Arbo!" Gladys yells. "He was just trying to help us."

"Help?"

"I know it's not right, but he was doing it for us."

"You're as crazy as he is. Listen to me. We wouldn't be here if it weren't for him. He's why we're orphans. Don't you get it?"

"You know what? Screw you. You're wrong. I know why it happened," Marcos says.

"All of a sudden, you know why. And it wasn't you? Right."

"It was your dad. He was in with them," Marcos says, looking Arbo straight in the eyes.

Arbo charges for him, barreling into his chest head first. Marcos tumbles backward, landing on one of our remaining four-liter jugs of water. Arbo crashes on top of him.

An explosion of water rockets out on both sides of Marcos. Arbo, either oblivious or blinded by rage, helicopters his arms, sending a barrage of blows downward, which Marcos blocks with his forearms.

"*Enough!*" I yell. This is what I feared—only worse.

I spring toward them to pull Arbo off, but before I can get there, Marcos lands a punch in Arbo's left eye.

Arbo screams and rolls off Marcos, landing in the wet dirt.

"My eye! You punched my eye, you *pendejo!*"

"You idiot. That was our water! Screw you! *¡Chinga tu madre muerta!*"

Arbo springs to one knee, to vault back toward Marcos. I try to hold him down, but I can't. My efforts send him sideways. He tumbles into Gladys, knocking her to the ground.

She screams as she falls. "Please stop!"

"Now look what you did!" Marcos says. He's pointing at Gladys, at the flattened plastic jug of water, at the weed, everywhere. He rushes to Gladys's side.

"Look what *I* did?" Arbo asks.

"Yeah, you, you fat freak!"

"How is any of this my fault?"

"Congratulations. You just killed us all." He grabs a chunk of wet sand and squeezes it.

"You landed on it!"

"Because you pushed me onto it!"

"Are you that stupid?" Arbo asks.

"Stop! Now! Stop!" Gladys shouts.

We all go silent and watch as the dirt between us morphs from wet to damp to simply discolored. The sandy ground soaks up our life before our eyes.

"If you hadn't brought that *mota*, none of this would have happened."

"Shut up. Why don't you ask your dad why all this happened?"

Again, Arbo tries to go for him, but this time I'm able to hold him down.

"Take it back," Arbo says.

"No. You know why? Because it's true."

"Whatever. You're nothing but a liar. *Vete a la chingada, mentiroso.*"

"Did you ever wonder where your dad got all the money for that nice *quinceañera*? For the ice sculpture? For the band?"

"From hard work, but you wouldn't know anything about that."

"No. From *narcos*. Ortíz knew it too. Do you remember when he came back with the newspaper with all of our pictures? Remember how he didn't have the article that went with it? You know why? Because it connected your dad."

"You're lying," Arbo says.

"Am I? Pato, you remember seeing me and Ortíz arguing, right?"

"Yeah."

"That's why we were arguing. I found out the truth when I snuck away, and then I started thinking about that paper. I asked him if he knew. He did. The whole time. And he didn't tell you. He didn't want you to think of your dads that way."

Dads.

I sink back.

Marcos continues. "So I promised him I wouldn't tell, unless I had to. Congratulations. Now you know the truth. How's it taste? You want to talk apologies? You owe me one. Your family got mine killed, *cabrón*. Which is kind of appropriate, given that you just finished us all off."

"You're lying," Arbo says again. Tears stream down his face. It's hard to tell if they're from the hit, or the accusations.

"I think you know that I'm not," Marcos says.

My mind is awash with memories, all gushing in at once, like pieces of a puzzle it's trying to assemble. *Do I believe this? Can I believe it?* Our fathers started their own construction business several years ago. They built houses. I visited them on job sites. I saw them do it. *Could they have done both? Houses and drugs?* I try to remember if I ever heard my parents have a single conversation about problems with money—I can't.

"The paper said my dad too?" I ask.

"Yeah. I'm sorry." Marcos looks at me. I can't look back. I can barely look at anything right now. The world is spinning. I want to throw up.

"They weren't selling drugs," Marcos says. "The paper said they did projects for the gangs...construction work...to hide drugs, secrets rooms and things like that. They got paid not to ask questions and not to talk. I guess they broke the rules. That's all I know."

I don't want to believe it, but the way he tells the story... It sounds credible.

I think back to what Sr. Ortíz said when he talked about his son, Diego.

Knowing what he was is a curse...

It's my biggest regret...

It spoils the memories...

Then I think about the care he took to tear our pictures out of the paper. It would have been much easier to grab the whole page, or the whole paper for that matter.

Sr. Ortíz knew.

It's as if every recollection I have of the past several years is suddenly discolored. When I was younger, I never had books. We went to the library. But over the last several years, my parents bought me a book a month. A new book. Any book I wanted.

I remember asking my father a few times on weekends if I could go to work with him. He always had an excuse. The last time, he gave me money for me and Arbo to go to a movie instead. I never questioned it. It never occurred to me to wonder why I couldn't go to work with him or how he had the money. I just took the cash.

I even think back to the "surprise" my dad had alluded to the night of the *quinceañera*, which he said wasn't really a surprise but "news...a change." *What was it?*

They were in business with the narcos. *And something was changing...*

I'm crushed. I was just beginning to accept that my future had been stolen from me, and now I'm being robbed of my past.

Gladys looks toward me. I can't meet her gaze. Not now. This is too much.

Carefully, Marcos grabs the flattened jug and guides the tiny puddle that lingers on top of it into one of our empty bottles. It's enough for a few sips at most. Then he begins scouring the desert floor and collecting—piece by piece—what's left of his marijuana.

"I'm not going with you if you bring that crap," Arbo says.

"Well, you know what? It doesn't much matter anyway. We've only got two liters of water left."

"Then leave it."

"Or what? You'll throw me on top of another bottle?"

Arbo moves to stand. I put my hand on his shoulder and stop him.

Marcos continues to gather the *mota*. "I'm bringing it. If we get out of here, somebody has to take care of us."

"I'm serious. I'm not taking a step with you. And neither is Pato."

They both look right at me. It's a moot point. We only have two liters of water. But if all this really did start with *mota*, I don't want it to end with *mota* too.

"I'm with Arbo," I say. "No drugs."

Marcos turns to Gladys, as if we're picking teams.

"Leave it, Marcos. We don't need it."

Marcos stands and chucks what he has out into the void around us. "Fine. But don't complain to me if we get out of here only to starve to death on the street."

— — —— — — —— — — ——

The problem with this fight is there's nowhere to go to calm down. Our options are to roast on our own beneath a fiery sun or to cram ourselves into a small patch of shade and swelter under the tension of being together. We huddle in an explosive mass. Limbs drift in and out of the sun and our bodies shift as we chase the slow-moving shadow beneath the tree. Nobody speaks. It's better this way. There's nothing good to talk about.

The reality is that we were in trouble with water before this ever happened. We were already going to run out. But this is devastating. Instead of relishing a sip every now and again, we suffer. We watch the sweat roll off us like blood dripping out of a mortal gash. Soon, it will run out, and so will we.

Sr. Ortíz's children wrote about wells, but we haven't seen

any yet—wet or dry. We'll either have to find water, or…
There's really not another option. We *have* to find water.

And as if this isn't enough, there are other problems on
the horizon—one of them, quite literally. The mountains to
our right continue to push us north and ever so slightly west.
We think we need to track to the east to hit Ajo, but we have
yet to find a good place to turn. We're hoping for a break in
the mountains, but that's all it is. Hope, which seemed easier
to hold on to before all of this.

I think Arbo is sleeping, but suddenly he turns to me. A
dark blue lump swells below his eye, pressing it partially
shut. He whispers, "Do you believe it?"

I nod my head.

He turns away as if I've thrust the final blade in his chest.
I wish I could have lied to him again.

I lie awake for a few hours, until my circling thoughts
finally exhaust me and I sleep.

POLLITOS

I feel a gentle brush against my forearm. I open my eyes.
Gladys is looking at me with her index finger pressed to her
lips. She's lying at my side, holding *Huckleberry Finn*. She
opens the book, grabs the pencil folded inside, and writes in
the margin of one of the pages.

Hi ☺

She hands me the pencil. I write back.

Did you sleep?

We pass the pencil back and forth, filling the slender
margins of many pages.

A little. No pillow. Oh, and sand and it's a million degrees.
Sorry I woke you. I don't feel like I can talk to you

when he's awake. →

She turns the book so the arrow points to Marcos. He's sleeping.

No kidding. This is awful.
I know. Nobody is talking! I want to talk with you. I miss
    talking with you.
Me too.
I'm scared.
Me too.
And thirsty. I bet I know what you're going to write...

I smile and mouth out, *Me too.*

I read what you wrote in here. I liked it.

I blush, trying to remember what I scribbled down while I was borderline delirious.

Thanks. I didn't mean for anybody to read it.
I figured that. But "you have to know when to break the rules."
Ha, ha.
I want to get to know you better. I like how you think,
    Pato. You're not like the others.
??
You think. Do you ever get the feeling you were born in

the wrong place?

No. You do?

Yes!

Why?

My mom wanted to be a doctor when she was little.
When she grew up, she sewed clothes. Dreams don't
happen there.

Is that why you want to be a doctor?

Maybe. I know that I say I want to be a doctor, but I'm
not sure.

So what do you want to be?

She blushes and hesitates. I grab the pencil back.

I'm going to guess. What do I get if I'm right?
I have something for you. A gift.
An artist.

She unfolds a small scrap of fabric torn from Marcos's
jeans. Weaved into the cloth is a variety of plant stems,
twisted together in an elaborate design, with varying shades
of desert green and brown ducking in and out of each other
amid the dark blue of the jeans. It's beautiful.

She motions for my hand. I hold it in front of her. She
wraps the band around my wrist and secures it by tying
together blue strands that extend from each end.

Wow! When did you make this?

Yesterday. When you were lost.

It's amazing. Where did you find all the plants?

They're everywhere. You just have to look. The world is
amazing. This has six different plants. I needed the
jeans to hold it together.

I love the blue in it.

Thanks.

I guess you proved my point. You should be an artist.

It's a hobby. It's not a job. Not where we're from anyway. You
work in a factory, you work in a field, you sew dresses.
You work. You don't play with colors and call it a job.

Who told you that?

How many artists do you know?

None.

Exactly.

But that doesn't mean you couldn't do it. Look what
you made in a place where there's NOTHING.
You're incredible. People like you go to college.
They move to bigger cities. Your cousins in Puebla
did that, right? You could study art.

I stop and realize that I'm writing about where we're
from as though it still exists for us. It's hard to let go even
when the loss is all I can think about. I twirl the pencil a few
times and redirect the thought.

Besides, your mom's work was art.

Thanks. I think she saw it that way. It was the best she could do with what she had. And maybe you're right. Maybe I could have left. Do you ever look at the stars and wish you could go there?

All the time.

Don't you think it's funny that people think that, and then they never leave the place that they're from?

I start to write and notice that she's wiping at tears.

What's wrong?

It's sad to think that my whole family had to die for me to have the chance to leave. If they hadn't, I would have stayed there. Maybe I could have left, but I don't know that I would have. I might have stayed and sewn dresses. Not become an artist. or a doctor. or whatever. Now, I feel like I really need to make it. My life can't end here. It's got to count. For them. For my mom especially. Because she never had that chance.

I think you'll be a great artist. I think you're already a great artist.

See what I mean? I like the way you think. What about you? What do you want to do?

??

No idea?

It's my turn to tear up, but I hold it back.

I always thought I'd work with my dad. Now I don't
    know what to think.
I'm sorry. Do you believe what Marcos said?
I wish I didn't.
Your dad will always be the person you want to
    remember him being.
Have you been talking to Sr. Ortíz?
??
Thanks.
We're starting over. You can be anything you want. So...
I'll get back to you on that.
Okay. Do you think we'll make it?
Yes.
Are you lying?
I hope not.
Me too. We need to think positively. Maybe we should promise
    each other that we're each going to make it through.
I promise.
Me too. There! Whew...

I smile.

And when we do, we have a small problem. I need your help.
??
Marcos thinks we should split up over there. He says that

La Frontera might be looking for us on the other side and that splitting up will make it harder for them to find us.

I don't want to leave you.

☺ Me neither. We need to change his mind, but don't say anything to him about this! He'll get mad, and everybody is already mad at everybody (except Gladys and P-P-Pato).

Pato!

☺ Let's try to talk about things that will work best when we all stick together. Like renting an apartment, maybe. It's cheaper with four people. We need to be smart. We can convince him.

I like the way you think.

She leans over and gives me a small kiss. As she pulls away, I see Marcos. He's looking right at me, with eyes narrowed like spears. He rolls over to face the other direction.

— — — — — — — — —

"What happens if we go too far north from here?" Marcos asks.

It's nearly dusk. We have a little more than a liter of water left. Because of this, we've decided not to walk until the sun is down.

"I don't know. We might miss Ajo," I say. Because I spent

an extra ten minutes with the letters and can find the North Star, I've somehow become the navigation expert. I've drawn the most basic of maps on a mostly empty page of the book to help lay out what little I know...or think I know.

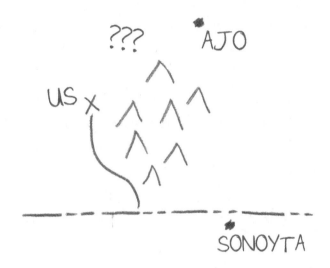

"And if we miss Ajo?"

"More desert, I'm guessing."

"So, you think it's on the other side of the mountains?"

"Probably. But I don't know. Maybe they turn. Or maybe there's a break in them. They didn't talk about climbing over mountains in the letters."

"That's because they weren't chased out of town, so they started out to the east of them," Marcos says.

"Maybe. We haven't seen the lights at night, so I'm thinking they're blocked out."

"You and your Ajo lights," Marcos says.

"I'm just trying to help," I say.

"And I'm just trying to make sure we don't walk off into the desert with one liter of water."

"We're not going to make it out if we don't find water."

"Tell us something we don't know," Marcos says.

"Give him a break. He's only trying to help," Gladys says.

"Great. Side with your boyfriend."

"Nobody's siding with anybody. We're trying to figure out what to do," she answers.

"Well, it doesn't feel like we're figuring much out."

"I'm guessing we hiked about fifteen kilometers the first day, then another fifteen yesterday," I say. "We're about halfway there. Which means we can walk for another night along the mountains to see if there's a better place to cross."

"And water?"

"Your guess is as good as mine."

"Great."

"Hey," Gladys says. "We're all in the same situation."

"Then maybe not all of us get it. We have one liter of water. That's not even going to last until midnight. And then, we *die*. We need to get out soon."

"That's what I said," I say.

"Well, you're not acting like it's a big deal."

"What do you want me to do?"

Marcos bangs his head against the tree. "I don't know. And it doesn't matter. It doesn't look like we're getting out of this place."

Arbo starts to laugh.

"What?" Marcos asks.

"We finally agree on something."

"And what's that?"

"We're screwed."

"I thought we were dead once," I say. "And we're not. So we still have a chance."

"Whatever," Marcos says. "Let's walk."

— — — — — — — —

Marcos packs his bag. Gladys sits, entranced, staring out into the sunset, as though she's enjoying it for the last time. In front of her is something new she's trying. It's a sand-scaped scene, but it springs up from the ground. A small collection of twigs, shrubs, bulbs, and other bits of nature are carefully stacked onto her three-dimensional canvas.

A tiny desert flower bulges out of the middle. As the sun drops from view, I watch her cover the petals with sand.

Marcos walks over to her.

Taking advantage of our brief separation, I pull Arbo aside.

"Hey, are you okay?" I ask.

"No, Romeo. I'm not. We're about to die."

"I thought you said you were okay about Gladys."

"I am. I don't know why I said that. I'm just…"

"You're what?"

"Done. I don't even care if we walk," he says.

"You want to sit here and die, like we were doing before?"

"That's fine by me."

"You want me to pee on your head now or later?"

I don't even get a smirk.

"Whenever you're ready."

"It doesn't change who they are, you know," I say.

"That's a lie. It changes everything. Do you know why everybody died? Almost forty people? My whole family? Your whole family? Our friends? Other families? Because of my dad."

"And mine."

"Fine. And yours. Our dads. Our *narco* dads."

"They weren't selling drugs, they—"

"I don't give a crap. They were in business with them. It was dirty money. Everything we had...dirty. I'm glad it's gone."

"No you're not," I say.

"Maybe you're not, but I am. I'm done with it."

"What would Revo tell you right now, Arbo?"

"Revo's dead."

"What?"

"You know what Revo did?"

"No."

"He fought bad guys."

"Okay."

"Well, they won. Actually, they were winning all along, and I had no idea."

It's eleven o'clock. We haven't had a sip of water since we started walking three hours ago. Marcos carries our remaining bottle in his pack.

The moon, dipping behind a mountain, presses us to an unsustainable pace, as we try to make as much progress as we can while we still have some light. My body is as devoid as the dim shadow lurking beneath me.

"There's no point in killing ourselves before we run out of water," I say.

"We can make it a little farther," Marcos answers.

We slog along for another minute or two.

"I can't do it, Marcos," Gladys says, stopping. "I need a sip."

"You know what, fine. I'm not the *jefe* here. You're all your own bosses. If you want water, bottoms up. Make it last however long you want."

He lets his pack fall to the ground. He puts the flashlight in his mouth, pulls the bottle of water out along with three empty bottles, and carefully fills them each with the same amount.

We all take sips, except for Marcos, who turns the light on his leg to inspect it. If it's still bothering him, he hasn't let any of us know.

I hold a small swig in my mouth and slide my tongue around, savoring the smooth glide across my teeth. I allow a portion to drop down my throat. I can feel it start to trickle downward before it's fully absorbed. It never makes it past my neck. I swallow the rest and exhale in delight. Then, as quickly as the relief arrived, it disappears. My mouth turns pasty again, and I eye the bottle, realizing that I could chug all that's left and still feel as dried up as the wilted bonds that are holding us together. I take one more tiny pull and hold on to it for even longer than last time.

Marcos tugs at my shirt.

"*Ven conmigo por un minuto*," he says.

I follow his instructions, walking a short distance away with him. We stop. He leans in close and speaks in a hushed voice. "If I see you kiss my sister again"—I can feel his breath, hot and putrid, punch against my face as he speaks— "I'll pick you up and throw you into a cactus."

He doesn't wait for me to answer. He turns and walks back toward Arbo and Gladys.

"Hey! We're not done," I say in a full voice.

He stomps back toward me. "Keep your voice down, and yeah, we are done."

"No. We're not even close. I'm not going to wait until your back is turned to talk to her, I'm not going to act like nothing is going on, and if I want to kiss her, I'll try to do it while you're not looking, but I'm going to plant one on her. You know why? Because we're dying, and this is all we've got. A few hours. A day maybe. And I'm done pretending." My voice has gotten louder by the word. By now, there's no doubt that Gladys and Arbo can hear everything. "So if you need to throw me into a cactus to speed up the dying and prove what a tough guy you are, then go for it. Pick one. They're everywhere."

He takes another step toward me. His nose nearly touches mine. The whites of his eyes hover like two rings, encircling the darkness inside.

"Don't. Push. Me," he says, making each word stand on its own, fully pronounced in a thick, slow, low voice. "I'm her brother, and I'll do what I have to do to protect her."

"I know," I say. "And I would too if I were you. But what I'm saying is you're not protecting her. You're hurting her. Can I ask you a question?"

"Go for it."

"How many boyfriends has she ever had?"

"None."

"And have you ever had a girlfriend?"

"Yeah."

"How many?"

"A few."

"I'm sure it's more than a few. How good does it feel?"

"What do you mean?"

"I mean, how great does it feel to have another person who wants you like that? Who loves you without you being family. Who tells you how great you are."

He doesn't answer.

"She's never had that. Neither have I, for what it's worth.

Not like this. And I think she deserves it. Before she dies. Before I die. Before we all die."

Again, he doesn't answer. He stares, long, like he's waiting for me to look away at some point. I don't.

He turns and walks back to the others.

I follow.

A soft hand reaches out from the darkness and squeezes my palm.

— — —— — — —— — — ——

I don't know what time it is. It doesn't matter. It's the middle of the night. The moon is gone. So is my water. I suck the air out of the bottle, trying to breathe in the moisture. Others do the same.

Marcos whispers something and passes his bottle to Gladys. She pushes it away. He shoves it back toward her. Neither will take the final sip.

We rest for a few minutes, then stand on shaky legs and press on.

— — —— — — —— — — ——

Arbo is the first to drop.

"I can't keep going. My legs are cramping."

None of us complain. We collapse alongside him.

"Maybe we'll be able to see something when the sun

comes up…" Marcos says. His voice fades in a way I've never heard it do. I don't know what he's hoping to see.

I reach into the darkness and grab Gladys's hand. She clutches back, and I close my eyes. If we're being watched, I don't want to know.

I let go of everything and drift into the night. I dream of a thunderstorm. A magnificent, pounding, rage of nature with gusting walls of water that slap against me, seeping into every pore of my body. As relief gushes in, a bolt of lightning explodes into the middle of us.

"Did you hear that?" Marcos whispers.

I wake in the windless night air. The first thing I feel is my thirst returning. It's not a longing. It's a pain. Then I hear the footsteps. Not right next to us, but not far away.

"What is it?" Gladys asks.

"I don't know," I say. "People."

"Shh," Marcos says.

We raise our heads and peer into the darkness. Shadows move. Many shadows. There's a flicker of light. Only for a moment, followed by a soft whistle. The footsteps stop.

"Shh," Marcos repeats, though so softly that I can barely tell he's doing it.

Did they spot us? Who are they?

My own quickening pulse fills my ears, blocking out their murmurs.

We lie low for an anxious stretch of minutes. Then one clear voice rises from the group.

"To the right. *A la derecha.*"

The footsteps resume—and become louder. We press our bodies low to the ground.

They pass within five meters and continue onward, oblivious to us. They march toward the mountains.

"Who are they?" Arbo asks as soon as the last of their group goes by.

"I don't know, but they seem to know where they're going," Marcos says. He starts gathering things.

"Do we follow them?" Gladys asks.

"It's that or lie here and die," Marcos answers.

I turn to Arbo for his reaction. He slowly pushes himself to his feet. The rest of us do the same, as quietly as possible.

"Who do you think they are?" Gladys whispers to me.

"*Un guía con pollos,*" I answer.

"What?"

"People like us, but they have someone showing them the way."

Following them is not as easy as we might have thought. We need to stay back far enough that we are neither seen nor heard, but close enough that we don't lose them in the darkness. And we can't use any light to guide us, not even Arbo's watch. We're back to Marcos waving a stick out in front of him, stopping and turning suddenly each time he strikes a target.

It's a sluggish pace, but fortunately the group is moving slowly as well.

My body still feels shriveled and empty, but the belief that we're now moving in the right direction lifts my spirits enough to lighten my feet. We don't talk, but I can sense that the rest of the group is feeling the same.

Soon the mountain begins its steep slope, and we all slow to a crawl.

"*Vámonos. Un poco más.* Then we'll go back down." The occasional voice echoes off the rocks, giving us clues as to what lies ahead.

Eventually.

Un poco más is like *mañana.* It's an intention, not a reality. An hour later, we're still climbing.

— — —— — —— — — ——

Dawn breaks, and with it, we lose our cover. We watch the group ascend in the distance until the *guía* finally delivers on his promise. The group drops over a ridge and out of sight.

We hustle up the steepening rise, winded but propelled forward by the fear of losing them. As we approach the ridge, each cautious step reveals a little more of what lies ahead. It's not what I expected. We are at the top of a hill, with more mountains beyond.

On the other side of our hill, we see the group snaking down toward an empty riverbed that forges a winding trail through the peaks ahead. I stare at the bed, wondering when, if ever, it brings water.

We rest until the group reaches the riverbed, turns around a bend, and moves out of view. Again, we follow their path.

All around us is evidence that we are going the right way—trash. It's clear that the group in front of us is not the first to pass along this ravine. Plastic and foil dot the landscape just as the prickly plants do. Empty soda cans taunt us. Shreds of other debris peek out of the sand in tattered strands. All of it looks dull and bleached, as if it were left here a hundred years ago. It's a cruel reminder of how quickly the desert destroys everything.

——— — —— — — ——

Walking in the riverbed feels both freeing and vulnerable. For the first time since we started our trip, we can move forward without fear of being jabbed or scratched, and we can take more than ten steps in one direction without having to turn. If we had any water left and weren't quickly withering away, I might even call the hiking easy. But it comes at a price. We are openly exposed to anyone in the area above, and to the group ahead of us if we're not careful. Even more than being spotted, we fear that the group will turn away from the riverbed and quickly disappear in the mountains. It's unlikely, but so was our finding them. Probability doesn't mean anything out here. You get one chance and you hope you get lucky. This is our opportunity to be led out of this death trap.

— — — — — — — —

The fire returns as it does every day, with an explosion of light and heat as the cloudless sky slings the sun over the mountains. The group stops, and we do the same. We're three or four hundred meters away from them, peering around the thick cacti and sprawling shrubs that line the edge of the riverbed. I try to count them. I think there are seventeen people total.

The cleverness I felt when I created our tree shelter disappears as we watch them unfold several small, tan tarps and drape them across a pair of *cholla* cacti, a towering mass of sprawling thorns that looks like what might happen if a cactus and a tree were to have a baby. They use its thick spines to anchor the tarps in place, giving them a broad swath of shade. Then, as we did, they huddle beneath it, too close for comfort, too hot to care. They pass jugs of water around and take long pulls on them. It's tormenting.

We backtrack until they're out of view and set up our own shelter.

"We need to make sure they don't leave without us," Marcos says.

"I don't think that's our biggest problem," I say.

He doesn't respond. Nor does anyone else. They don't need to. I look at Arbo. He's collapsed on his side, resting for now.

For now.

Gladys does the same. I feel the tickle of a headache in the back of my skull.

We won't last the rest of the day.

"We need water," I say.

"Okay. You have any ideas?" Marcos asks.

I turn and nod my head in the direction of the group.

"You think they're just going to give it to us."

"I don't know what other option we have."

Silence.

"We could steal it," Marcos says.

"There are seventeen of them," I say.

"They need to sleep. We could go in a couple of hours."

"They won't all be sleeping."

"They'll be trying to. Just one of us will go. I'll do it."

"*Güey*, they'll catch you, and then we're really in trouble," I answer.

"At least my way, they might not catch us."

"We can't steal their water. What would you do if someone stole our water?"

"And what would you do if someone walked up to us and asked for it?"

"I'd say I'd be glad they didn't steal it."

I don't say this. A coarse voice that comes from beyond our group does. We all sit up straight as two men emerge from behind a pair of thick shrubs that shield us.

"Settle down, and don't move," one of them says. He

wears a sleeveless flannel shirt that's partially tucked into his pants, revealing the upper half of a pistol.

"Anybody got any water we can have?" the other one asks, smiling through crooked teeth. He has a tattoo of three parallel bars that run up the side of his neck.

None of us speak.

"So, I'll take that as a no, huh? You want to tell us why you've been following us?" Flannel Shirt asks.

"We're lost," Marcos says. "We followed you because you look like you know the way out."

"We do. That's why you pay a *guía* to take you across. Anybody here a *guía*?"

We shake our heads.

"Every *pollo* pays the price... It's just a question of when and how much it costs you."

"I have money," Marcos says.

"Then why didn't you get someone from the start?"

"I don't have that much money."

"So, you don't cross. You wait until you do. There's a system, *güey*. You cross, you go through us. We're the ticket to the other side."

"Like I said, I have some money. Do you want to talk?" Marcos asks.

"Okay, *güey*. Let's deal. What do you have?"

Marcos stretches for his bag. Both men reach for their waistlines.

"Give me the bag. I'll open it."

"It's my bag."

"If we wanted to steal your bag, you'd be dead by now."

Marcos tosses his bag to them, a touch firmer than is necessary.

"It's in the pocket on the inside," Marcos says.

Flannel Shirt fishes out a small roll of money, counts it, then starts to laugh and shows it to Neck Tattoo.

"You want to cross for this? We can take you to the other side of the riverbed," he says, pointing about fifty meters away. More laughter.

"That's all we have," Gladys says.

"Do you see all those people over there?" Flannel Shirt asks.

They are blocked from view, but that's not the point. We nod.

"Each of them paid a thousand dollars. That's more than twenty thousand pesos."

"Can we just buy water?" I ask.

"And what happens when you try to follow us. All sloppy-like, and *la migra* finds you...then us. What happens then?"

"We won't follow you."

"There's only one way to go from here, *güey*."

I don't know whether it would help us, but I'll admit to wishing we had Marcos's *mota* right now. I wonder if Arbo feels the same.

They back away and talk quietly to each other.

"Stay here," Flannel Shirt says. He walks back to the

group. Neck Tattoo stays with us. He squats in the thin shade of a low bush a few paces away.

"How old are you guys?" he asks.

"Nineteen," Marcos says.

"All of you?"

We nod.

"You don't look nineteen. You look younger," he says.

"So do you," Marcos says.

He doesn't look much older than us, but the bars on his neck add a few years. Maybe that's the idea. I wonder what they mean, if anything.

"You. What happened to your eye?" he asks Arbo.

"He punched me," Arbo says, pointing to Marcos.

"Mr. Tough Guy, huh?"

"You want to find out?" Marcos asks.

He shoots Marcos an annoyed expression and quits asking questions. Several minutes pass in silence, then we hear footsteps. A different man appears. I recognize him from tracking the group—he's the one I thought was in charge.

He's probably twenty-five. He's wearing a beige T-shirt with some faded words in English. The stretched neckline of his shirt reveals a thin gold chain with a cross flopped over his neck. He looks us over from underneath a baseball hat pulled down nearly to his eyebrows.

"How old are you guys?"

"Nineteen," Neck Tattoo says.

"I didn't ask you," he says. He turns back to us.

"Nineteen," Marcos says.

Again, he looks us over.

"Why didn't you hire someone to take you across?"

"We didn't have any money."

"Lots of people don't. That's not how it works. You think those people over there have thousands of pesos lying around?" His tone is rhetorical. "They pick beans. They sell tortillas. They borrow the money."

"So, can we borrow it?" Marcos asks.

He chuckles.

"*No tienes ni idea, güey.* Did you just ride your bikes to the border and start walking?"

"No."

"Where are you trying to go?"

"Ajo," I say.

"Ajo. Ajo. So you do know something," he says. "Who told you to go to Ajo?"

"We read about it in a letter from a friend who crossed."

"Did your friend go through a *coyote*?"

"Yeah."

"Then why didn't you, *güey*?"

"Like he said, we didn't have the money," I say.

"But you did have some money, right?" He holds up Marcos's small roll of bills. "Which one of you had it?"

"I did," Marcos said.

"Can I talk with you for a moment, in private?"

Even Marcos looks concerned at this request.

"I'm not going to do anything. I swear. One minute and then we come back over here to your friends."

"What do you want to ask?"

"You're the money man. I have a couple of questions."

Marcos stands and they walk aside together. They never leave our sight, but they go far enough away that we can't hear them.

True to his word, they are back in under a minute. Marcos takes a seat with the rest of us.

"Okay. Let me explain how this works, since you apparently have no idea," he says. "There are two ways you can get a *guía*. If you have the money, you pay, and it's all good. But if you don't have the money, you ask *Sr. Coyote* to loan it to you. And he does, because he knows you're going to repay it. Do you know how he knows? Because he does his homework, and he knows where your family lives. That's trust."

He makes a point to look at each of us in turn.

"Can I trust you?"

We all nod.

"I'm tempted to. You look very nice. But to be sure, why don't we play a game called Confianza. It's an easy game. It's one question. Here's how it works. Everybody, point to your friend, the money man."

We all raise unsure fingers.

"Now, on three, everybody say his name."

Crap.

Marcos looks down. I know him well enough to recognize that look. He's been had. And so have we. At this point, we don't have much choice. Either we make up three names which won't match, or we all give the same name and hope that three out of four is a good enough answer. I hope Arbo and Gladys are thinking the same.

"One, two…"

"Marcos," Arbo and I say. Gladys says nothing.

He looks at Gladys with a stern eye.

"Marcos," she says in a low voice.

"Ah, Marcos. Everybody says Marcos…except for Luis."

"It's not Luis. It's Marcos," Marcos says.

"Why would you lie to me?"

"I don't know you."

"And yet, you ask me to help you."

Marcos gives a pride-swallowing nod.

"Let's play the game again," he says. "Now everybody point to him." He points to Arbo and we have no choice but to say his name.

Soon, we're all named.

"And on three, where are you from?"

This could get very ugly, very fast.

"Now, let's point again and tell me how old you are…"

Very, very fast.

"And where are your parents? On three…one, two…"

None of us answer this one.

"I said, 'Where—'"

"They don't know we came," I interrupt.

He stares at me and I stare back at him. As I do, Flannel Shirt returns. He's carrying a jug of brownish water.

"That's enough trust for now. You need water."

"Why is it brown?" Arbo asks.

"We hit an old well yesterday. It's not the best, but be thankful it had water. If it hadn't, you wouldn't be getting anything."

"So, you'll guide us out?" Marcos asks.

He nods back to us.

"How much?"

"We've got a couple of days. We'll figure it out," he says.

He turns and walks away. As he does, he says, "Come on over. There's a tree you can put your stuff on. But be quiet, our other *pollitos* are sleeping."

A
FAMILIAR
FACE

"I think he knows," Marcos says in a hushed voice.

Neck Tattoo lingers out of earshot while watching us gather our stuff.

"He might," I say. "He asked a lot of questions."

"But he could have been asking to make sure he'll be able to get his money," Arbo says.

"Yeah, but I don't like the way he ended it. He let it go too easily," Marcos says.

"What do we do about it?" Gladys asks.

"We can't do anything about it," I answer. "They have water. That's the only thing that's keeping us alive."

"That disgusting brown crap? You're calling that water?" Arbo asks.

"It's still water," I say. "And they know how to get out of here. We follow them. That's what we do."

"He's right," Marcos says. "We'll just need to figure out how to slip away once we get there."

"What if he doesn't know about us and he's really helping us?" Gladys asks.

"That's a risk I don't think we can take," Marcos says. "We already gave him all the money we have. That's enough," Marcos says.

None of us respond. Our silence is our agreement.

We walk the short distance to their camp where we find our tree. We make a plot of shade and sit, separated from the other people by about thirty meters of sizzling sand.

They look like us—everyday people, weakened from the trip, dazed from the heat. They're older, but not by much. Some sleep, some stare with blank eyes into the mountains. Most are men. I count only two women, and one of them has a baby. She's trying to nurse it under her shirt. I think about the strain my body is under and can't imagine what it must be like to be her.

I look at each one of them and wonder what drove them to make this trip. What did they have to let go of in order to come, and what, if anything, do they have waiting for them on the other side?

As I scan the group, I meet a pair of eyes. They are beneath a wide-brimmed canvas hat, folded down at the ears, buried deep in a tunnel of shade. They stare back at me and a lone finger rises to the lips beneath them, as if to say, *Shh.*

Then I recognize him. I don't know whether this is good or bad. It's the man from the motel porch. He continues to look right at me. It's not an aggressive stare, but more like he's trying to communicate. What I think he's telling me is, *It's okay, but don't act like you know me.*

"What are you looking at?" Marcos asks.

"Nothing," I say.

The man looks away.

"Well, you're looking pretty hard at nothing."

Marcos drinks the remaining swig of water from the jug and opens another one they've given us. We pass it around, ignoring the taste and taking mighty pulls as if a third one were on its way.

"We should try to get some rest," Marcos says.

We all lie down.

I consider waiting until the others are asleep to tell Arbo about the man, but I decide against it. He has enough on his mind. Instead, I keep it to myself. After the scene at the motel, I'm sure the man knows who we are, but—even though it doesn't make sense—I want to trust the person who warned me not to trust anyone.

— — —— — — —— — ——

I wait for Marcos to fall asleep, then I quietly lean over and kiss Gladys on the lips. Her eyes open and she smiles. She props herself up on one elbow and draws with a finger in the sand.

I think I love you.

I drop my finger next to hers and edit.

~~I think~~ I love you too.

We hold hands, close eyes, and sleep.

— — —— — — —— — — ——

It takes about three hours for the water to kick in. It starts with a small rumble. An uncomfortable gurgle. I shift from one side to the other, unsure of what's happening. I try to sleep again. I feel someone get up. I open my eyes and see Arbo darting away from the tree. He bolts toward a nearby bush in an antsy gallop, clutching the back of his pants. He collapses behind the shrub, dropping mostly out of view.

My rumble returns.

I'm five minutes behind Arbo. I speed past him to another bush and drop my pants just in time. Rockets don't launch with this much thrust. Every drop of water I drank feels like it's passing through me. It comes in waves every few minutes. It's not worth returning to the tree. I cram my back into the scratchy arms of the bush and try to hover under a slender strip of shade.

"I knew I shouldn't have drunk that brown crap," Arbo says. "Water shouldn't taste like anything."

I don't know what's grosser, the water or looking at Arbo right now.

"We didn't have a choice," I say.

My stomach cramps and I double over. It forces me out of the shade and into the full punch of the sun. My hands and forearms press into the scalding earth in front of me. Every part of me is miserable.

I spot a piece of foil wrapper from of a bag of chips, and I use it to clean myself. It's disgusting. I'm disgusting.

"How are you doing?" I ask Arbo.

"How do you think I'm doing? I'm th-quatting in a frying pan, peeing out of the wrong hole, and my dad sold drugs."

I turn to look around us and lower my voice.

"He didn't sell drugs."

"Whatever."

"There's a difference."

"Good. You can believe it then. I don't."

"What about the *guías*? What do you think about them? Good guys or bad guys?"

"I don't know."

"They found us dying," I say. "They threatened us, gave us bad water, and are forcing us to pay them whatever they want if they get us out."

"Okay. Then bad guys," he says.

"Well, we're taking their help, aren't we? And we even paid them."

"They took the money without asking."

"We told them we had it," I say.

"It's still different."

"Is it?" I ask.

"Yes."

"How?"

"We need it. If we don't have it, we'll die," he says.

"What if our dads didn't have a choice either? What if La Frontera came to them and told them to help, or else?"

"That's a nice story."

"Or what if they couldn't find other work? What if they needed the money so much, they had to take the deal?"

"You don't know any of this. You're making stuff up."

"I know my dad."

"And I thought I knew mine."

"He's still the same person."

"No, he's not. He's dead. You know why?"

I let it go.

When I return to the tree, Marcos and Gladys are gone. I don't look for them. I know where they are. We all drank the water. I grab a small plastic bag from our stuff and walk it over to Arbo. It's the best I can do for him. He grumbles in appreciation.

We pass hours between the tree and the bushes. As the afternoon burns on, Neck Tattoo comes over to check on us. He tells us in an unsympathetic voice, "You'll get used to the water."

We don't buy it. None of us touch it again, except to use sparse drops to clean ourselves. The sun is still near its peak,

242 | STEVE SCHAFER

and we're losing water fast enough without flushing our systems dry with that brown muck.

— — — — — — — — —

I drift in and out of sleep, though to call it sleep makes it sound more restful than it is. It's more like I pass out from exhaustion every so often.

We all struggle, though Marcos appears worse than any of us. He looks drained—when I see him, that is. He spends most of his time in the bushes. It requires less energy than going back and forth. Gladys suggests he take one of the bags from the tree. He does and keeps it propped over him like a small tent.

I don't talk much to Gladys. There's not much opportunity for romance. We give each other space to make the situation as private as possible.

— — — — — — — — —

"*Vámonos, chavos,*" Flannel Shirt says, spurring us all to move with a wave of his arm.

We're sharing our final sleeve of cookies and can of black beans, using whatever juice we can pull from a mouthful of beans to muscle the dry crumbs down. We're trying to fuel up, knowing that we have a full night of walking ahead.

The group is packing up. It's easy to understand where

all the trash comes from now. Discarded bags and cans now pepper the area, having quickly changed from life-saving vessels to desert carcasses. I grab the cookie wrapper at my side, put it in my bag, and slide the straps around my shoulders. The one benefit of no longer having any food or water is that my pack weighs very little. Still, I'd gladly trade the weight for clean water.

I try several times to look at the man from the porch, but I can't catch his eye. I don't have any specific reason to, other than to try to confirm that he's on our side.

Marcos finally returned from the bushes about an hour ago and is now sleeping at our side. Gladys gently rocks his shoulder. His eyes crack open into slivers that slowly scan around him while his head remains still.

"Come on, Marcos. We have to go," she says.

"¿Ahora?" he asks in a croaky whisper.

"Yeah. I'll help you get up."

She gives him her hand and pulls. He stays down. When I grab his other hand to help, I discover how much that awful water has affected him. His hand is cool to the touch. I've been here before, and I know where it leads.

Watching Arbo wither away was unbearable; seeing Marcos in the same state is a remarkably close feeling, one that comes with disbelief. How could someone so steely and unshakable be reduced to a stumbling lump? It reminds me of the old men in our town. I would hear stories about things they did, colossal feats, like lifting mud-buried ox carts that had tipped on their sides. But they never looked the part. Not when I saw them. They looked old, tired, and creaky. It was hard to imagine them in a different time, in a different body.

Marcos moves like he's eighty, or beyond. We get him to his feet, in a wide and wobbly stance. I hold on to his shirt. He takes a few deep breaths, removes my hand, and finds his balance on his own.

"*Vámonos*," he says, as he lumbers toward the others.

— — —— — — —— — — ——

We walk behind the main group, separated by a few paces, sometimes more, sometimes less. It's hard to tell if this happens intentionally or if it's because we're slow. We haven't had any more conversation with the leader of the *guías*. He walks in front of everybody. Neck Tattoo accompanies us in the rear.

People walk with jugs of clear water and jugs of brown water. They drink from the clear. It's apparent that the brown is there as a backup, or to give to the new guys.

Neck Tattoo gives us more of the dirty water to drink. Reluctantly, I take it. All of us do, except Marcos. I'm soon feeling the gurgle below again.

We stop periodically behind bushes and then struggle to catch up with the group.

I can hear Marcos breathe in and out of his nostrils with every step. It's an agonizing sound to hear, over and over. His limp from the cactus spine—which had almost disappeared—returns. I offer him my shoulder to lean against. He refuses. He simply puts his head down and hobbles. It's a superhuman effort, but two hours into our march, his humanity wins.

Marcos collapses onto his knees. He tries to stand and falls again.

Arbo and Gladys look like they aren't far behind him.

Neck Tattoo whistles. The leader comes back to visit us.

"It's the well water," I say. "It's making us sick."

Arbo is behind a bush and provides sound effects to reinforce my point.

"Can you walk?" the leader asks Marcos.

"*Sí,*" Marcos says. He tries again to stand and collapses.

The leader looks at each of us, then at his watch. It's nearing sunset. His eyes roll up and off to the side, as if calculating our progress. Then he turns to the group.

"We're going to take a break, *chavos,*" he says.

"How long?" someone asks.

"An hour or two."

"What?" says a guy who is standing between the man from the porch and the woman with the baby.

"Relax. We're okay on time."

The guy stomps from the front of the pack back to us.

"We paid you to take *us* across, not every *pobrecito* you find out here. Give them some water, point them in the right direction, and let's go."

"Listen up, *pollito*, you're all *pobrecitos* out here. You paid me to tell you what to do. I'm the reason you'll survive this trip. I've made it twenty-three times. How many times have you? So here's what I want you to do—sit, wait, and rest. We're climbing in a few hours. You'll need it. If I take somebody on, I take them across. You see these guys, they're with us now. You got it? Or, we can give you some water, point you in the right direction, and see how you do."

The man says something under his breath and walks back into the group. I try not to look at any of them.

The leader grabs the brown water out of my hands. He pops open the top and takes a big chug out of it.

"Your body gets used to it," he says.

He reaches into his bag and hands Marcos a full jug of clear water.

"But I still hate the taste," he says, then takes another gulp of the brown and sits down a few paces away.

We try to make it last, but between the four of us, the water goes quickly. Marcos refuses to take more than his share, but we make sure he gets it by passing it to him more often. He's too delirious to notice.

We're nearly done when the leader whistles to Neck Tattoo.

"Give them another. You're on the well water with me now."

Neck Tattoo looks at him like he's ready to throw a punch.

"You heard me," the leader says.

Neck Tattoo gives in and tosses me his jug as though it were a water balloon, hoping it might burst. We start guzzling it immediately, before anyone can change their mind. It's never enough. We could each get two gallons and still be thirsty. But it's something. You can't run on empty. Not out here.

Neck Tattoo stares at me with contempt while I drink. He paws at his neck as though he's trying to scratch away his art.

"*Gracias*," I say to the leader.

He waves back.

"How much farther do we have?" I ask.

"You'll make it," he says.

The final gasps of daylight fade, painting us all like shadows. We're nearing the end of our "break." Arbo, Gladys, Marcos, and I sit in a circle, like we did on the first night out here. We're separated from the rest of the group.

I feel the urge to pee for the first time in days. I walk to the other side of the riverbed. I don't get much more than a few drops, as though my bladder has shrunken from lack of use. I'm about to turn back when soft-spoken words emerge from the darkness.

"Don't worry about him."

I recognize the voice and turn to face him. The silhouette of his arm gestures toward the main group. "He's nervous because of the baby."

"Is the baby okay?"

"*Sí.*"

"Good."

"Is it true?" he asks.

"Is what true?"

"About your family?"

"*Sí.*"

"I'm sorry."

"Thanks."

"They came back to the motel after you ran away," he says.

"For our stuff?"

"No. For me!"

"What?"

"They saw me talking to you. They wanted to know everything I knew. They even thought I might be with you."

"I'm sorry. I didn't mean to—"

"I know you didn't. I'm only telling you so that you know why I don't want these guys to know that I know you. They put a gun in my mouth, *güey.*"

"Why?"

"To get the truth. Did you kill one of them?"

"Yeah. They were chasing us. They were trying to get us... And if they did, we'd die."

"I know."

"They told you everything?"

"No. I saw the paper they had. So after they left, I went and got it. You've got lots of people looking for you."

"Have you told anybody else about us?"

"*Güey*, I'm just trying to cross the border. The last thing I want is attention."

"Thank you. So... Why did you come to talk to me?"

"I've been waiting for a moment to explain myself. I like you. I feel bad for what happened with your family."

"Thanks. It's been..." I can't find the right word.

"At least you have your friends with you."

"Yeah. Did you meet up with your friend?"

"No. He sent a message saying that he found another way across. I'll see him on the other side, I guess. Actually, when I first saw you, for a moment, I thought one of your friends was him."

"Which one?"

"The sporty looking one."

My gut sinks.

It can't be. It must be a coincidence.

My mind races to think back through everything I saw.

"What?" the man asks.

I'm not good at acting, apparently not even in the dark.

"Um..."

"What?"

"We... We found a dead person right after we started walking."

"A guy? And you think it was my friend?"

I don't answer. I don't know how.

"Why do you think it was him?"

"He looked a lot like my friend Marcos."

"Oh my God. Where was he? How long had he been dead?"

"Just a few hours, I think. He had been shot. We saw him a few days ago, right after we crossed over the border."

"How many days ago? Exactly."

"It's all blurred out here." I pause. "Three days. We've been out here three days."

"Describe him."

"He looked like Marcos."

"Do better."

"He was maybe a little older, but not much."

"What did he have on him?" His voice grows more concerned. "What aren't you telling me?"

"Nothing. I don't know. He didn't have a bag, a wallet, or anything on him. He had on a plaid shirt and jeans. Do you know what your friend was wearing?"

"What kind of shoes did he have on?"

"Boots. Tan ones. They laced up high."

He falls to his knees.

"Are you okay?"

"I gave him those boots. They were mine. That's him. That's Victor. I know his family. I know his wife. I know his son. He's two. And he doesn't have a dad now."

I take a seat next to him.

"I'm sorry."

"¿Por qué, Victor? Why? I told him to meet me and that

I'd handle everything. But he was so concerned about the money. Always trying to look for a cheaper way to go. You don't mess around here. What did I tell you on that porch in Sonoyta? Do you remember?"

"Don't trust anyone."

"And how many times did I tell him that?"

I let the question hang, unanswered, like so much else.

"Why did you check for his wallet?" the man asks.

The space between us goes tense.

"Because we didn't want to leave him there, you know, without anybody ever finding him. We wanted to know his name so we could tell somebody."

"Victor. Victor Aguilar."

"I really am sorry."

"I know you are."

"You don't think they killed him because he looked..." I can't finish the sentence. I didn't even want to start it, but I had to ask. I need to know if his friend died because of us.

"Because he looked like your friend?"

"Yeah."

"I don't know. But it doesn't matter. What difference does it make? If he had stayed with me, he'd be alive. Maybe. Who the hell knows? What's wrong with these people? All of them. Money. That's all they're after. The holy dollar. And screw the people you need to step over to get it. They killed my friend. They killed your family. And they wonder why we don't want to stay here. All those people over there," he says and gestures in the direction of the group, "All they want to do is cross. They're good, honest people, and they paid more money than they've ever seen in their lives for a chance to live somewhere they can work hard to make something of themselves, while these *cabrones* on the border just want to find ways to screw them. To screw us. To screw everybody." He pauses and releases a long, frustrated breath. "I'm sorry. I'm upset, and I don't know what to say. And none of it makes a difference anyway. Victor is still dead."

I give him time to continue. He doesn't. "How well do you know our *guías*?" I ask.

"I don't. I went through my same *coyote*, but it's my first time with these *guías*."

"We're trying to figure out if they know who we are."

"I don't know. I'll listen. But I can tell you one thing for sure."

"What's that?"

"You know the tattoo on that guy's neck?"

"Yeah."

"It's a gang tattoo."

"Which gang?" I ask.

"Who knows? They're all bad news. I stay away."

"*Vámonos, chavos*," the leader says to the entire group.

"We need to go," he says.

"I know you said not to trust anyone, but I trust you."

"I trust you too. I'll help you where I can, but remember…

These guys don't know that I know you. It's probably better for both of us for it to stay that way."

"Okay. My name is Pato, by the way."

"I know," he says. "My friends call me Tito."

He drifts off into the darkness.

I return to my group. I don't say anything. I can't risk anybody else knowing. Arbo isn't subtle, Marcos is a wild card, and the last thing I need is for Marcos to see me telling secrets to Gladys.

We march. Again, the four of us bring up the rear, but the *guías* have switched places. The leader is now with us, while Neck Tattoo and Flannel Shirt are with the group ahead.

Marcos is better, though not by much. He shuffles and sways, but at least he can walk. That's progress. Gladys and I don't talk much. She's focused on Marcos. I get it. Arbo keeps to himself, either too consumed with the walk or with thinking about his dad to make any conversation.

Physically, I've caught a second wind. But mentally, I feel pounded into the dirt. My head is spinning after my talk with Tito. The only thing I can do with these unsettling thoughts is try to get some answers.

"What happens when we get to Ajo?" I ask the leader.

"You stick with me for a little bit," he says.

"For how long?"

"A few hours."

"Then what?"

"Then you go."

"Where?"

"That's up to you. I just take you there."

"Can we stay in Ajo?"

He chuckles. "*Güey*, you want to get out of there. It's a *pueblito*. Just a tiny, nothing town."

"So where do people usually go?"

"They scatter like little chickens. Where do you want to go?"

"I don't know. We don't really have a plan."

"You don't have family there? Who wrote you those letters?"

"They're in Canada," I say.

"*Es bien lejos.* Very far."

"We never talked about how much we'll owe you."

"We'll talk about it."

"Twenty thousand pesos?"

"We'll talk about it."

"Are you going to charge us more?"

"I said, 'We'll talk about it.'"

"It's not fair if you do," I say.

"Then I'll charge you less."

"Really?"

"*Sí.*"

"Why?"

"You ask a lot of questions."

"But you're not answering them."

"There are four of you. You get a discount. And if I

charge too much, you'll try to get out of it. That's bad for both of us."

"How much time will we have to pay?"

"You'll have enough time."

"But we don't know anybody. We don't know how to get jobs. We don't speak English."

"Relax, *güey*. I tell you what. I have an idea. I may know someone who can help you. When we get to Ajo, I'll call him. He sometimes helps me out by setting people up with jobs. I don't do this often. We'll call it a favor. No charge."

"Who?"

"Just a guy I know."

"Jobs in Ajo?"

"No, somewhere else."

"Doing what?"

"Can you wash dishes?"

"Yeah."

"Then you'll be perfect."

"Why did you give us the water?"

"Because you were going to die if I didn't."

"And you wouldn't get paid?"

"You got it."

"Thank you."

I mull over everything that he's said and done. It only adds up when I think about it one way: he knows who we are.

"Just remember, you need to stick with me the whole way."

"Why wouldn't we?"

"In case you're considering wandering off, the desert is a dangerous place. Things happen out here, and nobody ever finds out about them. You almost died once. You wouldn't want to do that again."

We both know what the other one knows.

———————————

The hours peel away in a monotonous trudge. We turn from the riverbed and start to climb again. A few hours before dawn, we reach a point where the slope no longer carries us up. Then I see it. A dim glow. The lights of Ajo lie almost due north. The town looks so close, like I could practically reach out and touch it.

"We're almost there," I say.

"Not tonight," the leader says.

"How far away is it?"

"Ten hours."

"But it looks so close."

"You don't want to try it. We've got to go around more mountains first."

With that, we turn to the east and follow the rest of the group, which has already started down the slope.

———————————

The sun bulges out of the earth like a giant stop sign. We're back near the desert floor, but elevated enough to appreciate the same vastness and nothingness that we had on the other side of the mountains. It's the mirror image of where we were when we started following the group—a steep climb to the west and a mind-numbing swath of drought stretched out to the east.

"A little farther," the leader says.

The words sting. I'm depleted and ready to rest. I could happily collapse right here, in a pile of sand and rocks. And I'm doing much better than some of the others. Despite the clear water, Marcos is still visiting the bushes often. He's thrown up a few times as well. He looks the part.

But for now, we defy the daylight and continue our slog forward. As I gaze into the baked gulf, wondering how much farther into it we have to walk, I see a brief pulse of light out of the corner of my eyes.

I look toward it. It flashes once more. It looks like a reflection, but I can't tell what's causing it. I squint and cup my palms over my brow.

Just as I recognize it, I hear the scream.

"¡La migra! Everybody down! Now!"

We all obey.

"Where?" Arbo asks.

"Out there. It's a car," I say.

"You saw it?"

"I think so... It looked like sun reflecting off a windshield."

"How many?"

"I only saw one."

"How far away?"

"I don't know. In the distance."

"Could they see us?"

"How would I know?" I ask.

The same conversation happens throughout the group in a low rumble.

"Everybody shut the hell up!" the leader barks in a low voice.

Again, we obey.

With faces buried in the hot sand, we can see nothing. We have no way of knowing if they're about to spring out of the nearby bushes or if they've moved on.

We lie still and hope, like a hunted animal hiding from the lion...in the den of the tiger.

I don't know how much time passes. The silence is torture. I think of what being captured means—the consequences get worse each step of the way. A beating. Then back to Mexico, to the home we don't have. Then facing the gang. Then...the end.

The leader crawls around, peeking from behind bushes and cacti until, finally, he calls out.

"*Paramos aquí.* Find a spot and stay low. There is too much *migra* on this side of the mountains for us to walk around in the daytime."

We crouch and move a short distance away to a large rock. It won't cover us for the whole day, but for the next few hours, it will keep the four of us in the shade. It also saves us the effort of making any kind of low shelter right now. It's a trade-off we're willing to make.

Again, we're separated from the broader group by a small gap. Neck Tattoo shuffles over to join us with a half-full jug of clear water and a peeved expression. He takes the cap off the jug and guzzles a good portion down. I catch a quick exchange of looks between him and the leader, and it's clear—the water was intended for us.

He puts the top back on and tosses what's left at my feet. It's barely more than a liter now.

"You don't get any more. Make it last," he says. "Unless you want more of the brown," he adds, looking at Marcos and laughing.

He sits alone several meters away. He's there to guard us, to make sure we don't leave, or even discuss leaving. It's concerning, but I'm too tired to care. We're not in any condition to wander off in the middle of the day. It's like the water that we don't have enough of—we'll deal with it later.

"If we make it out of here," Arbo says, "I'm never going to complain about being cold. Ever. No matter what."

"Or about rain," I say.

"Or any drink, of any kind. I don't even care if it's tomato juice," Gladys says.

"Or—" Marcos starts to say.

"Shut up and go to sleep," Neck Tattoo interrupts, pulling up his snarled lips enough to reveal his mangled teeth.

"Sure thing, *güey*," Marcos says. He shifts his head onto the corner of his backpack.

I stare at him and wish I had the old Marcos back.

— — —— — — —— — — ——

My eyes open. We're still in the shade, but something is off. I feel a weight on my feet. I look down. My pulse triples.

A rattlesnake slithers across my ankles. I try not to move. My body tenses. The snake stops.

Rattle, rattle.

Normally, people don't die from rattlesnake bites, assuming they are healthy and they can get to the hospital. But if I—or any of us—get struck out here, it's a death sentence.

I move nothing but my eyes to see if anybody is awake. I'm turned on my side and can only see Gladys. She's out.

Maybe if I just wait...

The snake stays put. I move my gaze down and watch its slimy little tongue zip in and out of its mouth. It's more than a meter long.

I start counting, hoping that it'll move along. *One, two, three...*

It doesn't move.

I can't stay like this. I've never been good at sitting still. All I want to do is shift. It's painful to remain frozen, like I'm resisting the urge to itch.

What if I kick really hard?

Its head lifts up off the ground and its body recoils slightly. It looks right at me, as if daring me to move.

If I kick, it will either hurl onto Gladys or turn to bite my leg. Probably the latter. It's faster than me. Much faster.

Rattle, rattle.

I'm at a loss. I don't want to call anyone's name. The noise might frighten it, as would any nearby movement. I don't want it frightened, like me. I move my head slightly.

Rattle, rattle.

It recoils a little more. It turns away from me and looks back at my leg, licking its lips in anticipation.

I'm going to kick. I need to kick.

I close my eyes and prepare. I think about *how* I'll need to kick. Up. So that it goes over Gladys. My knee is slightly bent, but I need to bend it more to get leverage. I gently scoot my body down while trying not to move my leg.

It doesn't like this.

Rattle, rattle, rattle, rattle.

This can't last long. I decide to scoot down and kick in one—hopefully quick—move. *On three. Uno, dos...*

Bang!

My whole body flails and my legs snap up to my chest in a clumsy panic. Gladys, Marcos, and Arbo all scream at once, along with others in the larger group.

The leader charges toward us.

Neck Tattoo is standing over me laughing. He's waving a gun at the snake, which is now missing its head. Its scaled body twists like an unwinding rubber band. To hit the snake's head, the bullet must have missed my leg by next to nothing.

"What are you doing?" the leader demands.

"Rattlesnake," says Neck Tattoo.

"You want to tell *la migra* exactly where we are?"

"It was on his leg, *jefe*. And *la migra* has already moved on," he says, smiling at me.

"I don't care where it was. Do you have any idea how much *migra* is on this side of the mountains? They're still out there! Somewhere."

"You said you wanted them alive," he says.

The leader gives him an awkward—and angry—look.

"Of course... I want everybody here to make it alive."

"So, look at him... *Está vivo*. Alive and well, for now."

"What's that supposed to mean?" I ask.

"Until another snake comes to get you," he says, chuckling and scratching at his scrawny neck.

"Shut up and put the gun away," the leader says. "We need to move. You don't make that much noise out here and stay in the same place." He turns to us. "Pack up your stuff."

He walks away and delivers the news to the other group. The grumbles are almost as loud as the gunshot. Neck Tattoo turns to fend off the nasty looks.

I lean over to Marcos and whisper, "Give me your knife."

"Why?"

"Just give it to me."

He pulls it out of his bag and slides it to me. I reach for the tail of the snake and make several quick slices. Then I grab the tip and slowly draw it back toward me, careful not to let it rattle. I empty the few remaining things out of my bag and roll the rattle up inside. I put all of it into Arbo's pack.

Neck Tattoo turns back toward us. I lunge for the snake and fling it away.

"Stupid snake," I say.

Neck Tattoo claps his hands in delight.

I grab Arbo's pack, and we all march toward the main group.

"Why?" Marcos whispers.

"I don't know yet," I say.

— — — — — — — — —

We walk for an hour, drifting away from the mountains. The morning sun no longer feels like morning. It already feels hotter today than it has any other day, if that's even possible. But it's all shades of fire anyway.

Again, Neck Tattoo walks with us in the back. At this point, he's probably better off back here. The others turn around occasionally and curse us with their eyes, reminding us that we're the reason they're walking right now—all of us. Even the baby cries, as if yelling at us.

"My wife needs to feed the baby. How much farther?" the father asks.

"Fifteen minutes," the leader says.

"Can we stop sooner?"

"No."

"You only stop for them? Is that how this works?"

"Relax, *amigo*."

"They don't have a hungry baby."

Nobody is relaxed.

Neck Tattoo turns to me several times during the trek, scratching at his neck and smiling. It's creepy. And his scratching isn't really scratching. It's more like he's playing with his...

Tattoo.

He's not scratching. He's pointing.

I think back to what Tito said. It's a gang sign. As I stare at it, I know which one it is. I even get what it means, I think. There are three parallel bars—two thicker ones separated by a thinner bar that runs down the middle. It's a border. The Border...La Frontera.

Despite the heat, a chill runs down my spine. I know this doesn't really change anything, but his presence feels more threatening now.

I need to tell the others. We have to get away. But how?

I don't have answers, and I don't even have space to discuss it. I feel like I haven't talked with my friends for days. We're under the microscope, our every word eavesdropped upon. It keeps us quiet. It keeps us apart. We walk side by side, yet I feel more disconnected from them now than I have at any other point in our trip.

There's only one answer. I need to wait until we rest and Neck Tattoo goes to sleep. This means I have to do two things that I don't want to. First, wait. Second, stay awake. I'm panicked, but I'm exhausted.

— — —— — — —— — — ——

He lies down facing us. His guard has become less subtle at every stop. Whereas before, we at least acted like neither of us knew the truth about each other, now it seems like that knowledge is an unspoken given. Neck Tattoo is here to make sure we don't leave.

His eyelids droop, then the moment I think he's gone, he looks at me again and fondles his neck. Gladys, Marcos, and Arbo have long since passed out. He's staying awake because I'm staying awake. It's now a contest. I need to let him win.

I close my eyes and do the only thing I can think of to keep myself from crashing into a deep sleep. I relive that awful night. I play it back in my head in miserable detail. I imagine horrible thoughts like what my parents' final words were, or if they were holding hands when they went down. I try to count the bodies scattered across the yard. I hear the shots fire. I listen, helplessly, to the screams again. I'm angered. I'm saddened. I miss my parents so much. But I'm awake.

I open my eyes a short while later and Neck Tattoo is out.

Quietly, I reach for my book. I look at Arbo and consider

waking someone else. But I don't. He needs to be rallied, and I need my friend back.

I tap his arm and hold an open page of the book to his face. I've written in the margin.

> That's a La Frontera gang sign on his neck. He knows. We need to do something.

He grabs the pencil and writes back.

> How do you know?

He keeps pointing at it and looking at me.

> That's not really proof.

It's three bars. The one in the middle separates the other two, like a border.

> Huh?

Never mind! He knows! They know! We need to do something!

> I don't remember my dad having a tattoo like that.

Stop it.

> Stop what?

This. It ends now. We need you back. Believe me, I get it. I'm the one person who really gets it. But we have to get out of here. If not for your dad, then do it for your mom. Or Carmen. Or anybody else who's not lucky enough to still be around. Okay?

He holds on to the pencil for a while. I give him time.

Okay. What do we need to do?

I don't know. That's why I'm writing.

I think we wait until we get to Ajo.

And then what?

Sneak away. What are our other options? Do you really want to run off into the desert?

Maybe.

And then what? Where do we go?

We can follow the lights to Ajo ourselves.

Where they'll be waiting for us. They'll get there before we do. And if that's really the only town out here, they'll know that's where we're going.

Good point.

If we wait, at least nobody there knows we're coming. We all get there at the same time.

It makes sense, but I don't like it. I wish there were a better option. But I can't think of one.

I'm going to tell M & G so they know. Or maybe they'll have another idea.

Arbo nods.

I turn and gently nudge both of them awake. I point to where they should start reading.

Read conversation on the next few pages between
   Arbo and me. They know. We need a plan. Agree?
   Thoughts?

Marcos barely lifts his head up off the ground. He grabs the pencil. Gladys reads over his shoulder as he writes.

Just one request.
??
I want to shoot him.
I think we're better off sneaking away.
You sneak. I'll shoot. Just the jerk with the tattoo.

Gladys gives me a concerned look. I turn to see Neck Tattoo shifting in his sleep. This could quickly get dangerous if he wakes and reads what we're writing. I keep a watchful eye on him.

That will make it harder to get away without being
   noticed.
They're going to notice anyway.
But it draws attention to us. We need to get out
   of Ajo fast and quietly.
How?
I don't know. I don't know Ajo.
Then I say we shoot him. One less narco. One less
   problem.

I stare at the page, unsure what I can write to take his mind off this path. I'm not sure I can. Fortunately, I'm not the only person who is reading this.

Gladys grabs the pencil.

> Making it out alive is more important than getting revenge.

Marcos glares at the page for a few seconds, then drops his head back onto the sand, closes his eyes, and gives a surrendering thumbs-up.

Gladys grabs the book.

> I'm worried about him.
> Me too.
> He can't eat anything. He just throws it back up.
> We'll be in Ajo soon.
> He can't die. I can't let that happen.

Tears drop onto the page.

> He's not going to. We're not that far away.
> Hug me. Please.

I slide over and wrap my arms around her. She buries her wet face in my chest. Her body shakes. She's trying to be quiet, but soft sobs escape.

I hold her until she calms.

She whispers in my ear, "It's not pretty anymore. I can't see it."

I don't understand. I stare at her, confused. She pulls away and reaches for the book again.

The desert. Around us. It's dark. It's death. I want out.

We'll get out.

I tried to sand-scape this morning and I couldn't. I wanted to tear it apart. All of it. I hate it. I can't stand feeling like this.

It will end.

Promise me.

I did. And you promised me.

We promised we'll get out. What about Marcos? Do you think he'll make it until Ajo?

He has to. And he knows that, so he will. He's tough. He'll find a way.

If he dies, I don't know what I'll do. He has to live, Pato.

I nod.

I'd trade places with him. I'd die for him. I would. He has to make it. I can't stand seeing him like this.

I know. I felt the same way when I was watching Arbo. But he's better now, so there's hope.

She leans back in and hugs me again. She whispers softly in my ear, "I'm not paying much attention to you. I'm sorry."

I turn my mouth to her ear and say, "Don't worry about it. We have the rest of our lives."

She reaches for the book and writes a final note.

⌣

— — — — — — — —

When I close my eyes to rest, sleep engulfs me. Dusk comes in a flash.

"*Cinco minutos*," the leader announces. Five minutes until we leave.

Gladys and Arbo both shuffle to the bushes, leaving Marcos and me sitting side by side. He looks at me with an expressionless nod. I hand him the water. He concedes to a few sips.

Neck Tattoo still hovers, but at a safe enough distance that we could talk. We don't. We watch silently as our camp begins to stir.

Shoes are laced, packs cinched, snacks eaten, as all prepare for the next step of the journey. Watching the others, I think about what Tito said and about how much I'd like to be with them in other circumstances. I wish I could hear their stories. Maybe it would make me feel better about mine.

After a few minutes, I get an uncomfortable feeling.

Something is off.

It's that gut voice. The same voice that told me about the black car. I can't place this feeling, but I'm not going to dismiss it this time. I focus. *What is it? What's off?*

That's when he catches my attention. Tito stares directly at me. We lock eyes and he holds my stare. Tightly. He's trying to tell me something, but I can't figure out what it is.

"What's his deal?" Marcos asks through an exhausted breath.

"I don't know," I say. "But we need to find out."

"Same guy who looked at you before. You know him, don't you?" Marcos asks.

I don't answer. I'm focused on Tito.

"Hello?" Marcos says.

Tito looks at the leader, then back at me. Then at Neck Tattoo, then back at me. Then he holds his stare.

I get it.

Where is Flannel Shirt?

I scan in all directions. He's not in sight.

Maybe he changed clothes?

I look at everybody in the group, one by one. None are him.

"The guide in the flannel shirt is gone," I say. Now I have Marcos's attention. He lifts his head and scans the crowd.

"Crap."

"Yeah," I say. "We're in trouble."

"We won't make it to Ajo," he says. "We won't even get close."

Neck Tattoo turns toward us. We both hang on to our thoughts for a moment. I try as best I can to look exhausted, not distressed.

He turns away.

"Thoughts?" Marcos asks.

"I have an idea…" I say. I walk him through it.

"I'm with you," he says. "But we do it my way."

I open my mouth to push back, then stop. His jaws pulse the way they do when he's locked on a decision.

I let it go.

PROMISES

As we snake out of our camp, I'm still hopeful that Flannel Shirt will appear. He never does.

We wait for dark.

It's almost an hour before I hear her scream.

"My ankle!" Gladys yells. She hits the ground with a thud.

"¿Qué pasó?" Marcos asks.

"I twisted it. I stepped on something," Gladys says, her voice dripping with pain. She screams again.

The two of them are surprisingly believable.

Neck Tattoo shines a light on her. Gladys is curled on the ground, clutching her ankle.

Quick footsteps approach.

"How bad is it?" the leader asks.

This is my opportunity.

I back into the darkness, taking slow, soft steps around the others in the group. The farther away I get from the lights shined on Gladys, the harder it is to see. The moon, low in the sky, gives me just enough light to avoid plowing into another person, or some other kind of trouble.

I gently tug at Tito's hand, and he follows me a few steps into the desert.

"How long ago did he leave?" I whisper.

"An hour or two before we started walking," Tito says.

"They're going to try to take us before we get to Ajo," I say.

"I think you're right."

"We need your help."

"Tell me what I can do."

I see them lifting Gladys to her feet. I don't have much time. I set down my bag and rush through the plan.

— — —— — — —— — — ——

I'm in the back now with Arbo. Marcos is in front of him and Gladys limps ahead of all of us.

I watch the moon and wait for it to touch the horizon. As it sinks, the faint light around us fades, thickening the shadows, plunging us further into darkness.

My palms sweat, the same as the rest of me. With each step forward, my pulse deepens, like the penetrating thump of a low drum. It throbs against my neck. I can hear the blood course through my ears. My breaths become short and loud. I wonder if I'll be able to hear the sound from where I am, above all the noise I'm making.

But when it finally comes, it's clear and unmistakable.

Rattle, rattle.

Rattle, rattle.

The woman with the baby shrieks.

Someone yells, "*¡Culebra!*" I think it's her husband.

Other shouts follow. I hear panicky feet stomping at the ground.

Neck Tattoo fires up his flashlight and charges by me, light in one hand and gun in the other. As he passes Marcos, he nosedives into the dirt. His flashlight bounces off the ground and tumbles erratically, finally coming to rest at an angle that points outward into the desert.

Neck Tattoo lies splayed on the ground in front of me.

Marcos leaps on top of him, blasting the wind from his lungs. The dark mass of their two bodies begins to twist violently on the desert floor.

A gut-wrenching thought cycles over and over in my head. *All we had to do was run away. We could have simply let Neck Tattoo join the snake hunt. But I gave in...*

I look at the group ahead of us.

Rattle, rattle.

The screams and stomps continue. A beam of light whips around at their feet.

And in front of me, the struggle continues. They grumble. They tumble. They bleed precious time from the clock. I'd help, but I wouldn't know how. It's impossible to tell who is who in the dark.

Rattle, rattle.

The sound is farther away now. Tito is moving to give us more time, but he can't do it forever. If it goes on for too long, they'll figure it out. For now, fresh shrieks emerge.

We need to go. Now.

I grab the flashlight from the ground and shine it on Neck Tattoo and Marcos. It's a risk, but I'm hoping the group ahead is too distracted to notice.

Marcos is on top with one hand planted in Neck Tattoo's face. Then I see what really matters. Neck Tattoo's gun. It's buried in Marcos's stomach, with the barrel pointed out to the side. They both have a hand on it. They rock back and forth, in surges, each fighting to take control.

I think back to Arbo's backyard, when I stood by and watched. I won't do that again. I have to help.

But I'm too late. When I'm about to lunge, Marcos flops onto his side. As he does, a bright flash of light pulses with a deafening bang.

Gladys screams.

I jump, and the flashlight falls out of my hands.

Again, the blasts continue. This time, they're muffled, as if pressed against something.

Neck Tattoo gasps.

Marcos jumps off him. "Let's go," he says.

"My leg," Gladys whimpers. She's sitting, clutching it with both hands. This time, she's not pretending.

My heart drops.

Arbo grabs the flashlight from the ground and shines it on her leg. Her thigh is bloody.

Another flashlight shines on us as a figure charges toward us from the group ahead.

"*¡Paren!*" shouts the leader.

Marcos shoots. It stops the leader in his tracks. The group erupts into chaos.

Marcos shoves the gun at me. "Take this," he says.

He slings Gladys up over his shoulder. Arbo lights a path into the desert and we bolt out into it.

The leader fires two shots. I hear one of the bullets whiz by, which must mean that it almost hit my head.

"Turn off the light!" I yell at Arbo as we all duck.

We're back in the dark. Gladys cries softly. I wish I could do something, but I can't. We can't. Not right now. First, we have to get out of this situation alive.

A beam shines in our direction.

"Shoot!" Marcos says to me.

I aim at the light and almost pull the trigger. Then I remember the other *pollitos*—they're all around him. I tilt the barrel up to the horizon. I'd love to knock him down, but I can't chance hitting one of them.

I fire.

"We can see you," Marcos yells. "Try to shoot us, and we'll shoot you first."

The flashlight turns off. We're left blinded, except for the dim shadows of objects immediately in front of us.

A shot blasts into the air. The bullet pings off a nearby rock.

We hit the ground and crawl. Marcos has Gladys flopped on top of him, like she's riding a horse on her stomach. I'm in the lead, shuffling forward on my knees with my backpack out in front of me, to take the sting out of anything I bump into.

Another shot sounds off from behind us.

"Shoot!" Marcos whispers.

"Then he'll know where we are," I say.

Another shot follows.

Then another.

And another.

It's terrifying. We crawl faster.

"You'll die out there on your own," the leader yells. "Then I'll find your bodies and turn you in just the same!"

I feel the ground sloping slightly downward. It leads into a dry creek bed. It's narrow, but perfect. It's the dumb luck we need.

We're back on our feet—three of us, at least—and the path ahead is clear.

"Gladys!" Marcos whispers.

"I'm still here," she answers.

"I'm so sorry. I'm so sorry. I got you shot."

You should be sorry, you idiot! Run. That was all we needed to do.

I want to kick him—and myself, for letting him have his way. We press forward.

I hear Marcos mumbling to his little sister, as the noises from the group fade into the distance.

A few minutes later, I stop. "We're far enough away now. We need to look at her leg," I say.

"Don't shine the light," Gladys says.

"We need to see it," Marcos replies.

"No. They'll see us. Just stop the bleeding."

"How bad is it?" Marcos asks. He's sobbing now.

"I don't know," she says.

"Use the watch, and we'll block the light," I say.

I take off my shirt and hand it to Arbo. He spreads it out in the direction of the others. Marcos shines the soft light on her leg. It's a dark, wet mess.

Marcos turns away and vomits.

We're left back in the dark.

"Where does it hurt?" I ask.

"I don't know."

I grab the watch from Marcos and shine it again on her leg. I see the hole in the outside of her right thigh. Blood flows out from the wound.

I want to vomit too. I want to scream.

This isn't real! It can't be.

I want to close my eyes, wake up back in Mexico, and discover that this whole thing is just a nightmare.

I want to shoot Neck Tattoo myself.

I want to shoot Marcos for messing everything up. I want to scream at him and ask him what the hell he was thinking.

Why did he have to be the hero? We were so close. All we had to do was run, but he couldn't let it go. We didn't need a hero. We needed to get away. Period.

And I let it happen. I let him talk me into it. I could have stopped this. I had my chance.

And now...

I want to give up. I don't see a way out.

But I don't want Gladys to know any of this. I want her to know that everything is going to be fine.

"It's okay," I say. "You're losing a little blood. We need to wrap it, that's all."

I turn off the light, and grab my shirt from Arbo.

"This is going to hurt, but you can't scream. Okay?"

"Okay," she says, as though she's already feeling what I'm about to do.

I feel for the bullet hole. She squeals under her breath. I want to yell for her. I wrap my shirt around her leg and tie it down as hard as I can.

"That's not wrapping it, that's a tourniquet!" Marcos says.

"We have to stop the bleeding," I say.

"She's going to lose her leg!"

"She's going to lose more than that if she doesn't stop bleeding." Immediately, I wish I hadn't said this.

"He's right, Marcos," Gladys says. "It's okay." There's strength in her voice, but I can tell that's not really what she wants to say.

"We need to get farther away without her losing more blood. We can clean it and rewrap it later," I say.

But it's a lie. We don't have any water to wash out her wound. We don't have anything remotely clean to press against it. And I have no clue what I'm doing. I only know we have to stop the bleeding.

I hoist her onto my back.

"No, I'll do it," Marcos says.

"We'll take turns," I answer.

She wraps her arms around my shoulders and I bend forward. Her tears roll down my neck, and her heavy breaths slap against my ear.

Each step is a small lunge. My legs burn with the fury of the midday sun. When I think it's too much, I focus on her breathing. I sync mine to hers. I think of what she would do for me.

She whispers this love to me from time to time. "*Te quiero, Pato. Te quiero.*"

I'll fall before I stop.

Grunt by grunt, we make our escape, stumbling away from a quick death and out toward a slow one.

"I think it's time to stop," she whispers in my ear. "We're far enough away."

We've only been walking for fifteen minutes, but they've

been crippling. My thighs ache like never before. I've carried Gladys the whole way. Arbo simply couldn't do it, and I didn't want to give Marcos the satisfaction of helping. He created this mess. But it's not like he could have helped anyway—he's a sniveling wreck.

I put my hand on her lower leg. It's soaked. Fresh blood still drips down.

I want to burst into tears.

"Gladys wants to stop," I say. "We need to get out of this gully in case they're following us."

I don't wait for a response. I turn to the side and climb up the shallow embankment.

The others follow.

Twenty meters of agonizing shuffles later, I crumble. I've hit my wall. Gladys rolls off me toward her good leg, while Marcos and Arbo help guide her down. We elevate her leg on a pack. Marcos cradles her head. It's a familiar scene, rearranged in all the wrong ways.

"What are we going to do now?" Marcos asks. It's not directed to anybody. It's rhetorical, and hopeless.

I don't have an answer.

I shine the watch light on her leg. The shirt is drenched.

"Should we wash off her leg?" Marcos asks.

"We don't have any water," I say.

"You didn't get the water?"

"No. I got a little distracted, okay?"

This was my role in the plan. In the commotion, I forgot

about it. That I could forget about water after all we've been through out here is unthinkable, but then, so is this. And I don't think that water will solve her biggest problem right now.

"Give me your shirt, Marcos," I say.

"Please don't touch it again," Gladys pleads.

"We have to stop the bleeding, or else..." I can't finish the sentence.

"Pato, I don't think..." she says, unable to finish hers too.

"Don't let her die, Pato," Marcos says, handing me his shirt.

"Nobody's going to die, okay?" I say. "I'm just going to put more pressure on it. Not much."

I turn off the light, leaving us once again under the faint glow of the stars. I push lightly into her leg and she inhales a painful breath.

Marcos leans over in the darkness and grumbles in my ear. "You have to save her. If we get out, you've got my blessing. You got that?"

I don't answer.

I don't know why this is on me. I don't want this responsibility. If anything, it should be on him.

"Look at the stars," Gladys says. "They're amazing."

"You told me not to do it," Marcos says. "You said revenge wasn't as important as getting away. You knew. And I did it anyway! What the hell was I thinking? Could I be a bigger *pendejo*?"

"It's not your fault," Gladys says. Her voice strains to get to a whisper.

Of course it is! Now that we're "safely" away, I want to reach out through the darkness and strangle him. But it's not worth it. For Gladys. For us. Blame won't change what happened. It won't get us out of the desert. It won't make anything better.

"Of course it is!" Marcos says. "All we had to do was escape. Quietly. That's it. And I couldn't do it. I could have let him run by, but I *had* to show him what I thought of him." The wet words slobber out of his mouth. "I'm such a *pinche pendejo*! I'm supposed to look out for you. And now you're...you're..."

"It's going to be okay," she insists. "I love you. No matter what happens."

There is peacefulness to her voice. Like she's happy. This is what she wanted. She's traded places with Marcos. And I'd trade places with her, if I could.

I'd like to say this revelation makes me feel better. It doesn't.

"We need to get help," Marcos says.

Nobody answers. There is no help. We are all we have.

"Did you hear me?" he asks.

Silence.

"Hello?" he says.

I reach for Gladys's hand. She squeezes it like she never wants to let go. I squeeze back. All I want is a moment alone with her. Leave it to my best friend to understand this.

"Let's take a look around, Marcos," Arbo says.

"For what?"

"For anything. We're looking for a miracle at this point. Maybe we can at least find a rock to climb on to see if there is anything around here."

There is a pause while Marcos thinks it over.

"Or, we could sit here and do nothing," Arbo adds.

Marcos kisses Gladys's forehead.

"I'll be back in a couple of minutes," he says.

The blue light fades out into the night. I ball up my pack and put it under her head.

"P-P-Pato," Gladys says.

I lay my head on her shoulder. "I don't know what to say. I feel like I should have the perfect words, but all I want to do is cry."

"Don't. I found it again. Beauty. Art. This place. Look at where we are."

"I need to put pressure on your leg again."

"You just did," she says. "It can wait a few minutes. Let's look at the stars for a while."

I feel her arm gesture upward, and I track it with my eyes.

"They're amazing. I could stare at them forever," she says.

"I could too."

"Show me a constellation."

"I don't really know the official ones. I only know the ones that we made up."

"So show me one of those."

The first one I spot is directly overhead. I smile. I hope she can sense it.

"You're not going to like it."

"Why?"

"Right above us is the Wrestler."

She lets out a soft, airy laugh.

"Where? How?"

I press my cheek to hers, raise her arm into the air, and point with her finger.

"You see those four stars that look like a box?"

"Yeah."

"That's his head. Then, go down to the left and to the right. You see the brighter stars there?"

"Yeah."

"You make a triangle from his head to those lines and that's his cape."

"Where is his body?"

"He doesn't have one. He's a head and a cape. That's it."

"What about that star down there? That could be his leg."

"Then he only has one leg."

"I hope you don't have a problem with that," she says, pinching at my neck.

Ugh.

"I'd take you with no legs."

"Like your wrestler. Are there others?"

"Yeah. They're mostly Revo stuff though."

"We should make our own," she says.

"I'd like that."

"Let's do it now."

"Okay. You're the artist. What should we make?"

"I don't make it. It's already there. I'm just open to seeing it. But I don't think it should be something random. It should be something meaningful to us."

"Like what?" I ask.

"We'll know when we see it."

"It's a big sky. Where do you want to look?"

"North."

I roll fully onto my back and lay my head in the crook between her chest and shoulder. My head rises and falls with each breath she takes. We stare together into the endless possibilities.

"I've got it," she says. "It's perfect."

"Where?"

She guides my hand and points. "Do you see it?"

I stare at the jumbled mess above and fail to connect any meaning from the shape.

"No. I'm sorry. I'm trying."

"Look from the North Star, up and to the right. You see that other bright star?"

"Yeah."

"Now, use the stars on top of it and the ones below it... You can make an arc."

"Yeah, I see it. It kind of looks like a C."

"Except it's not a C."

"What is it then?"

She takes my hand back down and places it onto her chest. My palm wraps around her breast.

"Do you need another hint?"

"It's a boob?"

"Just one."

"I love it."

"Thanks. It's ours now. Forever."

"I have an idea," I say.

"Okay..."

"You see that reddish star way below the boob?"

"Yeah."

"I think that's her leg."

"Her one leg?"

"Yeah. Her one leg."

"I love you, Pato."

"Me too. *Yo te amo también.* So much."

"Thank you," she says.

"For what?"

"For making the worst week of my life one of the best."

We kiss. Salty tears roll into our mouths and moisten our lips.

"I need you to make it," she says.

"Don't say that. You're going to make it with me."

"Pato..."

"Stop!" I whisper.

"It's okay. You've made it okay. You've made it great."

"You promised me. Remember?"

"I'm going to be with you. In here." She touches my chest. "In here." She touches my head. "And out there." She points to the stars.

"Don't do this. Please. I can't make it without you."

"You can. And I need you to. You have to help Marcos."

"This is all his fault," I say.

"Don't take this out on him. Please. I need you to help him. We all did our best. It's not any of our faults. We were just caught in the middle."

She presses her palm to my cheek. I nod. I'm sobbing over her. I don't know what to say. I don't want to accept this.

I feel her hand begin to slip. Softly, I press my forehead to hers.

"Thank you too," I whisper to her.

She tries to whisper back, but the words slur, sliding out in a slow, draining breath. Her last.

Footsteps approach along with the soft, blue glow of the watch.

"How is she?" Marcos asks.

I pull away and stand.

Marcos moves closer to her.

I walk away.

"Gladys?"

I walk.

"*Gladys?*"

I stop. There's nowhere else to go. I have to face it.

"Gladys! No! No!" His voice booms. If anyone is nearby, they surely hear it. And I don't care.

"What did you do to her?" he screams.

"I couldn't save her. I'm sorry."

"No! Save her. Now!"

"She's gone. I'm sorry. I'm so sorry."

"No! She can't be!"

"Marcos..."

"Don't give me that. You were supposed to save her. We were gone for five minutes. What did you do?"

"Nothing!"

He reaches for his shirt on the ground and hurls it at me.

"You didn't wrap her leg?"

"She was dying, Marcos."

"Maybe she wouldn't have if you had done what you were supposed to do. *¡Cabrón!*"

"I didn't want to put her in more pain."

"Well, congratulations. I'm glad it was easier on you. And now she's dead because of it!"

"Stop yelling at him!" Arbo says. "He didn't kill her."

"Stay out of this," Marcos says.

Arbo tries to answer, but I cut him off. "You're blaming *me*?"

"You were the one who was with her. And what about water? Why didn't you grab the water?"

"She didn't die from thirst. You know why she's dead? Because of you! You got her killed!"

"Don't say that! He shot her. Not me."

"No! You said it yourself—all you had to do was walk away. And you couldn't. And now she's dead!"

"Stop!"

"No! You need to know it. You need to live with it." Even as the words come out, I can't believe I'm saying them. It's the last thing she'd want—it was even her dying wish that I help him—but I can't stop myself. The wound is too deep. "I hate you! You've been an *hijo de puta cabrón* this whole trip. And now you've killed her. It should be you! I wish it were you!"

He shoves me so hard my feet leave the ground. I land flat on my back, breathless. I pick up my head, unable to charge back but still trying.

Arbo whimpers. He's on the fringe, in tears.

It's ripping us all apart.

I stare at the shadowy outline of Marcos with the same fury I bore into Rafa in the backyard. And I'm back to wishing it had all ended there, so I wouldn't have to be where I am right now.

VULTURES

Denial prevents all conversation. To talk about her death is to acknowledge it. To talk about anything else would be...absurd.

It's as if we've all been thrust outside the backyard again, only this time there's no urgent reason to leave—no danger to run from and no safety to run toward. So we sit, immobile, slowly moving toward wherever Gladys is now.

La Frontera has won. The desert has won. At this moment, I think of them as one—a boundless, gripping, unforgiving, armed force that will not cease until we're all dead.

I don't see a way out, but I'm not looking hard either. I don't have it in me. If I look anywhere, it's to the newest constellation in the sky, but I can't stare at it for long. It's a reminder of a future I no longer have. If I have one at all.

— — —— — — —— —

"Do you hear that?" Arbo whispers.

Low voices come from the direction of the creek bed.

"Yeah," I answer back.

"Do you think that's them looking for us?"

"I don't know," I say.

I reach in my pack for the gun and wrap my hand around the cool metal. I'd never held a gun before in my life, and in the past few hours, I've done it twice. I slide it out of the pack and turn softly toward the noise. I see several quick pulses of a flashlight. I wonder if they tracked the blood. I soften my breathing. We fall silent and listen.

The sounds fade into the distance.

Whether they're people like us passing through or people hunting us down, it's impossible to say. I don't think we have it in us to move anywhere tonight, but if anyone had been considering it, this puts a hard stop to those thoughts. We're better off remaining still.

Dawn is many hours away. I keep the gun outside the pack, reaching for it every time the desert rustles. It's a long night.

— — —— — —— — — ——

Fiery streams of reds and yellows spill in from the east, warning of what's to come. The morning shadows stretch over us. The mountains have moved slightly farther away, and the bushes are a bit sparser, leaving open gaps of nothing.

Everything else looks the same as yesterday. The same as every day.

Arbo lies near me, on his side. He looks less like he's sleeping and more like he's passed out in the same surrendered pose we found Sr. Ortíz in when we first walked into his house.

Marcos is awake, holding Gladys's head off the ground and cradling it, just as he has all night. He rocks back and forth, looking down into her lifeless eyes.

I don't think either of us slept.

I look at her body in the soft light, and all I want to do is hold it like he is. I want to walk over and touch her once more. But I can't. It's not even worth trying.

I think a million things as I stare at her. I think about our plan. I blame Marcos. I blame myself. I question whether she's really gone. I want to try ridiculous things, like giving her water that we don't have. *Maybe Marcos was right, and that's all she needs... A few sips and she'll be okay.* I talk myself out of the absurd. I think of what she'd do right now. She wouldn't be festering in this misery. I try to imagine what she would tell me at this moment, but I'm no good at it. All it makes me do is wish she were here to tell me herself.

I look at my wrist and notice the bracelet she made from Marcos's jeans is missing. It must have fallen off last night.

Everything about her seems to be gone.

I close my eyes and weep again, until sleep finally sweeps me away.

— — —— — —— — — ——

The shade retreats, and the heat jars me from my sleep. I fight it. I roll from side to side, letting the sky and the ground take turns searing me. I take in the burn, on the outside and the inside. Rage fills me. My legs kick, my fists pound, my body twists, my thighs slam down. I try to hurt this beast that's killing us, knowing it feels nothing and knowing it's a fight that can't be won. It's a fitting end.

But it's not the end. That's the problem. When it's over, when I flush this moment out of my system, I'm still here, lying in the grit, awake, overwhelmed, disgusted, mourning…aware that I need to do something, and unwilling to acknowledge it.

Arbo still lies beside me. I check his breathing and place a hand on the back of his neck. He's boiling. From the little I know now, this is good. He stirs as I paw over his body.

"What time is it?" he grumbles.

No trace of morning remains.

"I have no idea."

He doesn't respond.

"We need to move to the shade," I say.

He opens his eyes. I watch them track toward Gladys, then close tightly. It hurts almost as much to watch him confirm it.

"Come on, Arbo," I say. I reach for his hand to pull him up. He doesn't take it. Instead, he belly-crawls about five meters to a creosote bush with some shade beneath it. I follow. We cram our bodies together into the tight space.

"We're dying," he says. "We're just next in line."

He's right. We have no water left. No food left. The only salvation we know of is at least five hours away. And even if we could make it there, it's teeming with scumbags eager to turn us over to angry *narcos*. I know that's what we signed up for when we made our escape from the group, but the naive hope that we'll all make it is gone now. Reality has trounced optimism.

"I want to let it go, Pato, but I can't. I'm trying so hard. I don't want to die angry, but I'm still so mad at my dad."

I wish I knew what to tell him, but I don't. My head is too cluttered. I don't know why I'm able to let go of my dad's role in this and he isn't. Maybe I've only distracted myself with Gladys.

"All I want right now is to forgive him before I die, and I can't do it. Every time I look at her, I think that it's all his fault," he says.

He balls up like he does when he's upset, and I watch him suffer. I watch. I can't believe I just watch. Like I have no other choice. Like I've given up and I'm letting whatever happens, happen.

A haunting voice whispers inside my head, pushing me forward. It's hers.

"Then maybe we don't die," I say.

"How?"

"I don't know, but we need to do something. We have to walk out of here."

"I can barely move, Pato. I don't have much left in me."

"You have to. We have to try."

"He's not going anywhere," Arbo says, pointing to Marcos.

"Maybe you're right, but we can't leave him," I say.

"So... What are you saying?"

"I don't know, Arbo."

He closes his eyes and leans into the creosote.

"Okay. Let me know when you're ready," he says.

I look at Marcos. The last thing I want to do is talk to him. Maybe I should have more sympathy. No, I *should* have more sympathy. But I don't have the space for it. I'm still too filled with disgust.

I stand and walk over to him.

I sit down several feet away from him. He doesn't look up. He sways gently over her, as if he could tip at any moment and join her. His bloodied shirt still lies at her side, leaving his thin frame exposed. I spent so much of the night building him up as the bad guy that I'd forgotten how withered he's become.

"We need to go, Marcos."

He doesn't answer.

"Marcos, we need to go. We can't sit here."

Nothing.

I scoot closer.

Then closer.

"We need—"

"I'm not leaving," he says. It's a whisper, yet as commanding as a roar.

"Marcos—"

"No!"

"So what, you're going to die here?"

"Isn't that what you want?"

"Marcos…"

"I died last night," he says.

"No. *She* died last night."

"We died."

"That's not what she'd say."

He finally looks up at me, drilling his eyes into mine. "*Cabrón*, don't tell me what my sister would say. Okay?"

"What do you think she'd say then?"

"I'm not playing this game. I'm staying."

"It's not a game. We're going to die if we don't go," I say.

"Then go," he says.

"Marcos."

He stops answering.

— — — — — — — —

We continue to roast. I watch Marcos, wondering if he'll move. He doesn't.

The lip of shade under the creosote bush slowly retreats.

There is no other shade nearby. Soon we will be exposed. Several vultures circle above, reminding us of what awaits.

Her voice, inside my head, won't quit.

I stand. There's one last thing I can do. I go back to Marcos.

"You don't have to listen to what I say. Read what she wrote in her own words."

I swing the book in front of his nose and point to where I want him to read. He turns his head away.

"Read it."

"No."

"Fine. Then I'll read it to you. This is what she wrote yesterday morning." My voice trembles. I pause. I didn't consider how hard this would be. "'If he dies, I don't know what I'll do,'" I begin. "'He has to live, Pato... I'd trade places with him. I'd die for him. I would. He has to make it. I can't stand seeing him like this.'" I set the book down at his side with the pages open, pressed into the earth. "She traded places with you, Marcos. And it made her happy. Don't let her down by being a stubborn *pendejo* who dies for nothing."

I walk away.

I wait.

He grabs the book.

Our shade is gone. More vultures have joined the deathly circle above us, sweeping lower, like anxious chefs, peering in the oven as their main course bakes to perfection.

Marcos has set the book down and picked it back up several times. He doesn't stop at the page I showed him. He thumbs through more. Then more. I feel as though he's reading my diary. It's embarrassing. But if it works, it's what she would want. That's what matters.

Of course, even if I get us all to move, it would solve little. There's still the question of where to move to. And where to find water. For now, I take this one step at a time.

Each time he sets down the book, he looks like he's teetering on the edge. I'm teetering too. If we're going to move, we need to go.

I start to stand when a black streak bombs down from the sky.

Marcos jumps back as the vulture lands nearly in his lap. The huge bird latches on to Gladys's face and rips off a chunk of skin.

I look away.

Marcos screams.

The vulture's broad wings beat in a powerful whoosh as it makes a quick exit, flaps of flesh dangling from beak and talons.

Another bird swoops down from the sky, crashing into her. This time, Marcos is prepared. As its talons grip, Marcos charges. Wings flap, but not quickly enough.

Marcos drives his foot squarely into the vulture's chest. The bird tumbles a body length away, landing on its back with a dull thump and an ear-piercing screech, its wings spastically slapping the ground, trying to right itself, squawking in pain.

Marcos takes no pity. His next kick crushes the vulture's wing into its body. It snaps and feathers explode, launching into the breeze so that they drift into me like a floating, black rain.

The animal hobbles a few paces away, then drops to the desert floor.

Marcos's eyes narrow on the fowl. He knows he's won. He draws the knife from his back pocket and slowly approaches. He drops to his knees, shirtless. His back arches, and he raises the weapon until the blade hovers high, glimmering above his head. Then he plunges it down.

More feathers fly.

Again, he hoists the blade and thrusts it into his prey.

Another vulture squawks and dives toward the ground in a steep pitch.

"Marcos!" I scream as the bird lands.

He turns. His face and chest are smeared with blood. His eyes are crimson.

Between us, the vulture spreads its wings and hisses at Marcos. He leaps to his feet and rushes at it. The animal flies away, narrowly missing a punt.

Marcos turns back to the feathery carcass and clutches it

by the neck. He swings the limp body around and slams it into the ground.

Half-crouched and scanning the sky, I bolt through a fresh cloud of feathers toward Gladys. I slide onto my knees, nearly crashing into her. Her face is torn open—it oozes, as if trying to bleed. It breaks my heart all over again.

As I'm about to embrace her, Marcos barrels into the tight space between us and swats my arm away.

"Don't touch her!" he barks. He grabs his shirt and covers her face.

"I'm trying to protect her!" I plead.

"That's my job! That's my job. That's my job," he repeats, over and over, sinking down each time, until his face is buried in her stomach. "And I couldn't do it," he finally says, his words packed with so much pain they're barely understandable.

He pushes away.

"Everything I did was wrong. And now she's gone. Because of me. All I wanted was to save her."

He flops into me. I hold him. His body convulses against mine.

— — — — — — —

The buzzards continue to circle, but they keep their distance now.

Arbo asks for the knife. He leans over Gladys and makes

304 | STEVE SCHAFER

a small slice in his index finger. Drops of blood splatter onto Marcos's shirt, which covers her upper body. He bows his head.

"To the one of us who most deserved to make it."

He backs away.

I take the knife. My hand shakes as I try to cut.

"To love. Then. Now. Forever. I'll see you in our stars. Always."

Marcos follows. "To a little sister with more courage and heart than her big brother could ever hope to have."

We are—and always will be—bonded together. By tragedy. By triumph. By our very blood.

— — — — — — — —

Not staying here to die with Gladys is one thing. Leaving her here this way is another.

"What, do you want to let these filthy birds eat her?" Marcos asks.

"What else can we do? We can't take her with us," I say.

"We could bury her," Arbo says.

"With what?" I ask.

"Good point. It was just an idea."

"I'm not going to turn her into vulture food," Marcos says.

"We could cover her," Arbo says.

"They'll pull away whatever we put on top of her," I say.

"Not if we use rocks," Marcos replies.

"We can barely walk and we don't have any water. We have to go, or we're all going to be vulture food," I say.

Marcos opens his mouth to speak, but Arbo cuts him off.

"Do you guys hear that?"

There's a whining in the distance. It's hard to identify, but it's getting louder. Quickly.

"It's a car," Arbo says.

"It's not a car... It's something else," I say.

"It's more than one," Marcos adds.

We lower our bodies. Whatever it is, it sounds like it's passing through the creek bed...until, abruptly, it turns toward us.

Engines rev. Bushes rustle.

"Run!" Arbo yells.

We all take to our feet—even Marcos. We sprint away from the noise, as if it could be outrun. It can't. Within seconds, two four-wheelers blast through the brush.

"*¡Manos arriba!*"

We freeze.

A cloud of dust floats across our faces, blurring our view. I squint but only see forms. Then the dust passes. There are three men. Each holds a massive rifle. Each points at one of us.

"I said, '*¡Arriba!*' Now!"

I know the voice. We raise our arms high in the air. He slides off his four-wheeler, lifts his sunglasses from his face, and flashes a victorious grin.

It's the gunman from the backyard. Rafa's brother.

"*Hola, chavos.* Remember me?"

None of us answer.

"I'll take that as a yes. Funny bumping into you out here." He looks up. "Vultures never lie."

I glance at the other two men, who carefully climb off the second four-wheeler while keeping their aim on us.

The leader of the group we escaped from smiles and waves.

"Ah, and I think you know my friend here too," Rafa's brother says. "Small world, really." His smile is at full gloat.

I don't know the third man, but I recognize what's on his neck—three bars, side by side.

I scan around us. There is no escape. No options remain. Death is finally certain and near. And faced with this, I realize how much I don't want to die.

I look at Arbo. He's resigned to it. I turn to Marcos. He's looking away in disgust, like we're about to meet the one end he dreaded most.

I can't bear it either. I have to do something.

Our gun.

I spot it. It's on the ground by the creosote bush, ten to fifteen meters from us. I stare at it. Before I even have a chance to try to hatch a plan, I give myself away.

Rafa's brother turns and sees it.

"Oh, that's a shame. You have a gun, but it's so far away. You can go get it if you want. I'll trade you. You get the gun, and I shoot one of your friends. In the *huevos*." He grabs himself, as if we need the reference, and laughs.

My stomach turns thinking about what is mere moments away.

"Do you have any idea how much I've fantasized about this?" he continues. "I crossed the border for you. I don't cross. But for this... Oh, this is going to be worth it."

We stay silent.

"Hey, look at me when I talk to you," he says to Marcos.

Marcos ignores him.

"I said, 'Look at me,' you *pinche culero*."

"You don't exist," Marcos says.

"Oh, I exist. Believe me. You're going to know that soon enough."

"So do it already and shut up."

He laughs. "Don't you wish I would, *pendejo*. I'm thinking maybe I have other plans for you. Like shooting you in the kneecaps and leaving you out here for them to eat. Alive." He points up. "Maybe everybody gets a little revenge today," he says, looking at the bird carcass between us.

Marcos doesn't respond.

Rafa's brother walks over to Gladys and pulls the shirt from her face.

"Wow. Somebody got a mouthful. Literally!" Again, he laughs at his own words.

I can hear Marcos's breathing intensify.

"Ignore him," I say under my breath. I don't want Marcos

to go charging him. Or provoking him at all. I need time to think. To come up with a plan.

"What a shame. She looks like such a delicate little flower. Maybe it's for the best. I've always had a hard time shooting little girls."

He pulls out a stack of hundred dollar bills.

"And shooting three out of the four of you isn't bad. But before I do, I want you to see something. This is my lesson to you. This is what it's all about." He fans the bills in the air. "Ten thousand dollars," he says. "Twenty-five hundred for each of you, and twenty-five hundred for the dead girl. That's what it cost me to get you. That's what your lives are worth. This. We always win, because we have *this*. Lots of this. When you see your daddies, remind them of that."

He walks over to me, stopping close enough that I could take a swing at him.

I ponder it.

He peels away one of the bills.

"Look at it. Smell it." He holds it in front of my nose, then slowly crumples it into a ball. "Die with it."

He flicks the money in my face and walks away. He tosses the stack to the leader of the *guías*, then turns back to us.

"I own you. And now it's time to die."

I need to think.

Think.

Think!

It's not happening. My mind races in circles. It's all panic, not coherent thought. If we run we get shot, if we stay we get shot, if we charge them we get shot.

I should at least have swung when he was close enough for me to hit him. What did I have to lose?

It ends here.

I stare down the barrel of one of the rifles, and a switch goes off in my head. The fear vanishes. I forget about Rafa's brother and the others. I forget about everything.

I close my eyes and find her voice.

If this has been my final week on earth, then that's fine by me. We made the most of what we had.

It's not apathy. It's contentment. In some ways, this has been the best week of my life. I open my eyes, look beyond the horror in front of me, and bask in the searing glory that devours me. I, too, now choose to see the beauty.

I look into the sky. My only wish is to see our stars one more time.

A twinkle catches my eye.

I'm awestruck. And bewildered.

Did I imagine that?

It pulses again. This time I see where it's coming from— the horizon.

I snap back to here. Present. Grounded. With one last hope...

"One question," Rafa's brother says. "Which one of you shot my brother?"

Marcos opens his mouth. "I di—"

"Shut up, Marcos," I interrupt. "You like to take credit for everything. Not this time. This *cabrón* gets the truth." I start laughing.

Marcos and Rafa's brother both look at me, confused.

"You're too late," I say.

"What do you mean?"

"She's right over there. That 'delicate little flower' shot your brother."

"You're lying."

"No, I'm not. And that's not even the best part. She tricked him into getting on his knees to beg. She said she wasn't going to do it... Then she shot him in the throat. He suffocated." I fall to my knees and laugh harder. "You came all the way across the border to get revenge for your brother's death, and these dirty, filthy birds got to her before you did. You can't even shoot her now."

"You want to bet?"

He aims the gun and pulls the trigger. He hits her in the head.

"Ooh, one bullet." I laugh one more time, with everything I have. "And I almost forgot. She peed on him."

"What?"

"You heard me. That 'little flower' peed all over Rafa. I think he was still alive too."

It's gross. It's not Gladys. But I need to push him, hard.

He takes the gun and fires. Six times. Her body bounces with each shot. It's surreal. I know she's no longer there, but

THE BORDER | 311

with each tiny twitch of her body, it looks like she's flinching, in pain again, and ripping at my heart, again.

"Now you're going to shut up. It's your turn," he says, pointing the rifle at me. "Actually, I like you the least. So I'm going to have you watch me shoot him instead." He turns the rifle to Arbo.

No! Not yet.

I look up. The vultures still circle, pointing us out from above.

We need more time. I need one more small distraction.

Rafa takes aim at Arbo. He drops to his knees.

"Why did you do it?" Arbo asks. "Why did you attack the *quince*? I want to know."

"Ask Daddy. Oh wait, he's dead."

He puts his finger on the trigger.

"No. Tell me! You can shoot me, but I need to know first. Please!"

I'm desperately scanning the horizon.

Nada.

Seconds cling to the clock like the sweat sticking to my body.

"Didn't you pay attention earlier? Money, *gordo*. You're as stupid as you are fat. No, you're as stupid as your dad."

"I don't get it. Tell me why. What did he do?"

"He forgot the number one rule—it's all about money. Money wins. And you never talk to the police, no matter what."

"He went to the police?"

Rafa's brother is about to answer when the leader cuts him off.

"¡La migra!"

Sirens blast just beyond the bushes. The gunmen turn and we run. There is no discussion.

Rafa's brother tries to mount his four-wheeler while firing at us.

I leap for cover behind the nearest bush. Arbo tumbles into me. Bullets fly through the brush. Engines whine. The four-wheelers race away as two *migra* jeeps burst into view and turn to follow them, as they all try to weave their way across the dotted landscape.

I look at Arbo. "Are you okay?"

"Yeah," he says.

I scan for Marcos. I don't need to look hard. He's charging across the area where we were. I know where he's headed.

I jump to my feet in pursuit.

He reaches the gun and points it in the direction of the four-wheelers. It's already a long shot to where they are. That doesn't seem to bother him. He takes aim.

I barrel into him from the side. We both crash into the dirt.

"No!" I yell.

"What are you doing?" he barks.

"It's time to go. We need to get away."

He raises the gun back into the air.

"I said no!" I grab his arms and force them down, sliding my hands on top of the gun as I do. "It's not worth it. Do you want to let the *migra* know there are still people back here? We have to go. Now!"

We lock stares.

"Don't fight me for it," I say.

He tries to raise the gun. I push it back down.

"Let go," he commands.

"No. You got your way last time. Remember what happened?"

He almost punches me. He clenches his jaws so tight his face looks twice as wide. I clench back.

We both stand firm. The chaotic pursuit resounds in the distance while we remain stock-still. Not blinking, not budging—nothing.

Until finally, he says, "Fine." His arms go limp, and I take the gun.

"Good. Let's get out of here."

"Where?" Arbo asks.

"It's an easier run in the gully."

Marcos goes to get his pack. He kneels over Gladys. We need to hurry, but I give him the moment.

I throw the gun in my bag and am about to follow Arbo, who is already running away, when I see the little green bill in the sand, crumpled, where it fell after bouncing off my nose. I dart over and grab it. I've never held so much money in my life.

Thirty seconds later, we're all back in the creek bed, racing once again, away from one danger and toward another.

PERSPECTIVES

Adrenaline carries us farther than what our thirst, hunger, and exhaustion should allow. The dry creek bed helps, as it's a hard-packed mix of dirt, sand, and pebbles. But nothing out here is easy. It's a grueling slog. My legs are still drained from having carried Gladys, and every other body part feels almost the same. The mere thought of water is painful. If I could have only water or air right now, I'd debate the choice.

We rest for a moment. We can only go for a few minutes at a time. That's the most we have in us. I put my hands on my knees and look cross-eyed at the sweat collecting at the tip of my nose, then dripping off me to boil on the ground below. It's like watching a slow leak in a bucket. I put my tongue out to catch a drop. I know it's salty and I'm not supposed to, but even that one tiny splash in my sandpaper mouth is enough to give a few seconds of relief. Enough to push off my knees and stand upright one more time.

I listen for the sound of anyone following us. Nothing. Still, we need to get farther away.

"Come on," I say. "A little more."

Trudge.

Rest.

Trudge.

I turn from time to time to make sure we're still together. And when I do, for a split second, I look for Gladys. Like some part of me can't remember that she's gone.

Other pain distracts me from the hurt. In spite of its next-to-nothing load, my pack is nearly unbearable to wear. It rubs my sunburned shoulders raw. The shade it gives my back isn't worth it. I take it off and clutch it in my arms, opting to take on the sun. That's what this whole journey has felt like anyway—us, taking on some massive, tortur-ous, cosmic force that's out of our control.

Rest.

Trudge.

Rest.

Trudge.

Fold.

We push until we have nothing left, inside or out. We reach the end of the creek bed. Within a few hundred meters, it evaporates into the desert floor in a lattice of jagged cracks. After many cycles of filling and drying, it's fully baked, like the crust of a loaf of bread. The bushes thin out and the horizon stretches into nothing.

We collapse onto the crispy ground.

"I can't go any farther," Arbo says weakly.

Marcos's eyes roll up into his head as if to say the same.

That makes three of us.

We've given all we have, then more.

We try to huddle under the thinnest bush I've ever seen. It doesn't help. I push myself up to look for something, anything. There is no substantial shade nearby. No trees, no rocks. There is nothing.

We sprawl out, depleted and exposed.

I place my pack over my face. *Only for a moment*, I think. I pretend it covers my body.

— — — — — — — —

I open my eyes. I don't know how long they were closed. I don't remember choosing to close them. I slide the bag from my head. It's blindingly bright. The piercing rays stab into my skull. Everything is fuzzy and washed out. I put a hand to my forehead to block the sun. Slowly, my focus returns. I see Marcos and Arbo sprawled out next to me, baking in the dirt. They're breathing, but there are no signs of life beyond that.

I need to do something.

There's still not a scrap of shelter to be found. I sit up. I think I spot a tree in the distance.

Then it's gone.

Then it's back.

Shade. Oh, sweet shade. Maybe there's even fruit on that tree?

No. Stop. Think clearly. Think clearly.

I poke Arbo.

"We need to go, Arbo."

He grunts but doesn't move.

I press my palms into the flaming ground and push. I make it to my knees and stare at the shimmering skyline. I pause in the slim space between my will to push farther and the temptation not to. The wind whips a small dust devil in the distance. I turn back to see how far away the mountains are, and...

Wait. There is no wind.

The air is stagnant, scorching. Dead.

I look again toward the dusty cloud. I stare at it. *Is it real?*

It's moving. In a straight line. Tight at the front, then bleeding slowly into a long, wispy trail. And just ahead of it...a car.

A car?

I watch it slide across the horizon, sure it will disappear like the tree. It never does.

I stand on wobbly legs and charge toward it, dashing clumsily with everything I have. I feel like Arbo back in the alley in Sonoyta. My limbs don't work together. They flop, barely keeping me upright. I trip, roll over, and lunge forward again. I repeat.

I wave my arms and yelp an airy screech. But I'm probably half a kilometer away. It's a losing battle.

I trip one last time and watch the car drift out of view. It's a bitter loss, but not a hopeless one. It was traveling far too straight and steady to be on the desert floor. It was on a road.

I stumble back to the others.

"Arbo! Marcos! Get up. There's a road!"

They respond with groans.

"Come on! There's a road! There are cars! We can get help!"

I grab Arbo's arm and yank him. His eyes, half open, look at me as though I'm bothering him.

"Get up!" I kick at him.

He shakes his head a few times. "Where?" he asks.

"Just over there. It's a five-minute walk," I say, minimizing the distance. It *is* only a five-minute walk, but for us, in our condition, it will take longer.

He throws an open hand toward me. I hoist him to his feet. Marcos sways on his knees. He leans back over the ground.

"Are you okay?" I ask him.

He, too, holds out a hand for me to grab.

Soon we're all staggering toward the road.

— — — — — — — —

We tumble into a shallow ditch on the side of the dirt road, panting and choking with throats so dry we're unable to speak much louder than a whisper.

"What do we do now?" Arbo croaks.

"We wait," I say. "For someone to come."

"What if it's *la migra*?"

"That's a chance we have to take."

We sit on the side of the road. And wait.

Hope cools me. Or at least it helps takes my mind off the heat. I turn in shifts, staring to the north and to the south, looking so deep that the tiny ripples of heat morph into vessels of all kinds, all coming to save us. But each time my heart leaps and I'm ready to announce our salvation, the mirage fades, and I have to face the agony of falling back to mere hope. And I do. Over and over. I don't know for how long. I don't look at the time. That would only make the wait feel longer.

After a while, it ceases to feel like we're waiting and begins to feel like we're just sitting, cooking, melting, dying.

— — —— — —— — — ——

None of us have spoken for at least an hour. Arbo taps my arm and I turn to him.

"What did he mean about our dads talking to the cops?" he whispers.

I shrug my shoulders.

"Do you think our dads tried to turn La Frontera in, or do you think the cops came to our dads to try to scare them?" he asks.

"Right before the *quince*, my dad said he had a change to tell me about. He said something was going to change."

"What did he mean?"

"I don't know. He never got to tell me."

We fall silent for a moment, then a faint smile appears on his face.

"I think our dads knew they were on the wrong side. They tried to switch. That's why the *narcos* attacked. That was the change... Maybe they couldn't even do construction anymore and were looking to do something else. They were going to leave it. Yeah."

"I think you're right," I say.

He closes his eyes and the corners of his lips drift upward. Watching this makes mine do the same.

But it's short-lived. I look at the three of us, lying in the dirt, passing the time, and it makes me think back to those long, idle stretches with Gladys. Holding hands, sneaking kisses, passing words back and forth. It fills me with regret. I wish I had appreciated those moments more while I had them. I open the book and try to read our notes. I can't. My eyes won't focus. I strain, blink, squint, but it's no use. It's all a blur. I wish I could go back to when I was with her.

I feel like I'm crying. Again. I reach to wipe away the tears, but my eyes are dry.

I'm empty.

— — — — — — — —

"Car!" Arbo whispers. It's so faint the first time, I barely hear it. "Car! Car!"

I look in the distance and see the familiar trail of dust swirling out from the road.

We scramble to sit upright.

We wave our arms.

We scream with raspy cheers.

We wonder if it's *la migra*, and we let that fear go. We'll worry about that after we get out of this place.

The car nears us. It's not slowing down. I'm not the only one who notices.

We stretch our friendly waves outward, as if to shout, *Stop! Please!* We press our palms together and cross our fingers on our knees.

The car speeds up. It whizzes by, smothering us in a cloud of dirt.

"Why?" Arbo asks.

The question goes unanswered.

We sit, stunned, as the dust settles.

I crawl out into the road.

"It won't happen again," I say.

I stretch out across the center. Arbo follows. I slide to the far side.

There is no way to go forward, other than to go over us.

Marcos stays in the ditch.

The sun kisses the earth. We haven't moved for hours.

I draw my hand to my cheek. My skin feels cool. I look down my body. I've started to turn pale. *Am I becoming a ghost already?*

Everything is foggy. I turn my head north. It takes all I have to do so. I stare down the road, wondering where it leads and how long it takes to get there.

Maybe we should start walking. Night will be here soon. Maybe one last push is all we need to finally get out.

The thought seems absurd. I can barely lift my head.

Then suddenly, I do. I press my hands into the dirt, push up, and start moving. My feet are light. Fresh. As if they're not my own, or as if they are my own, but from weeks ago. I run. I sprint. The ground slides effortlessly beneath my feet. I throw a tight trail of dust behind me.

Then I remember—Arbo! Marcos! I've left them behind.

How could I be so selfish? I need to get them!

I turn. I've run so far they aren't even in sight. My spry legs turn to jelly. I fold. I try to stand, but now I can't even peel my face from the dirt.

I'm alone.

Am I?

I blink and Arbo is next to me again, with Marcos nearby in the ditch.

And then, they're not.

I'm not dreaming. I'm not awake. I think I'm somewhere in between.

I hear sounds. Familiar sounds, but I can't tell what they are. My lungs fill with dust.

"*Hola?*"

"*Hola?*"

Something icy bursts against my neck. *A drip?* It throws my whole body into a small spasm.

Two people hover above me. I stare at them. They look angelic and alien at the same time, looming over me, silhouettes cast against a mesmerizing kaleidoscope of colorful swirls.

One of them—a man—holds out a bottle of water that drips so temptingly with condensation that it looks like a scene from a television ad.

"*Agua?*"

He leans down and extends the water bottle to me. I grab it, still unsure if this is real. It's so frigid that it bites my hand. I sling it to my lips. It unleashes an explosion of cold inside of me. I can feel everywhere it goes. I track it down into my innards. I swear it blasts right past my stomach and fills into the rest of me.

The other person—a woman—says something. It's gibberish. I can tell it's a question. Beyond that, I'm lost.

She looks nervous. Her hands shake. She alternates between glancing at me and at everything else around us.

I stare at her, confused.

"*Está bueno?*" the man asks.

I don't feel bueno, I think.

"No," I try to say, but it comes out stretched with more vowels than it should.

Arbo!

I point to my side, as if they can't see that someone else is there.

They leave me. She goes to Arbo and he goes to Marcos. They both stir with the same delirium as I did.

Soon we're all staring at each other, unsure of what comes next.

"*Por qué?*" the man asks.

There's no way to answer the question I think he's asking: Why are we here like this? I just point to the water in my hand. They nod, as if I've told them something that isn't obvious.

Again, the woman looks around us with anxious eyes, like she's expecting someone to leap out at us. After all I know about this place, I don't blame her.

I finish my water.

He goes back to their vehicle. It's a pickup truck with a shell on top, like it's toting a small room on its back. He climbs into the front of the truck, slides open the small window in the back of the cabin and climbs through it, disappearing into the covered space in the bed of the truck.

The woman looks nearly panicked while he's gone and steps back toward the truck.

He emerges with more water and hands each of us a fresh bottle. I grab it. If it were any colder, it would be ice. It hurts to drink. It's the most wonderful pain I've ever felt.

We drink and he retreats to the truck.

The man and woman confer with each other. Back and forth, back and forth. I understand none of it, but I get the gist. They have no idea what to do with us. They pause. They look at us. I catch the man's eye for a moment.

"*Por favor*," I say.

They understand. They look back at each other. The debate continues, but now it's less a discussion and more an argument.

She finally disappears behind the truck. I hear noises as she fumbles with something. She reappears several times, leaning two bikes against the side of the vehicle. She retreats once more then returns with a small cooler in hand.

She opens it in front of us, showing us what's inside— bottles of water and a few sandwiches. She says something I don't understand, but I'm pretty sure it's "Sorry."

She goes back to the truck. The man leans against the hood. He appears conflicted.

I look at Arbo. I look at Marcos. I look all around us.

Sandwiches and a few bottles of water buy us time. But time for what? To walk until we run out again? To follow this road to Ajo, if that's even where it leads? To encounter La Frontera, *la migra*, *las guías*, or everybody else out here who doesn't want us to make it?

No.

This is our chance.

I try to push myself to my feet, but I can't quite get there. So I crawl. All the way to the front bumper of the truck.

If you're going to leave us here, you might as well run us over, because we'll die just the same.

I know they won't understand me if I say it, so instead I do it. I lie down underneath the front wheel and look up at the man.

He turns to the woman.

Again, they go back and forth.

"*Por favor. No te vamos a hacer nada. No sabes lo que nos ha pasado. ¡Por favor!*" I plead, knowing that all they'll get is the desperation in my voice.

She climbs into the passenger side and shuts the door.

He looks back down at me and holds out his hand, helping me to my feet. I shuffle to the back of the truck with him.

I peer inside. It's a cross between a tiny kitchen and a bedroom. It has cabinets, a small stove, coolers, a slender bench lining one side, and a crawl space with a slim mattress above the front cabin of the truck.

Through the window to the front, I can see the back of the woman's head. Her hand is pressed to her temple. She's not happy about this.

He grabs my attention. "*Está bien*, okay?" He points to himself. "David," he says. Then he points to the truck cabin. "Karen."

"Pato," I say. "*Gracias.*"

He motions that he's going to get the others. As soon as he leaves, I remember my book. I made it this far with it. I'm not going to leave it behind.

I lean away from the truck and walk very slowly back toward the others. My legs are nowhere near steady, but it's amazing how quickly the water has improved how I feel.

As I reach my pack, Karen rolls down the window. David goes to talk with her.

He points to my bag. "*Qué?*"

From her expression, it's clear what they're asking.

I pull the book out and dump the bag upside down, showing that it's empty. As I do this, something nags at me...

The gun.

It isn't in my bag. But I put it there. Which means it has to be...

As soon as I think this, Karen's eyes drift to Marcos's pack, which lies by his side. She nudges David.

"*Qué?*" he asks again, pointing to the other pack.

I stare at Marcos and he stares at me. Some arguments don't need words. I'm hoping we both know what needs to be done.

He slides his hand toward the bag.

I want to yell at him. *Don't be stupid! Let it go! We're getting out!*

But I can't.

He has to get it on his own.

His hand grips the top of the bag. He squints at me. We both freeze.

Then he waves it off, as though it's empty and worthless, and he starts to crawl toward the truck.

If I never see a gun again, that's fine by me.

Soon we're all loading into the back of the truck. I see a map folded open on the bench. I grab it. David points to a spot on it, which I assume is where we are right now. On the page, it looks exactly like it feels in person—like it's in the middle of nothing.

"*¿Por qué están aquí?*"

He seems to get what I'm asking. He grabs a book and points to the title, *Organ Pipe Cactus National Monument*.

I don't know what this means, so I look at him with a confused expression.

He gestures like he's riding a bike, then opens the book to show me softly lit photos of people posing with cheerful expressions among cacti, desert flowers, and mountainsides.

We're fighting for our lives out here. They came to ride their bikes. I don't know how to make sense of this.

I settle into the bench, next to Arbo. The air-conditioning from the cabin trickles in enough to keep it from being hot. It's not cold, but just minutes ago mere shade felt blissful—this is way beyond that.

David closes the door, then secures the bikes to the back of the truck.

I stare out the window as the sunset dims and we're whisked away from all of this. I want to feel good. I want to feel thankful for being as lucky as we are. But I've never felt so guilty.

"Phoenix," David says from the front.

I look at him through the window. He points down the road and repeats it. It sounds familiar.

Marcos sits next to me, unresponsive, as if he's barely interested in what's going on.

Arbo shrugs.

"Okay," I say.

I crawl up into the space above the front cabin and curl into a ball, looking for an escape from our escape. But I can't sleep through it. The best I can do is close my eyes and weather it.

— — —— — — —— — — ——

"Shit!"

My eyes open. I only know a few words of English, and this is one of them.

David says it again.

Karen responds, sounding frantic.

"*Policía!*" David says.

A red-and-blue flicker of lights shines through the tiny back window, faintly glowing in our trail of dust.

David yells something else, but this time I can't understand it.

I hear the click of a buckle, and Karen crams her torso through the cabin window. Her arms flail and she screams. I'm looking down at her, while Marcos and Arbo are looking up.

The truck starts to slow.

She screams louder. As the lights get closer, we can finally see what she's doing—she's pointing up to me. Arbo gets the hint. He starts up and she shoves his tail end the rest of the way. Marcos piles in after him.

The truck stops.

She slides back into the front cabin. The window between us slams shut. Moments later, we hear a booming voice.

David answers.

"Can you understand any of it?" Arbo whispers.

"No," I say.

"Shh!" Marcos hushes us.

The conversation directly below us continues.

Our limbs press uncomfortably into each other. There are no windows up top where we are. I have a slim view down into the space below. Beams of light pass quickly through.

They exchange a few more words, then I feel David put the truck in drive.

We move for several minutes before the window opens, the signal we've been waiting for to untangle ourselves and climb back down.

Karen is crying in the front.

"*¿Qué pasó?*" I ask.

David makes a pistol shape out of his hand and says, "Boom, boom." Then he cups his palm around his ear.

I take this to mean that the police heard gunshots and were checking with anybody in the area. It's only a guess, and I don't know if these shots have anything to do with us. As far as I'm concerned, it's just another night on the edge of the border.

— — — — — — — — —

Karen's sniffles continue. David calms her.

I'm half-expecting the truck to pull over and for us to be dumped back into the desert with a cooler full of sandwiches.

But the truck keeps moving.

When I'm tempted to drift off to sleep, I feel a nudge inside me. It's the voice of Gladys telling me to pay attention. Not so much to what they're saying, but to who they are. I'm still feeling the firm grip of so much that is vile in this world, but they are a reason to reaffirm my faith in people. A reason to hope. Two back-road drifters who stumbled upon three half-naked kids on a road in the middle of nowhere. And they dropped everything and helped. Even if reluctantly.

Thinking about them—focusing on them—makes me reflect on others like them. Sr. Ortíz. Tito. I consider the fact that there are good people everywhere. To the south, to the north, and in between.

I can't say this makes the ride much better though. Knowing and feeling are two different things. And I mostly feel miserable and broken.

— — —— — — —— — — ——

The truck stops. We're in a parking lot. I climb down to sit next to Arbo.

The dim lights of a two-story motel shine through the windows. I peer out at it. In its simplicity, it reminds me of the motel where we stayed in Sonoyta. This, however, looks clean and well kept.

David gets out of the truck. He removes the bikes and opens the back door. After we step out, he climbs inside and rummages through a canvas bag. He pulls out three T-shirts and hands one to each of us.

I put it on. The soft, clean cotton makes me feel even filthier than I am.

Karen says something. She stretches an arm through the cabin window to give something to David. He passes it to us. It's forty dollars. He points to the lighted motel sign, which reads $39.99.

Karen looks back at us with a soft smile.

"*Gracias.*" I don't know what else to say. I wrap my grimy arms around David and give him a hug. He doesn't see it coming, but he hugs back.

Arbo follows suit. Marcos half follows.

Then, as quickly as they entered into our lives, they vanish.

— — —— — — —— — — ——

We close the door to the motel room and crumble into the beds.

"We made it," Arbo says.

"No, *we* didn't," Marcos answers from the other bed.

I think we'll each wrestle with the right perspective on that for a long time.

MOVING ON

The draft from the window unit air conditioner sweeps across my body. I bury myself in a cave of covers. I've been sweltering for so long, I can hardly believe I'm cold. I shiver in awe, the same way that I stare at the faucet that runs water endlessly at the mere twist of a wrist, or at the thick curtains that block out the fierce light of a new day. They masquerade as conveniences, but I know better.

I dreamed of Gladys throughout the night, of wild twists and turns that saved her. Now, I curl up, awake to reality and alone in my thoughts.

Arbo lies next to me. I haven't felt him move since we turned out the light. I heard Marcos, however, spin like a tornado all night. His bed is empty now. I don't know where he is.

— — — — — — — —

I take a shower, standing under the water until long after my fingers prune, still gawking at the never-ending stream that pours over me. It's as mocking as it is refreshing.

Marcos returns and Arbo wakes. Marcos has seen a break-fast special nearby—all-you-can-eat pancakes for $4.99. We're starving, and we have the hundred-dollar gift from La Frontera that I plucked from the desert. It's a quick yes.

Our waitress is Mexican. She looks at us and doesn't even bother to speak English.

What little conversation we have stays on food. I think back to our first morning at Sr. Ortíz's house. We've trav-eled so far, but in some ways it feels like we've arrived at the same place, just at a different table, full of sadness, regrets, and survivor's guilt. And we still don't know how to deal with any of it.

"I miss her," I say.

"I don't want to talk about it," Marcos answers. "There's nothing to say."

I let it go. Maybe there really isn't anything to say.

It's hard to stay angry with him. I still blame him, but it's as if I'm mad at a different Marcos—the cocky, brash guy who thought he could do anything, not the puddle of a person who sits across the tower of pancakes from me.

The waitress returns to check on us. We ask for more pancakes.

"Also," I say to her, "do you know how far Denver is from here?"

She looks at us with empathetic eyes. She knows. Not who we are, not the details, not our story... But she gets it. She's been there. I can tell.

"Maybe fifteen hundred kilometers? You can take a bus there. The station isn't far from here. I'll draw you a map," she says, then flips a paper menu on the table and sketches out quick directions. "It's a thirty-minute walk," she adds, sliding the sheet toward me.

She doesn't ask any questions about us, and we don't ask anything about her. She hustles back to tend to her other tables.

"Why did you ask about Denver?" Arbo asks.

"The man who helped us escape the *guías*—Tito—that's where he lives. He gave me his address, and he said Denver is a good place to get started."

Arbo opens his mouth to speak, but Marcos cuts him off.

"I think we should split up."

"Why?"

"Aside from you hating me?"

"Marcos—"

"In case you forgot, we still have a bounty on our heads and an army of gang members looking for us."

"But if we go to Denver—"

Again, he interrupts, lowering his voice. "We've killed three of them now. They crossed the border and found us in the middle of a desert. Do you think they're going to stop looking just because we go farther north? No. They want blood. And if we stay together, we're more obvious. It's harder to hide. If you guys want to stick together, that's your choice. But we should split."

"But you won't have anybody then," Arbo says.

"No offense, but I think that's already happened," he answers.

Silence.

The new pancakes arrive.

"Maybe we all go to Denver, and then we split," I say. "At least we'd be in the same city."

Marcos doesn't answer. I want to take that as a good sign, but I can't read him right now. I doubt he can even read himself.

— — —— — — — — ——

"We don't have to go to Denver," I say. "It's just an option. I really don't know anything about it other than what Tito said."

Arbo and I are outside on the balcony. It's night. We've spent most of the day inside, sleeping off the desert and the pancakes, then refilling our bellies on canned food and watching TV to take our minds away from where they naturally wander.

Marcos has gone out. Somewhere.

"Where else are we going to go? Canada? I think we've crossed enough borders for right now," Arbo says.

"Yeah, I guess you're right. We should still get in touch with Sr. Ortíz's kids though. Maybe we could go there eventually."

"Maybe so."

Both of our thoughts drift to the same place. Arbo voices it.

"I miss her too," he says.

"Thanks. I know you do."

I leave it there. I'm the one who doesn't want to talk about it now. I can't wrap my thoughts around missing her. I look out into the sky and spot our stars, nearly washed out by the city lights. I like that Denver is to the north.

"Do you think Marcos will come with us?"

"I hope so," I say. "When he gets back, I'll try to talk him into it again. We all need family."

The halo around the dark curtain wakes me. It's a little after eight o'clock in the morning. I look at Marcos's bed. It's still empty.

As I walk to the bathroom, I stop. There's an envelope propped up against the base of the TV, with our names written on the front.

I slump onto the bed.

"What is it?" Arbo asks.

"He's gone."

"What?"

"There's a note for us by the TV. He must have dropped it off in the middle of the night."

Arbo looks at the note, unopened.

"How do you know what it says?"

I stare back at him. We both know.

"I didn't hear anything," Arbo says.

"I didn't either. I don't think that was an accident."

I think about what I said to him in the desert. I wish I could take it back. I don't know if it would have changed anything, but still, I feel like I've failed Gladys. My heart sinks.

I reach for the envelope. Inside is a letter wrapped around three crisp hundred-dollar bills. I read the note aloud.

> I'm sorry it has to be this way, but I think it's for the best. For what it's worth, I think your dads would be proud of both of you.
>
> This should be enough for two bus tickets to Denver. Please use it. We all need a little help sometimes.
>
> Your friend,
> Marcos

I set it back down on the table. Arbo and I stare at it for a while.

I don't speak. I know we'll take the money—we need it too much not to. But I can't be the one to grab it. I need for that decision to be his.

— — — — — — — —

The money sits there.

We shower.

We gather the few things we have.

We avoid each other's eyes.

We open the door to leave. We both stare at the table.

At last, Arbo grabs it.

We walk to the bus station.

— — —— — — —— — — ——

I flip through a rack of postcards. We have a brief wait before our bus leaves, and I want to make sure we send this from Phoenix. I find one with a golden bird rising out of the desert toward the sky. I fill in Sr. Ortíz's address and write three words.

We made it.

It's a half truth, but it's the half I want him to have.

— — —— — — —— — — ——

I scan around me while we wait, hoping to see Marcos. In my heart, I know he won't come, but still, I hope. I wonder where he'll go. I wonder what he'll do. I wonder if I'll ever see him again.

I wish the best for him. Really, I do.

— — —— — — —— — — ——

The bus pulls onto the highway, and we settle in for a twenty-two hour ride. I pull out *Huck*, ready to get lost again in his adventures and forget about mine for a while.

Thumbing through the pages to find my place, I stumble across an image. In the blank space below a chapter's end, there is a sketched drawing of a superhero-like figure. He's wearing a wrestling mask with a peace sign and has a stethoscope wrapped around his neck. Below him, his name reads: El Revolucionario, the peaceful wrestling doctor.

I show Arbo.

"When did she do it?"

"I don't know. I just found it."

"I love it," he says.

I stare at the picture, and with it comes a wave of memories.

"I keep thinking about a conversation we had back in the desert," Arbo says. "You and Marcos were arguing—about her. And instead of focusing on that, she tried to help me. She started telling me about all these amazing things she remembered my dad doing. One after another. He built her a rocking horse when she was a kid. And for her fifteenth birthday, even though she didn't have a *quince*, he gave her a gift... an artist's easel that he made." He pauses. "I didn't want to listen. But now, it's all I can think about. It's like I had forgotten how much he liked to build things and then give them away. She helped me remember who he really was."

"I'm sure she loved the easel."

"She did. My dad was a good man."

"Yeah. He was," I say.

"So was your dad."

"They both were."

Arbo looks down at the picture again.

"It's perfect."

If you ask me, that sums up everything about her. I break. "I don't know how I'm going to do this."

"I'm here for you. Like you were for me."

He puts his arm around me.

"I know. I couldn't do it without you."

"You could, but you don't have to," he says.

I look out the window. As we leave the city, the desert landscape zips by at speeds that feel absurd.

I promise to never take this for granted. To always remember what that walk was like, and what it cost us to get here.

I don't know what we'll do in Denver, or wherever we end up. Truth is, I don't know how I'll face tomorrow. Each breath is still hard. But I've been through enough to know that we have an opportunity. And we owe it to ourselves and to all the others to make the most of it.

AUTHOR'S
NOTE

February 16, 2017

Several years ago, a good friend of mine lost a family member in northern Mexico. He was kidnapped. Ransom calls followed, but then they suddenly stopped. No one knows what happened or why, and attempts to discover the truth only resulted in threats against the family. I couldn't stop thinking about this tragedy, and I found myself asking: What would I do if I lived there and something like this happened to my family? This question sparked my initial idea for *The Border*.

  While the opening scene in this novel is more extreme, it is no less real. The drug war and lawlessness along the U.S.– Mexico border has produced a violent, inhospitable climate. From 2007 to 2014, it's estimated that anywhere from fifty-five to ninety thousand people were killed in Mexico's drug war.[1] Many were innocent victims caught in the cross fire, including one thousand children and sixty-seven reporters.[2] There is conflicting evidence as to whether this level of violence is currently decreasing or persisting. Time will tell, but for now, it creates a compelling reason for people to search for something better. Desperate situations provoke desperate measures.

The long trek through the Sonoran Desert is a passage so brutal that it has earned the nickname the Devil's Highway. It is littered with real-life tales of tragedy. Thousands have died. Many go unnamed. In January 2013, the state of Arizona held almost eight hundred unidentified bodies of would-be immigrants who tried to cross but failed.[3] Those who undertake this journey truly gamble with their lives. At the time of writing this, there's talk of building a wall. Who knows what may happen, but in my opinion, Mother Nature has constructed a far more formidable obstacle in the Sonoran Desert.

---

1. Jason M. Breslow, "The Staggering Death Toll of Mexico's Drug War," PBS.org (July 27, 2015), http://www.pbs.org/wgbh/frontline/article/the-staggering-death-toll-of-mexicos-drug-war/.

2. Anne-Marie O'Connor and William Booth, "Mexican Drug Cartels Targeting and Killing Children," *Washington Post* (April 9, 2011), https://www.washingtonpost.com/world/mexican-drug-cartels-targeting-and-killing-children/2011/04/07/AFwkFb9C_story.html?utm_term=.a83c52d3d2b5; "The Violence of Mexican Drug Cartels," IShotHim.com (January 6, 2013), http://visual.ly/violence-mexican-drug-cartels.

3. Robin Reineke, "Arizona: Naming the Dead from the Desert," BBC.com (January 17, 2013), http://www.bbc.com/news/magazine-21029783.

I have always been interested in stories of immigrants coming to the United States, but this specific journey fascinates me. For me, it's impossible to hear about someone's experience making this passage and not admire their determination and perseverance.

I grew up in Texas and am an adventurous traveler. I speak Spanish and have lived, worked, volunteered, and traveled throughout most of Latin America, including northern Mexico. I've faced some dicey circumstances. I have been lost and alone at night in the backwoods of Paraguay, and I have been stranded in the highlands of Bolivia. I have never, however, made this harrowing trip through the Sonoran Desert, nor have I had an experience that comes even remotely close to it. My travel has been that of privilege, not necessity.

While I've gained a deep cultural appreciation and perspective from my experiences, I needed much more than that to write *The Border*. Crafting an authentic story, characterization, and setting required an education from a plethora of sources, from the Internet to books to anecdotal accounts from conversations I've had.

Two incredibly valuable resources were *The Devil's Highway* by Luis Alberto Urrea and *Clandestine Crossings: The Stories* (published online) by David Spener. Urrea, in particular, deserves an enormous thank-you. His graphic depiction of twenty-six immigrants' ill-fated passage in 2001 was instrumental in helping me to accurately understand the terrain, the voyage, and the social structure involved in crossing.

Although this story is fictional, I wanted to make the journey as factual as possible. Sonoyta exists, as does Ajo, and I have tried, to the best of my abilities, to capture the exact route Pato, Arbo, Marcos, and Gladys might have taken. To do so, I blended some real-life accounts with conjecture. Here is a copy of the map and notes I originally used to plot their trip.[4]

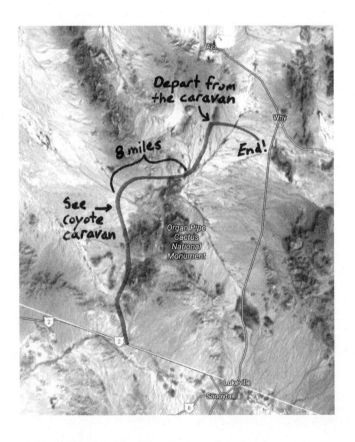

4. Satellite imagery © Google 2017.

One irony I've always struggled to reconcile is the presence of Organ Pipe Cactus National Monument, 517 square miles of national park that lie in the middle of the madness in the map above. Although violence in the region has reduced park attendance, tourists still visit. How many? According to the U.S. National Park Service, in 2016, more than two hundred thousand desert-lovers savored the majesty of this terrain.[5] The contrast between the experiences of the immigrants and the tourists who essentially coexist in this same area astounds me. The encounter between the mountain bikers and the teens at the end of *The Border* is my attempt to push these two competing forces to come to terms with each other. It also represents one of my principal motivations for writing this novel, which feels more relevant with each passing day.

We've recently entered a period of heightened debate about immigration, especially about illegal passage along the U.S.–Mexico border. This political discourse often loses sight of the individuals at the heart of the issue. To generalize, they are people in need—in Sonora, and elsewhere. Survival at home is grueling; bettering their own lives there is unlikely. They leave desperate situations to find an opportunity for a better life. And they risk everything along the way.

---

5. "Annual Visitation Report by Years: 2006 to 2016," accessed March 2, 2017, https://irma.nps.gov/Stats/SSRSReports/National%20Reports/ Annual%20Visitation%20By%20Park%20(1979%20-%20Last%20 Calendar%20Year).

My hope for anybody who reads this novel is that it inspires you to take a moment and imagine what drives someone to come to this country and what that journey is like, whether legal or illegal. Empathy begins with the recognition that everyone has a story.

ACKNOWLEDGMENTS

While I'm very proud of this novel, the amount of guidance and support I needed to arrive at the final product was more than enough to keep me modest. I'm forever indebted to all of the amazing people who provided this help.

Any list must begin somewhere, and it's right to begin this one with Chris Gardner. He is the busiest person I know and incredibly generous with the time he doesn't have. He's my Yoda, strong with the literary force and there when I need him most. As if this alone weren't enough, he also recruited his high school English students to review early versions of *The Border*. Their combined feedback had a significant impact on the shape of this story. In no particular order, thank you to: Natali Morriss, Aliya Fantauzzi, Josh Gonzales, Hanna Malott, Megan Reyna (plus her grandmother, Susan Baker), Claudia Norman, Kylie Newsome, Christian Aguirre, Liliana Palacios Herrera, Sabrina Spracklen, Greg Meinhold, Alex Moore,

Samantha Garcia, Michaela McClanahan, William Guthrie, and Karina Bustos.

Along with Chris Gardner, I had two family members on my core feedback team—my creative and articulate brother, Billy, and my thoughtful and understanding wife, Lisa. They deserve many rounds of applause for enduring endless revisions and my accompanying neuroses.

I'd like to profusely thank Adrienne Rosado, my spectacular and persistent literary agent, who has tirelessly critiqued and pitched my work for way too long without receiving anything in return. Her support and dedication to helping me has been a constant force in my growth as a writer. Adrienne also introduced me to Dani Young, who deserves significant credit here as well. Her early editing and suggestions took this story to another level. Without Dani's insightful recommendations, I can confidently state that this book would not have been acquired by Sourcebooks.

And on that note, I can't say enough positive things about my experience with the entire team at Sourcebooks. Huge thanks to my phenomenal editor, Annette Pollert-Morgan, who shepherded this rookie through the publication process, made me a part of her team, and showed me "just" how much better this story and my writing could be. Further credit and appreciation goes to Michelle Lecuyer and Claudia Guadalupe Martinez, who each brought a thoughtful and invaluable perspective to the novel. And I'd also like to thank Cassie Gutman, Sarah Kasman, and Lynne

Hartzer, and all the others behind the scenes who believed in this novel and helped bring it to market.

Others who reviewed portions or entire versions of this novel and provided valuable feedback include Chris Cassell, Mark Trahan, Mark Berry, Abby Ford, and Kelsey Ortinau. Also, Karen Mendoza was an invaluable consultant to help make the Spanish more authentically Mexican. Thanks to all of you.

I owe Mark Wachlin much gratitude for several clutch suggestions when this novel was only a one-line idea. Top among these, I had originally conceived of four *boys* traveling. Mark suggested making one of them a girl. It's hard for me to imagine this novel without Gladys.

Last, but far from least, I'd like to thank my parents for giving me remarkable opportunities to explore different cultures. Without these experiences and the perspectives gained from them, this novel wouldn't exist. An additional thank you and giant hug to my mother who has reviewed nearly everything I've ever written and—despite this—has an unwavering belief in my scribblings. I can write no stuff written badly in her eyes, even this sentence. In the marathon of writing a novel, she is a carton of energy bars. And I needed every one.

ABOUT THE AUTHOR

Steve Schafer is an avid cultural explorer, animal lover, bucket-list filler, and fan of the great outdoors. He has a master's degree in international studies from the Lauder Institute at the University of Pennsylvania. He lives in Philadelphia, Pennsylvania, with his wife and two children. *The Border* is his first novel.

FIREreads

 ━━━━━━━━ ⊗ **#getbooklit** ━━━━━━━━

Your hub for the hottest young adult books!

Visit us online and sign up for our
newsletter at FIREreads.com

 @sourcebooksfire

 sourcebooksfire

 firereads.tumblr.com